Fury of the Phoenix

Fury of the Phoenix

Cindy Pon

WITH CHAPTER DECORATIONS BY THE AUTHOR

GREENWILLOW BOOKS
An Imprint of HarperCollins *Publishers*

Fury of the Phoenix

Copyright © 2011 by Cindy Pon

All rights reserved. No part of this book may be used or reproduced in any manner whatsoever without written permission except in the case of brief quotations embodied in critical articles and reviews. Printed in the United States of America. For information address HarperCollins Children's Books, a division of HarperCollins Publishers, 10 East 53rd Street, New York, NY 10022.

www.harperteen.com

The text of this book is set in 12-point Weiss
Book design by Paul Zakris

Library of Congress Cataloging-in-Publication Data
Pon, Cindy (date).
Fury of the phoenix / by Cindy Pon.
p. cm.
Summary: When Ai Ling leaves her home and family to accompany Chen Yong on his quest to find his father, haunted by the ancient evil she thought she had banished to the underworld, she must use her growing supernatural powers to save Chen Yong from the curses that follow her.
ISBN 978-0-06-173025-2 (trade bdg.)
[1. Supernatural—Fiction. 2. Voyages and travels—Fiction.
3. Fathers and sons—Fiction.
4. China—History—Xi Xia dynasty, 1038-1227—Fiction.] I. Title.
PZ7.P77215Fur 2011   [Fic]—dc22   2010011700

11 12 13 14 15 LP/RRDB 10 9 8 7 6 5 4 3 2 1
First Edition

 GREENWILLOW BOOKS

For my mommy, Margaret,
who showed me what it means to be a heroine

CHAPTER ONE

Chen Yong was already on board the ship.

Ai Ling stumbled when her spirit touched his, and she caught herself against a merchant's bamboo stand. The old woman gave her a curious look as she set out eggplants and carrots. Ai Ling murmured an apology and veered off, the pungent scent of cilantro following her.

She couldn't feel the spirits of others near the port yet. She was still too far away. But she was drawn to Chen Yong as if she had been starved for months for warmth and light. She closed her eyes for a moment, trying to slow her racing pulse. His face filled her vision: his inquisitive amber eyes; the strong lines of his jaw and cheekbones; his mouth curved into a smile that made him look boyish.

She *had* to get on that ship. His life depended on it.

It was barely dawn, and the large seaside city of Yuan Hai clamored to life. As Ai Ling approached the harbor, the hubbub of vendors in the narrow streets was punctuated by the cries of seagulls soaring above. Boys darted like sardines through the crowds. Women dressed in the same grays and blues as the men chorused in singsong voices; hawking sticky rice filled with pickles and minced pork, candied yams, and hot soy milk to start the day and drive the cold away. Ai Ling's stomach growled, but she didn't stop.

Slipping from the labyrinth of buildings that leaned like haphazardly stacked dominoes, she finally stepped onto the broad main street. The seafront shopkeepers had already laid out their merchandise: embroidered handkerchiefs and slippers, fans adorned with lotuses and dragonflies, gold earrings and jade bangles. She smelled dumplings and custard buns steaming, scallion flatbreads being fried.

The sight of the massive port took her breath away. Ships larger than Ai Ling could have imagined swayed like giant monsters, creaking against the gentle lapping of the sea. Smaller boats bobbed in their shadows.

Triangular pennants in a rainbow of colors fluttered above ocher sails, as the sun rose like a ripe persimmon on the horizon. Men shouted at one another while they unloaded cargo and checked lines that were as thick as her wrist. Tasting the sea's salt on her lips, she hurried toward the water.

Ai Ling, clutching her satchel to her side, maneuvered among the sailors. She had limited herself to a few changes of clothing, a light blanket, and dried foods. Also her sketchbook, which she couldn't leave behind. This time she had left willingly, with a large pouch of gold coins from her monthly widow's allowance. It was a generous allowance, as Zhong Ye had been the highest-ranking adviser to the Emperor. Ai Ling's scalp crawled, and she shivered.

She could almost see his pale gray eyes, felt as if it were yesterday their spirits entangled when she had killed him. No matter how often she tried to push Zhong Ye from her mind, he lingered, festering like some dark wound.

She pulled her square cap lower, her single braid tucked inside a slate blue tunic, and cast her spirit forward, let it skim over the merchants and sailors surrounding her. She imagined tenuous threads coiling from her navel, searching and connecting to hundreds of others. She had never opened herself so completely—she had shut herself away these past months, trying to control her ever-growing power. But today she wielded it as a master painter would a brush. And it was far too easy.

"She's one hundred and fifty feet, made from teak and camphor wood," a man called Tien An said. "This will be her sixth journey to Jiang Dao."

A boy, Xiao Hou, exhaled, wide-eyed with wonder.

They both were out of earshot, but Ai Ling gathered their conversation and feelings as easily as plucking peach blossoms in bloom. A brush of the shoulder, a graze of the arm were like leaping into someone else's skin. She hummed tunelessly to quiet her mind, concentrated on the giant sails snapping like dragons' jaws. Stopping just short of her destination, she tilted her head back. The *Gliding Dragon*'s rounded bow was hewn with images of the Immortals and swallows. Giant eyes were carved on the prow, and the three huge sails flapped in the breeze. Magnificent. No wonder the boy had gawked.

Tien An and Xiao Hou were carrying chests and crates aboard, and she watched them from beneath the rim of her rough cap. The fragrance of sandalwood and jasmine drifted to her from the stack of cargo. More sailors disembarked to help, their brusque voices as loud as their thoughts. It was the boy's first time traveling so far across the sea, and his excitement was a bright whorl in his chest.

Ai Ling threw her spirit aboard the ship. Thirteen men and two boys composed the crew. Chen Yong was there, and she avoided him. She had once trespassed on his most private dreams and had promised herself never to intrude again. And she would keep her vow. It was too humiliating not to; she knew he loved his childhood sweetheart still. He couldn't know she was here. He'd send her home immediately, like she were an annoying little sister.

Ai Ling pressed her fingers to her chest, as if it would ease the dull ache. The *Gliding Dragon* would sail soon. Chen Yong was speaking to the captain and pilot inside the bridge near the stern. Anxious to glean the ship's layout, she delved into the pilot's mind. There were two different hatches that led to the compartments below. She would hide below deck until the ship sailed.

"Please, everyone, join me for the *Gliding Dragon*'s blessing," the captain said. Peng was his name. Ai Ling held a light touch on his spirit, on every spirit aboard the ship. She saw Chen Yong through Peng's eyes, so handsome in a deep scholar blue tunic, the stiff collar around his throat drawn closed with a single pearl button.

Someone grabbed her elbow and wrenched her

around, twisting her shoulder violently.

"What're you doing skulking about?" The brute squinted at her, his broad lips squashed together as if he had just sucked on a lemon. "A girl! You thinking of stealing?" His free hand slapped against her torso, her hips and breasts.

Her face flushed with anger. She tried to yank her arm free. Still connected to the men on the ship, she could smell the sandalwood incense wafting over the small altar laden with fruit and cups of wine. A golden effigy of the Queen Empress of Heaven sat in the middle of the altar, a serene smile etched on her face.

"They don't deal lightly with thieves!" He felt the hilt of her jeweled dagger beneath her tunic. "What's this?"

"Let go!" Ai Ling tried to punch him, but he swiped her arm out of the way. They struggled as he yanked at her tunic. She kicked him hard in the shin, but his grip only tightened. Ai Ling released her touch on the crew and threw a coil from her spirit to her attacker's. She possessed him instantly. His shin throbbed, but greed and excitement pumped through him. She enveloped his spirit in hers, forcing him to release her wrist.

Mouth slack, he stood motionless for a long moment. He had felt her intrusion. "Go away," she said. "Or I'll make you jump into the sea." She unsheathed her dagger

and pointed its tip at his throat. "And you can't swim."
Surprisingly, her hand did not shake.

He sneered, even as the stench of fear rolled from him.
"Sorceress!" He spit at her feet, then ran.

Ai Ling threw her spirit back toward the *Gliding Dragon*.

A sailor slit the throat of the chicken tucked beneath
his arm and drained its blood into a silver cup. He paced
the deck, chanting blessings.

Ai Ling ran toward the ship, but the gangplank had
been drawn. Firecrackers popped above, the acrid smoke
curling toward her. The ship slid from its berth as she
watched, aghast, cursing the stupid oaf who had delayed
her. Panic surged through her. Chen Yong would die if
she didn't get on board.

Her mind cast wide, she raced along the wharf and
skidded to a stop in front of a small fishing boat with a
single square cabin. Its wooden sides were so bleached
by the sun they appeared white. A fisherman was gnaw-
ing on the end of a pipe as he watched the *Gliding Dragon*
take to sea. He scratched his bearded chin, then glimpsed
her from the corner of his eye. "She's a beaut, yeah?"

"Can you overtake her?"

His bushy eyebrows lifted. "If we set sail now. Not
once she gains momentum in the open sea." He gave her
the once-over. "Why?"

She took the pouch of gold coins from her satchel.

The old fisherman extended his hand, and she plopped it in his palm. He peered inside and whistled. "Stolen?"

"No." She touched his spirit, knew his thoughts. His calloused hand bobbed, as he considered the weight. He would help her for that amount of coin—stolen or not.

"Hop on. We'd best move." She jumped on board, and he pulled anchor. He acted fast, adjusting the single sail to harness the wind. "She isn't full speed yet. Pray to the God of Luck we'll catch her."

"The God of Luck has mocked me all day," Ai Ling said.

"Aiyo. The Queen Empress of Heaven will look after us."

They sailed swiftly over the waves, but so did the *Gliding Dragon*. Ai Ling willed the tiny boat to go faster, even as she wobbled on unsteady legs. The larger ship left a trail of sea foam in its wake, and they chased it.

"Sit," the fisherman said.

She thudded onto a hard bench.

"What you after?"

"A friend." It hurt to say it. Her feelings for Chen Yong had not lessened during their time apart, as she had hoped. In truth, they had deepened with each polite letter she had received from him. And with all the ones she had written, divulging her feelings, her dreams, and her fears. Letters he would never read because she had never sent them.

He whistled again between his teeth. "Must be some friend."

Ai Ling's gaze never strayed from the *Gliding Dragon*. The wind whipped across her face, tearing strands of hair loose from its braid. "Faster," she said under her breath, as if the gods could hear her. "Faster."

As if they cared.

"Faster!" She shouted into the wind, and it swallowed her words. They slammed over a large swell, and the spray soaked her tunic. She wiped the salt water from her eyes as the fisherman chuckled.

They were gaining on the larger ship. Almost there. "They can't know I'm coming on board. They'll never let me stay, so close to shore."

He snorted. "I can get you near the ship. But on board? I didn't promise that. You'll have to climb, and you'll have one chance." He glanced at her dubiously. "Your arms look thin."

"I'll manage."

He huffed. She cast her spirit over the *Gliding Dragon*. Everyone was gathered at the stern, letting the giant sails catch the wind as the captain dictated his rules for the voyage. They—thank the goddess—appeared not to have noticed the little fishing vessel.

"Go to the front of the ship," she said.

He mumbled something about half-mad girls but guided his small boat near the *Gliding Dragon*'s bow. The ship loomed over the fishing boat, and the fisherman deftly maneuvered the rudder so they could stay near the ship without surging in front of it.

Ai Ling glanced up and gasped. "How do I climb on?" Her heart was hammering.

The old man nodded to a thick length of rope coiled on the bottom, the tip ending in a sharp four-pronged grapple hook. "Throw that."

"What?" She gaped at him. Her throwing was even worse than her embroidering. But she grabbed it anyway. The hook was much heavier than she would have guessed. She tossed it into the air, and it plunged into the sea.

"Aiyo!" the fisherman grumbled. "Try again. Quick!"

Ai Ling fished the hook from the water. She whispered a prayer, then threw the hook upward with a desperate strength she didn't know she had. It traced an arc against the pale blue sky and flew over the ship's railing.

She stared up at the *Gliding Dragon*. All was quiet. No one had noticed. The fisherman tugged on the rope and nodded. "I'm impressed." A smile creased his sun-darkened face. "Climb fast. Go. Go!"

She gripped the rope, catapulted off the deck, and tried to haul herself up the side of the ship. She didn't budge.

The fisherman growled. "Walk your feet up the side!"

He wrapped his arms around her waist and pushed her with astounding force. Ai Ling suppressed a cry and pulled with all her might, planting her cloth shoes firmly on the ship's side. "Hurry!" He gave her rump a shove for good measure.

With trembling arms, Ai Ling took agonizingly slow steps upward. The ship rocked across the sea, riding over a large wave so its bow slanted to the heavens. Ai Ling was flung backward and dangled helplessly, the sky filling her vision, then was bashed back into the ship's side. Unable to breathe, she squatted like a bruised toad against the ship as it slammed down, and the water surged up to meet her. Focus. One hand over the other, then shuffling with her feet. The rough rope bit into her slick palms. The crew would disperse soon. She began to shake with the effort and bit her lip hard. She would get on board this ship or die trying.

Mustering a final burst of energy, Ai Ling dragged herself over the side and somehow landed noiselessly,

limbs askew. She stood and quickly saluted the fisherman, then threw the hook overboard, her arms feeling
like overcooked noodles. She turned too fast and slid,
landing so hard her teeth clacked. She rolled behind a
rowboat and, when she rose to her hands and knees,
discovered she was smeared in the fresh chicken blood
that had been sprinkled to bless the ship. Ai Ling could
almost hear the God of Luck laughing. She crawled to
the hatch near the bow and crept below. Incredibly, no
one had seen her. Her tunic wet from the ocean and
streaked with chicken blood, she gripped the railing and
scanned the darkness for a hiding place. She couldn't
come out until the evening, until they were well offshore.

She cast herself into Captain Peng to catch a glimpse
of Chen Yong. They were studying the maps and discussing the journey. Chen Yong was taller, broader than
she remembered, with the same intensity in his amber
eyes. Her heart was in her throat when she forced herself to reel back. She had missed him so.

Throughout the day Ai Ling huddled below deck in
one of the dark cabins and drank warm water from her
flask. The constant roll of the sea had robbed her of any
appetite. Afraid she might fall asleep, she cast her spirit
around the ship, learning what she could.

She fingered the jade at her neck and ran her thumb over the carved spirit character. Her father had offered to buy her a new pendant, as this one had clouded over. But she had refused. No powerful spirit sent by the Immortals protected her any longer, but she still felt an attachment to the piece.

What had her father thought when he found her letter? Her parents had not chased her. Two days into her journey, and she had still been able to sense their spirits. Her father sent his love and strength, touching her mind like shining pinpricks. It was impossible for her mother to rein in her anxiety and agitation, but beneath their nettle was a surge of love for her rash, stubborn daughter. Ai Ling smiled to remember it.

She jumped to her feet. Yen, the pilot, was climbing down the steps. He walked along the corridor, past her dark compartment. Her heartbeat pounded hard in her ears.

Now he was coming back, and the compartment door opened, bringing a whiff of the sea and a halo of lantern light into the cramped space. The small cabin had a wide berth, a rough square table, and a lop-legged stool. She pressed herself against the wall behind the door, cursing the God of Luck for his tricks. Maps were stacked high on the table, and Yen riffled through them, his muscular body seeming to take up half the cabin. She fought the urge to squeeze her eyes shut.

Finally finding what he had been searching for, he turned to leave. He froze when he saw her. The small lantern swayed in his hand. She opened her mouth, but no sound came out.

"Who are you?" He stared, his flare of incredulity almost pinning her against the wall. He had dropped the map, and a dagger had replaced it. Around twenty-five years, he had high cheekbones and deep-set eyes, his features emphasized by the fact that his head was shaved. He set the lantern on the table and reached over to remove her cap. "A girl?" He shook his head in disbelief. "You'll have to come explain yourself to my captain."

The sun hovered low on the horizon, but Ai Ling still shaded her eyes when she emerged from below deck. All she could see was a glittering, endless blue. She lurched on unsteady legs toward the stern, with the pilot close behind, and the crew gawked in astonishment. Captain Peng stood outside the bridge. Although Xian, he had his hair cut short at the ears and trimmed close to his neck in the back, a hairstyle Ai Ling had never seen. He also wore strange clothing: tight black trousers, a white shirt with billowing sleeves, and a black sleeveless tunic over it.

His surprise was controlled, almost compartmentalized like the chambers of his magnificent ship. She felt his amusement and curiosity, his consternation. He strode forward to meet them. "I asked for a map, Yen."

The pilot handed him the parchment. "She was hiding in my cabin."

The crew had gathered around them, far enough away to be unobtrusive, but near enough to hear the conversation.

Peng scrutinized her. "I hope you can swim. Toss her overboard."

The men murmured in excitement.

"You jest!" Ai Ling's face felt cold and hot at once. They were leagues from shore.

"Ai Ling?" Chen Yong spoke from behind her.

Her skin tingled at the sound of his voice, and she turned, swallowing hard. He had pushed himself to the front of the crowd. Ai Ling met his golden gaze for just a moment. She felt as if her heart would leap from her chest.

"You know the stowaway?" Peng arched one dark brow.

Chen Yong was shaking his head. She wound her spirit tight within herself. Still, she felt his confusion, his anger. "I do. She's my . . . sister."

"Sister!" The captain flicked his dark eyes from Chen Yong to her. "I guess we can't throw you overboard, then?"

Chen Yong didn't respond, and she gritted her teeth. All this to save *him*?

"I am called Ai Ling." She tilted her chin.

"Why are you here, Ai Ling?" the captain asked.

It was a reasonable question, but so direct it caught her off guard. "I—I wanted to travel with . . . my brother. To help him find his birth father."

"Why didn't you tell me?" Chen Yong asked.

"You wouldn't have agreed." She glared at him.

"We've never had a girl on board, much less a stowaway," Peng said. "Very well. You can share your brother's cabin."

Feeling the heat creep up her cheeks, she stared at her feet.

"Yen, clear out your cabin and switch with Chen Yong. Yours has the wider berth," Peng said. Yen nodded, his face inscrutable. "Not exactly following the rules of decorum for brother and sister to share a cabin and bed, but you probably bathed in the same tub as babes."

She caught a spike of amusement from Peng and snapped her head up. But his expression was cold, revealing nothing.

"You'll help with tasks to earn your passage—like the rest of the crew."

"I can earn my keep." She made certain she spoke in a loud and steady voice.

"Indeed? I'll see you at dawn tomorrow, then."

Peng made to leave, then paused. "Go to the galley and get some ginger. You're looking slightly green." He wrinkled his nose. "And get yourself cleaned up. You smell like a butcher."

He did not wait for her reply, and the crew scattered like embroidery beads when the captain disappeared back into the bridge.

CHAPTER TWO

Three Hundred Years Past
In the Sixth Moon and Forty-first Year
of the Son of Heaven, Da Qian
Year Six Hundred and Thirty-three
Within the Palace of Fragrant Dreams

Every available space in the giant banquet hall was taken.
Guards dressed in black lined the walls, competing for
room with guests who had yet to find seats. It was an
invitation-only event to celebrate the Emperor's forty-
first year. Guards at the front entrance stopped those
who did not carry the gold invitation.

Zhong Ye had not been invited, but in his plain
gray tunic and trousers he passed as a servant easily
enough. It'd been almost two years since he'd joined
the Emperor's household as a palace eunuch, swear-
ing his fealty. A huge banquet had also been given for
the Son of Heaven's thirty-ninth-year celebration, but
Zhong Ye had been too busy emptying latrines, his

first official task. Even now he could recall the stench.

He had soon been promoted from latrine boy in the servant quarters to one in the private chambers of the concubines. From there he was made a palace messenger. He had been searching for lychees for a high-ranking concubine when he impressed the royal chef with his intelligence and demeanor. This was how Zhong Ye had become the recipe keeper, ensuring that all the necessary ingredients were at hand for the dozens of dishes served to the Emperor each day. Early in the morning, before dawn, and even late at night, near the thieving hour, he still made himself available to the whims of the concubines, often fetching treats from the kitchen or fabric and new embroidering thread from the royal sewing quarters.

Two years on four hours of sleep each night at best, and it was time to set his sights higher. Zhong Ye stood still, willing himself invisible behind the guests who all were finally seated, their chatter surging with the day's languid heat. Sweat collected at his nape, trickled down his back, but he didn't twitch.

A gong reverberated across the hall. Everyone stopped speaking in mid-sentence, but the rustling of silk, the snapping of fans, and coughs could still be heard. The Emperor entered, trailed by his main consort and eight guards. They paraded down a red carpet embroidered with golden dragons to a massive dining chair. He was attired in black stitched with crimson and gold designs and, despite the heat, wore a black and red cap encrusted with gold, rubies, and pearls.

Zhong Ye followed the Emperor with his eyes. He'd learned much about the Son of Heaven's routine through his time in the royal kitchen. He knew his likes and dislikes from gossip among the concubines. His Empress, dressed in deep purple, stepped daintily up to the throne beside him, her head held high despite her heavy bejeweled cap. She had given the Emperor one son and one daughter, but both were pale and meek, their voices as thin as their faces. Zhong Ye knew she was trying hard to become with child again.

The gong sounded twice, loud enough that he felt it in his teeth. He allowed himself one full breath. The stout banquet master stood by the Emperor's throne, intoning salutations and blessings for a most prosperous forty-first year in this earthly realm. He had quick hands and was known to fondle handmaids throughout the palace. All the girls tried to steer clear of him. The banquet master flourished those hands now as he spoke.

Finally, he stilled, drawing his arms to his side, and the gong sounded three more times. He gave a sudden clap, and servers emerged from side entrances and began placing dishes covered with lacquered trays before the guests. Zhong Ye wove between them, along the length of the opulently laid table, toward the Emperor's chair. He slammed into a wall of armored chests several feet from his destination.

"You're not the Emperor's server," one guard growled.

"No, but I have reason to believe that at least one of his dishes has been poisoned," Zhong Ye said in a steady voice.

The guard's mouth dropped open, and in three strides Zhong Ye was beside the Emperor, who had just picked up his solid gold eating sticks to try the marinated cold cuts. The guard whispered in his ear. The Emperor cocked his head, cast his eyes in Zhong Ye's direction. He gave a slight nod, and the guard waved his hand. Zhong Ye dropped to his knees beside the Emperor's ornate dining chair.

"Your most humble servant, Your Majesty," Zhong Ye said in a clear voice, so he could be heard. He was crouched low against the ground, and the din of festival guests seemed especially loud.

"What's your name?" the Emperor asked.

"Zhong Ye, Your Majesty."

"And you think my food has been poisoned?" The Emperor's boots were also embroidered with pearls and rubies. His foot shifted as he spoke.

"Yes, Your Majesty."

"All the dishes served to me are tested by a taster." He tapped one jeweled boot. A hush spread among the guests closest to the Emperor; the clink of eating sticks against porcelain was like musical notes.

"Get him up," the Emperor said brusquely.

Zhong Ye felt himself being pulled by the stiff collar of his tunic, the guard clutching a handful of his queue at the same time.

"You imply that my dish was poisoned somehow between being tested by my taster and arriving at my table?" Silence rippled like a wave across the enormous hall.

Zhong Ye clenched both hands, felt the slick of his palms. He had to have timed this perfectly; it was his only chance. "Yes, Your Majesty. The foreign enemy has an expert assassin within your court. I bid you with my own life to take caution." He would have fallen to his knees again if the guard hadn't gripped him by one arm.

"Very well then. Prove your claim." The Emperor picked up a slice of beef tongue and whisked it in the soy and chili sauce. Gasps and murmurs rose until the Emperor slanted one look at his guests. The hall quieted. Zhong Ye gulped, his throat much too dry, as the Son of Heaven fed him the piece of beef tongue as tenderly as a mother.

It was delicious, the perfect mixture of salt and spice, with a hint of sweet and sour, garlic and chives. He chewed as if it were his last earthly act. The Empress pressed one hand against her delicate mouth, and the other gripped the curved armrest. He swallowed and felt his stomach grumble. He hadn't eaten since before daybreak.

The Emperor leaned back in his chair and crossed his arms, his silk sleeves swishing. "Release him." He nodded at the guard. "How do you feel?"

Zhong Ye unclenched his fists and bowed his head. "Perhaps I was wrong—" His knees buckled as heat blazed from his chest outward to each limb. The world turned black, but he could still hear. His face was pressed against the cold stone floor, and hands grabbed at him. Voices sounded like distant echoes.

"Take him to the royal physician," the Emperor said.

It was the last thing he heard.

Zhong Ye opened his eyes to a blurred world, light and dark spots skittering across his vision. He squeezed his eyes shut again, his head spinning.

"Drink this." A man's soft voice. The physician brought a steaming bowl to Zhong Ye's lips, and the bitter stench of medicinal herbs filled his nostrils. He would have jerked his head away if he'd had the strength. He took a sip. The dark brew hit the back of his throat, and he gagged, but he forced himself to swallow. He had to be back in perfect health as soon as possible, and the royal physician knew what he was doing.

"More. Drink it all." Zhong Ye opened his eyes and looked at the physician. He had a thin face, and he squinted back at him with curious intensity. "You're fortunate to be alive. Most victims who ingest dragon's rue do not live to see the next day."

It had gone as Zhong Ye had planned. The maiden's slipper, a wildflower with blooms shaped to inspire its name, mimicked the symptoms of dragon's rue, but merely put its victim out for a few days, not forever. From his studies of herbs and medicine, Zhong Ye knew the only difference between the two was that the maiden's slipper increased one's heart rate before consciousness was lost, while dragon's rue slowed one's heart until it stopped. He had forced down a cup of hot tea brewed with crushed maiden's slipper flowers before the banquet, hoping that it would take effect at the right time.

"You're fortunate I was at hand to attend you." The physician placed the empty bowl on a lacquered table beside the bed.

"I'm grateful. I owe you my life, Royal Physician—"

"Kang. Royal Physician Kang." He leaned over to touch Zhong Ye's brow with the back of his hand. "You're not as hot as before. This is good news. Rest."

Zhong Ye wondered how long he had been unconscious. He didn't want the Emperor to forget him and his act of bravery.

When Zhong Ye next awoke, both his vision and head had cleared. A lotus-shaped glass lantern sat on the table beside him, and the summer air did not stir. He struggled to sit up, wiggling himself against the cushions he rested on. He blinked into the dark corners of the sparse chamber. The window panels were shaded so it was difficult to tell what time of day it was. He swallowed, the taste of the bitter medicine still in his mouth.

A panel scraped against the stone floor, and he shifted his arm closer to the lantern, the nearest weapon. Zhong Ye looked down at the dirt brown tunic someone had changed him into. His legs were bare beneath the thin blanket.

He heard the rustle of a robe before he saw the low light catch the glint of gold and silver embroidery. The Son of Heaven settled on the stool by the bed, one foot casually propped on a low wooden rung. The Emperor rubbed one smooth cheek with a hand, head slanted, and studied him, his dark eyes shrewd. The Emperor was not dumb, just too easily distracted by his vices, drink and women.

"Well done, Zhong Ye. I hope you're feeling better?" He raised his dark brows, and Zhong Ye wondered if he truly cared.

"I am, Your Majesty. If it weren't for Royal Physician Kang, I would be roaming the underworld."

"Yes, he tends to me and is the best. I owe you that much, after forcing you to eat the beef tongue." The Emperor smiled. "I had your records pulled to learn more about you. It's important for me to know the history of the man who saved my life."

"I come from a very humble background, Your Majesty."

"Farmers. Not the most clever of people—" The Emperor paused, and anger seized Zhong Ye. His father's greatest possession was his dull-witted oxen. Zhong Ye had spent the last seven years of his life trying to escape being a farmer's son.

"But the backbone of our kingdom," the Emperor added.

Zhong Ye exhaled and nodded. "My family works hard."

"Tell me what you know of this conspiracy to murder me," the Emperor said. His hands were in his lap now, the fingertips pressed together.

"There was a new boy in the kitchen these past two weeks. Looking not more than twelve years but not acting at all like a boy. Everywhere I turned, he was beneath my feet. I found him skulking in the storage room one morning when I was taking inventory." Zhong Ye's voice was hoarse, and the Emperor waved one hand. A petite handmaid emerged from the shadows, cupping a small bowl. She proffered it, and Zhong Ye took a sip and couldn't stop himself from grimacing at the taste.

"That morning the kitchen was in an uproar preparing for Your Majesty's banquet. The boy slipped out when he thought no one saw, and I followed. He ran quick as a rabbit into the Garden of Tranquility. I saw one of those foreigners from across the northern mountains hand him something. Something small."

"Did you catch a good glimpse of the man?"

"No. He was draped in long folds of dress like those from Alban, a cowl drawn over his face. They exchanged few words, and the boy darted back toward the kitchens." Zhong Ye took another long draft of the medicinal brew, the warmth zinging a path through him. "I wanted to chase after the foreigner, but it was near banquet time, and I feared what the boy held in his hand, what he might attempt."

"How did he slip the poison into the food?" The

Emperor leaned close, and Zhong Ye could smell the liquor on his breath. "How was it that my taster was unaffected?"

"The boy was nowhere to be found when I returned to the royal kitchen. I watched the taster test your first two dishes, and when he approved, the chef plated them. But the tray was knocked over by a kitchen hand I didn't recognize. The boy I had been following reappeared and was asked to clean the mess, while the other who had knocked over the food was taken out to be whipped. When I saw them replate your food, I felt unease." Zhong Ye, exhausted from speaking, slumped against the cushions. He had hired the "suspicious" boy himself, paid him to appear and then disappear. The knocked-over dishes were pure luck; he couldn't have asked for a better scenario.

"You mean to tell me you risked ruining my banquet on a hunch? That you actually saw nothing?" He could feel the Emperor's eyes on him.

Zhong Ye closed his own, knowing he looked as weak as he felt. "I don't question my intuition, Your Majesty. I've survived and advanced this far because of it."

"But what if you were wrong?"

"It was worth the risk. My humiliation would be nothing. I was scared for Your Majesty's life." Zhong Ye's voice was barely audible now, and it was no act.

He was asleep before he heard the Emperor's response.

Zhong Ye strode down a long hallway lit with blazing lanterns. Anticipation rushed through him, and he quickened his pace. The Emperor had promoted him the previous day, his first day back in full health. He glanced down to admire his new robe, a deep sapphire blue embroidered with yellow, befitting his new rank.

He paused in front of a red paneled door, accented in gold and carved with seven fierce dragons. Four guards flanked each side of the door. Zhong Ye knocked and bowed his head. The panel opened after a moment, and a giggling girl peered up at him.

"It's Master Zhong, Your Majesty," she called.

The concubine jutted a dainty chin toward the main chamber, indicating that he should enter. Her brocaded robe slipped to expose a creamy shoulder—not by accident. Zhong Ye bowed lower and lower still, until he glimpsed the concubine's silk slippers peeping from beneath her sleep dress. Foolish girl, to flirt with him with the Emperor so close.

"Hurry!" The Emperor's voice was deep and impatient.

Zhong Ye walked with quick, confident steps into the Emperor's pleasure chamber. It had been specially created for his dalliances. The Emperor could take his women anywhere, of course. And it wasn't uncommon for him to indulge in the imperial gardens, barge in upon a handmaid's chamber, even corner servants in the kitchen. The only place that remained sacred was the Temple of the Sun.

He was sprawled naked on the massive bed. Sumptuous brocades hung from the ceiling along its sides, and star-shaped brass lanterns cast a warm, muted glow around the chamber. Two concubines pressed themselves against the Emperor, each seeking his attention. He was no longer in his prime, but still strong, virile. He pushed both women off and smiled, his eyes heavy-lidded from drink and pleasure.

"Congratulations, Zhong Ye. You've caught my attention, and I hope I wasn't wrong to promote you."

Zhong Ye fell to his knees, pressing his brow to the ornate rug. "I am honored, Your Majesty."

"As well you should be. Remind me, boy, whereabouts did you start? I hadn't seen you until this past year."

He kept his head pressed to the ground. "As latrine boy, Your Majesty."

The Emperor barked a laugh. "Latrine boy! Well done! Perhaps one day you can rise high enough to clean the Son of Heaven's shit." A deep chortle and the resounding sound of flesh being slapped. "Rise," the Emperor said.

Zhong Ye leaped to his feet. One of the concubines was pouting, rubbing her full hip. He could smell the Emperor's deep musk of pine, citrus, and sweat. Zhong Ye didn't let his nostrils flare, kept his face a neutral mask.

"I'm bored with my favorites. Find me a new girl." Unabashed in his nakedness, he leaned back into the cushions. "Someone special."

Zhong Ye bowed, never letting his eyes stray from the Emperor's face.

"You're cockless." The Emperor sneered. "Can I trust you to still have good taste in women?"

Zhong Ye bowed deeper. "You won't be disappointed, Your Majesty."

Zhong Ye flew through the corridors, out into the night air, heart pounding hard against his chest. This was his chance, his opportunity presented so soon. He couldn't make a mistake. His mind raced, thinking of all the concubines he knew, the new ones, the young ones, some barely fifteen years. The older ones, at nineteen or twenty, more refined, confident. More womanly.

He burst into the bedchamber of one of the concubines, Mei Gui. She sat at her dressing table, a handmaid behind her, brushing her long hair. Both women turned to him with wide eyes.

The quarters were small; she was a low-ranking concubine, unlikely to ever cross paths with the Emperor. Still, the women had decorated the chamber with deep purples and opulent greens. The faint scent of roses filled the chamber.

Mei Gui stood. "Master Zhong." Her voice was small, trailed off. News of his promotion had already spread among the concubines, just as he had orchestrated.

"Strip."

Her mouth formed a circle.

"The Emperor is asking for a new lover tonight. Let me see you!"

The handmaid quickly drew her mistress's robe from her shoulders and folded it over a slender arm. Zhong Ye met her eyes for a brief moment, before she dropped her gaze to the floor. Distracted, he shook himself.

"Arms raised." He gestured with an impatient hand for her to turn.

Mei Gui had been clutching herself, covering her breasts. At his command, her porcelain face paled even more. She stretched her arms and rotated: it was almost comical. She was nearly eighteen years. Her eyes were light brown, slender and tilted slightly upward. Her face flushed with embarrassment, and the color spread to her neck, down to her chest. Alluring.

"When was your last monthly letting?"

Her mouth dropped again.

"Two weeks past, Master Zhong," the handmaid said. "She is ripe."

Mei Gui's handmaid was petite, curvaceous, with wide-set eyes in a heart-shaped face. Stunning, really. Why hadn't she been chosen as a concubine?

"Your mistress is a virgin?"

Mei Gui nodded. At least she knew that much.

"Has she been taught?" He directed the question at the handmaid.

"Yes, master."

He narrowed his eyes and deliberately said nothing.

"By me, sir. I was a song girl before I entered the palace."

No wonder. A used girl, not worthy of the Emperor.

"Taught well then, I hope. If Mei Gui gains the Emperor's favor, we shall rise in status with her."

Zhong Ye grabbed the robe from the handmaid and threw it back on Mei Gui. "What are you called?" he asked the handmaid in a brisk tone.

"Silver Phoenix, master." She bowed elegantly, bringing to mind an orchid swaying in the breeze.

CHAPTER THREE

Ai Ling followed Chen Yong through a cramped passageway into the galley, which was bigger than she would have guessed, with a large rectangular dining table and crooked stools scattered around it. The cook, a gaunt man with a sun-wizened face, offered her a hot brew of sweetened ginger. She sipped the drink, grimacing at the spiciness of the root, and avoided Chen Yong's eyes. His anger and bewilderment were as sharp as the ginger.

"Let me show you to the cabin," Chen Yong said finally, when she was done.

She trailed behind him. Yen was just leaving, carrying a large stack of books. He nodded to them without speaking. The cabin had been cleared of his belongings.

"What are you doing here?" Chen Yong asked, before he even shut the door.

"I dreamed of Li Rong," she blurted.

He sat down on a small stool. "What?"

"He came to me and said—told me to travel with you."

"But why?" His features were hard, guarded; his amber eyes, dark.

"He said you were in danger." She knew how ridiculous she sounded, how superstitious.

"You came because of a dream?"

"It felt real. I was worried for you!" She wanted to kick the stool, remembering how terrified she had been for Chen Yong when she had woken. The dread had crushed her for days, really until she had touched his spirit this morning.

His expression softened. "Did he appear . . . well?"

"He did."

Chen Yong turned his face away. It still hurt her, too, to think of his brother.

"Your parents let you come?"

She clasped her hands and stared at the bare wall behind him. "I left them a letter."

"They'll be sick with worry," he said. "This journey is long and dangerous. No place for—"

"A girl?" She let herself become angry, so she couldn't

feel anything else. "You seem to forget our last journey together." Her tone was sharp. This wasn't at all how she had imagined their reunion would be.

Chen Yong winced, but it was fleeting. He stood, and there was no space in the cabin to back away. "I'd feel responsible if anything happened to you." His voice was low.

He was close enough for her to smell the faint lemon scent of his skin. "It was my choice to come. If you're somehow in danger, I . . ." she stammered, not knowing how to finish.

The corner of his mouth twitched, though he would not meet her eyes. He wasn't pleased to see her. She was a burden.

He tilted his head as if remembering something. "I never wrote you the name of the ship that I would be traveling on."

"No. Li Rong told me in my dream," she said. "The *Gliding Dragon*, and the day that you would sail."

Captain Peng was already seated at the head of the table when they returned to the galley. Yen sat to his right, and Lao Lu, the cook, was beside the pilot. The rest of the crew had eaten earlier.

The captain rose to his feet, and the other two men

followed suit. "Ah, our guests have arrived. How are you feeling, Ai Ling?" He pulled out the stool to his right. She touched him with her power and gathered nothing but amusement again. Feeling a little embarrassed, she walked to the table on rubbery legs and managed to sit down without incident. Chen Yong sat beside her.

"Lao Lu has prepared steamed fish and stewed beef along with chicken soup. A celebration for smooth winds thus far." He raised his wine cup.

Lao Lu was a good cook, to judge by the mouthwatering scents that rose from the bowls and plates. Ai Ling searched for tea and, finding none, lifted her wine cup as well. She sipped when the men did, felt the unfamiliar taste of the wine cut a quick path to her stomach.

She kept sneaking glances at the captain as she ate. His hands were well groomed, tan from the sun. His clothes were impeccable. Peng caught her eye, and she hid her face in her soup bowl. The broth was warm, and it soothed her. It reminded her of home.

"Have you studied Jiang as your brother has?" Captain Peng asked.

Ai Ling swallowed too fast and put her bowl down. "No."

"You'll take lessons in Jiang with us each morning then." Peng wiped his mouth with a silk handkerchief.

"After your assigned tasks." He leaned forward, and both Ai Ling and Chen Yong straightened on their stools. "I don't mean to be harsh, but I run a disciplined ship. It would set a poor example if you did nothing after sneaking aboard."

She pulled her shoulders back. "I understand."

The merriment in Peng's dark eyes didn't reach his mouth. "You'll help on deck each morning at dawn. And anything Lao Lu requires of you in the galley. The emptying of the chamber pots"—he sat back in the only proper chair at the table—"has already been assigned to one of the boys."

Chen Yong ducked his head to hide a smile, and she nearly crossed her arms in a show of indignation but refused to give either man the satisfaction. "Certainly."

"You may join us after finishing your tasks," Peng said.

"Do you all speak Jiang?" She looked from Yen to Lao Lu.

The reticent pilot nodded, and Lao Lu shrugged his thin shoulders. "Enough to get by, miss. I can haggle for a better price at the markets."

"One hour each morning," Peng said, as if the matter were settled. "What can you teach me in return?" He raised a dark brow, and Ai Ling looked away. She could sense his mirth and began reciting a poem about plum blossoms in the snow in her mind.

"I can offer to teach shuen," said Chen Yong.

"Shuen. Really?" Yen leaned forward, interested in the conversation for the first time.

Chen Yong poured the pilot more wine. "My family is known for its ability in the art."

"That seems a more than fair exchange," Peng said, lifting his cup. "And what about you, Ai Ling? Will you learn shuen with us?"

"Why not?" Then, remembering she was supposed to be Chen Yong's sister, she added, "My father only taught my brothers." She wouldn't be intimidated; she had chosen to come on this journey. Peng toasted her and smiled.

Ai Ling prepared for bed in the small latrine. It was so cramped she could barely turn around. The smell was already too strong; what would it be like after two months? She hurriedly rubbed coarse salt over her teeth, wet her washcloth with water, and wiped her face and neck. She yearned for a bath.

She leaned into the sway of the ship as she shuffled back down the passageway and almost convinced herself that she was becoming used to it. She pushed the rough cabin door open and caught sight of Chen Yong's bare back. He was stretching his arms over his head, and the wavering light flickered across the taut muscles of his shoulders and biceps. She froze.

Chen Yong quickly crouched and retrieved his sleep tunic from his trunk. "Knock next time?" His expression was unreadable as he pulled the garment on.

Ai Ling nodded.

"Could you close the door?"

She stared at it in surprise, then shut it.

He crossed his arms as he surveyed the tiny cabin. "I could sleep on the floor." The double berth was barely wide enough for two, but it took up most of the cabin. There was a small gap beside it. She didn't think he could lie flat in the narrow wedge of floor between the bed and the wall.

"No. We can share," she said. She climbed onto the right side of the berth, which was pushed flush against a wall, and lay down, drawing her soft blanket from home up to her chin. She smelled the familiar scent and was grateful.

Chen Yong snuffed the lantern and eased into bed beside her. Her entire body flushed. Their shoulders just touched, and his arm pressed warmly against hers. She could feel the rise and fall of his chest in the dark.

"Do you truly believe I'm in danger?" he asked.

"The dream was so real. I woke with a strong sense of

urgency. I had to come." Her words sounded thin. Why *had* she come? "I'm sorry," she whispered.

He shifted, his thigh brushing hers. The air seemed to crackle between them, and he tensed, became dead still. "We need to be vigilant then."

Ai Ling felt light-headed.

"Your power can help warn us of any danger?"

She turned a hot cheek toward his voice.

"Is it the same as before?" he asked.

"Stronger," she whispered. "Too strong."

He was silent for so long she began to wonder if he had fallen asleep. "A peaceful evening," he finally said.

She almost laughed but sensed he had wanted to say more. The unspoken words hung between them. She wished she knew what they were as she wound herself tight, away from the brightness of his spirit. "A peaceful evening," she murmured.

She stared wide-eyed into the dark, trying to draw deep breaths to slow her hammering heart. Chen Yong's breathing matched her own. She closed her eyes, and the image of his bare back bloomed beneath her lids.

Dear goddess.

She prayed to the Goddess of Serenity for sleep, and in answer the ship rocked and Chen Yong was thrown against her, pinning her to the wall.

He cursed.

She blinked; a gasp caught in her throat.

He edged from her as the ship rolled the other way. "Sorry," he mumbled.

They didn't speak another word that night, although she remained awake for a long time after.

Somehow Ai Ling did finally fall asleep. When she woke, she was lying in the exact same position, her hands folded over her stomach and her arm still touching Chen Yong's. There was no way of telling if day had arrived. But footsteps in the passageway outside and the shutting of doors let her know that the crew had already risen.

She wondered if Chen Yong had woken. "Is it day yet?" he asked in a thick voice, answering her question.

"The crew seems to be up," she whispered for some reason.

He slipped off the bed, and the cabin door opened, letting in dim light from the lanterns in the corridor. He brought a lantern into their cabin in exchange for the extinguished one hanging in the corner, then grabbed some clothes from his trunk.

"I'll change in the latrine," he said.

She sighed as he closed the door behind him. This

would take some getting used to. She dressed in peach-colored trousers and tunic, long sleeved to protect her from the sun and sea salt. She loosened and brushed her hair, running the wooden comb through it again and again. Her mind wandered, and she heard a crew member ask in the galley if they'd be given more dried beef for breakfast. She felt his hunger and became aware of her own. To clear her mind she recited a stanza of poetry, her favorite one about a lotus in bloom on a deep pond.

Eventually she eased the narrow door open and peeked outside. It was quiet. Chen Yong and Captain Peng were still eating in the galley when she arrived. Lao Lu filled a bowl with hot soy milk for her and was about to place a steamed bun on a chipped plate when Peng raised a hand. "She's late," he said. "We'll go directly into lessons in Jiang after your tasks, Ai Ling."

She gulped the soy milk, telling herself her face felt hot from the steam rising from the bowl. It was past dawn when she climbed onto the deck. Tendrils of mist were just beginning to wither, and the air was cold and damp against her skin. Xiao Hou was pushing a wide flat broom across the wet deck. "We've already scrubbed the deck," he said.

Sailors stood below each of the three masts, wrangling with lines. They shouted at one another, synchronizing their motions as they set the enormous sails. Xiao Hou followed her gaze. "My pa said he'd teach me when I'm bigger."

She returned his toothy grin, his cheeks rounded with obvious pride. "I'll be on time tomorrow." Her stomach growled in reprimand. It wouldn't do to be denied another meal.

The boy showed her how to push the broom toward the sides of the ship, then left her to the task. The Sea of Seven Stars spanned forever. It seemed nothing existed in this world except the ship and the endless water. Ai Ling paused when she finished her task to admire the view. The sunrise had cast the clouds in a deep golden pink. I've always wanted to travel, explore the world, she thought, then blinked. It was as if the notion had dropped into her head from the ether. *Had she?* Her scalp tingled.

Xiao Hou scuttled back and took the long-handled broom, startling her. He scanned the deck and finally nodded in approval. "Not bad for a first go," he said.

She smiled. "Am I dismissed?"

He cocked his head, in a gesture that reminded her entirely of her cat Taro. She almost expected his ear to twitch. "I s'pose. See you tomorrow, miss."

She bowed. "At dawn."

She climbed below deck and returned to the galley. Only Peng and Chen Yong, both engrossed in books, remained at the large table. Peng barely glanced up when she entered. "Done? Lao Lu was kind enough to wash up for you today. So we can begin our lesson."

She turned to the cook and smiled gratefully. He gave a curt nod. Ai Ling tried to catch Chen Yong's eye, but he didn't acknowledge her. He had not spoken to her since their brief exchange that morning.

Peng asked Lao Lu to bring a pot of hot tea. "Chen Yong is advanced in his knowledge of the language. We can converse during our free time. It's important you understand elementary phrases at least." He unbuttoned the silver clasps on his cuffs and rolled up his sleeves.

Lao Lu returned with tea, along with a small tray holding a long white feather, a corked ceramic pot, and sheaths of thick parchment. Captain Peng picked up the feather and uncorked the ceramic pot. "The Jiang don't use calligraphy brushes to write. They use quills." He dipped the feather into the ink. "Their language is formed by twenty-eight letters, strung together to make words."

He scratched in a neat hand on the thick parchment. "This means a peaceful morning."

Ai Ling stared at the small scribbles stacked next to one another and furrowed her brow.

Peng pronounced the phrase for her, enunciating slowly. "You say it," he told her. He spoke the phrase again, and she watched his lips purse together, heard the strange rolling sound of his tongue.

She tried to repeat it.

A smile flitted across his mouth; then he cleared his throat. "The roll of the tongue is the hardest to learn. We don't speak like this in Xian."

And so they spent the next hour. Peng proved to be a good and patient tutor, and soon she had the twenty-eight letters and their sounds memorized. Chen Yong's head was bent over a text the entire time. They ended their first lesson with a conversation in Jiang. Amazed by Chen Yong's knowledge of the language, Ai Ling couldn't help staring at him.

Even the captain nodded in admiration. "I know you've been learning for six months, but your pronunciation is truly impressive. Well done." He rose from his chair as Yen entered to whisper in his ear.

Peng bowed to them. "I'll see you this afternoon for our lesson in shuen, Chen Yong? You'll be joining us as you promised?" He slanted a look her way, and Ai Ling recited the Jiang phrase for "thank you" over and over in her mind. She managed a small nod of her head.

"I think you'll also make great improvements in the language over the next months, Ai Ling," Peng said.

"Thank you for teaching us," Chen Yong replied.

"Of course. It helps me to practice as well." He smiled and left them.

He must be wed. But if so, where was his wife? She shook her head slightly when she realized where her thoughts ran.

They converged near the bow an hour after the midday meal. Ai Ling had thought it would just be the three of them, but the pilot, Yen, was also there, along with five other crew members.

"There are many interested in learning shuen, Chen Yong," said Peng. "And your family's reputation has traveled far."

Chen Yong bowed low to everyone. "It's an honor."

He began by showing them the basic Horse Riding stance. He had pulled a thin bamboo rod from nowhere and tapped each person on the thigh as he walked past. "Wider stance. Drop lower." He strolled the deck with confident ease, the dazzling sunlight catching the hints of deep bronze in his black hair.

Chen Yong paused in front of her. He tucked the bamboo beneath his arm and assessed her in silence. She forced herself to remain steady. Her thighs began to burn. "What is it?" she asked through gritted teeth.

To her annoyance, he didn't reply. Instead, he walked a slow circle around her. She clutched her spirit tight, and his gaze rippled like pinpricks across her body. Finally, he stood in front of her again. She clenched her jaw, refusing to rise a fraction, even as her legs began to tremble.

"It's perfect." He met her eyes for the first time that day, jolting warmth to her cheeks. He tapped the deck with the bamboo rod. "Show me how long you can hold it," he said.

Chen Yong asked everyone else to rise and began demonstrating the first basic punch, Jade Serpent Steals Breath.

Was he punishing her? Ai Ling's legs began to bounce like a puppet's. She closed her eyes for a moment, lifted her chin to catch the sea zephyr across her face. The salt tang mixed with her own sweat.

"She's risen a bit," one of the boys shouted.

She flinched, swallowed a nasty retort.

Chen Yong threw her a glance. "Lower. Sit back into it."

She went deeper into the stance. Sweat rolled from her hairline, trickled down her back. She tried to distract herself by watching Chen Yong as he punched his fist in one fluid pantherlike motion. The other men tried, but they looked like bumbling kittens. He strolled across the deck, adjusting the height of the men's arms, even how they formed their fists.

The ship rose over a large swell, and she fell backward, thumping onto her rear.

Chen Yong turned and smiled, amid laughter from the men behind him. She would kill him! "Well done, Ai Ling. Join us to learn this first technique."

She pushed herself to her feet and walked on wobbling legs to the end of the line, standing next to the boy who had snitched on her. He grinned up at her, and she narrowed her eyes. She would show this little Yam Head.

Zhong Ye peered through the peephole into the Emperor's chamber. The Emperor was on top of Mei Gui, his body obliterating hers. He saw her feet, the toenails painted crimson, and one pale hand with fingernails the same color clenching the Emperor's shoulder. Zhong Ye grimaced in distaste, but still felt a faint tingling, from phantom parts he no longer had. He smiled wryly.

Mei Gui had managed to keep the Emperor's interest, and Zhong Ye had been relieved. Silver Phoenix had trained her mistress well. He felt an unexpected rush of pleasure when he thought about the handmaid.

He forced his mind back to the task at hand. It wasn't like him to let it wander. The Emperor had rolled off Mei Gui, and she rose to pour him a cup of wine. He hoped she would be with child after a few more visits. When the concubine returned to the massive bed, the Emperor was already snoring. She stood at his side, her expression unreadable.

Zhong Ye wondered what she felt, what she thought. Her sole purpose in life was to please the Emperor, hope that she made herself alluring enough to catch his eye, to be bedded by him, to have strong sons. She and Zhong Ye both had sacrificed themselves in different ways to gain the Son of Heaven's favor.

Mei Gui shivered and hugged herself. He took in her nakedness with detachment. He had been propositioned before by concubines, beautiful women who, unlike Mei Gui, would never be brought to the Emperor's bed-chamber. He had always deftly demurred, believing those entanglements to be more bad than good for his ambitions.

Zhong Ye tilted his head back and then from side to side. He had been standing for at least an hour. And he would remain there until Mei Gui was excused. She knew what she had to do: wake the Emperor and seduce him. He wondered how much longer he'd have to crouch in the secret passageway, his brow pressed to the wall, his thoughts always wandering to Silver Phoenix.

Zhong Ye was woken by the sound of the Emperor's lovemaking. He had no inkling what time it was until he peered into the bedchamber and took note of the wan daylight filtering through the lattice windows.

They were done, and as if on cue, a sharp rap shook the doors. The Emperor said, "Enter," and a handmaid slid the panel aside, revealing for a moment the guards in the corridor. How did they enjoy safeguarding this particular chamber? At least they did their job in shifts, Zhong Ye thought, rubbing his sore neck. But one didn't rise to power in shifts.

The girl entered with her head bowed; she held a lacquered tray laden with fruit. Another handmaid, indistinguishable from the first in posture and dress, followed, carrying a tray with tea. Zhong Ye smelled jasmine and was thirsty and hungry at once.

The Emperor rose, and a third handmaid wrapped around his shoulders a silk robe of imperial yellow, embroidered with the symbol for longevity. He took the opportunity to pull the girl to him, pressing against her.

She looked down and stood still, no fool was she. Zhong Ye contained a smile. The Emperor's vice was obvious. The way to control him, and most likely his downfall, would be through his weakness for carnal pleasures.

Mei Gui was dismissed after she had fed the Emperor fresh slices of mango and pineapple. The Emperor liked her well enough to return the favor, and they sipped tea together at a small round table, the Emperor praising her for her beauty and Mei Gui smiling and looking demure at the right moments.

Zhong Ye was relieved when she was finally sent away. He arrived outside the Emperor's reception chamber as a guard ushered Mei Gui out.

"Good timing," the guard said in a gruff voice.

Zhong Ye took her by the arm. She was swathed again in the robe that he had swaddled her in the night before. She smelled of sweat and sex mixed with the delicate perfume of roses. He swallowed and tried not to wrinkle his nose. If he was exhausted, how did the girl feel?

"Well done, Mei Gui," he said as they walked through corridors lit with golden lanterns. "The Emperor is pleased with you. If we are fortunate, he'll continue to ask for you."

"Thank you for choosing me, Master Zhong. I've done my best, remembering everything that Silver Phoenix has taught me," she said in a quiet, determined voice. The determination was what surprised him. Perhaps she was more clever than he had given her credit for.

He led the concubine back to her quarters. Silver Phoenix was waiting. She took Mei Gui's hand and guided her into the bedchamber. Zhong Ye followed, although he had no reason to. Their business was done.

"Did you have any further need for us, Master Zhong?" Silver Phoenix asked as she sat her mistress in front of the mirrored dressing table. "My mistress has had a long night."

Zhong Ye almost snorted. "Indeed. She did admirably. The Emperor has been pleased, as am I. You taught her well." A hint of a smile lingered at the corner of Silver Phoenix's small, full mouth. He caught himself staring. "May I speak with you alone in the reception hall, Silver Phoenix?"

She turned to her mistress, who nodded, and they stepped out into the cramped hall together.

"Yes?" Silver Phoenix tilted her face to his, and he saw how dark her eyes were: nearly obsidian.

He was flustered and caught off guard. Beautiful women surrounded him, but none had ever held his attention until now. "I—I wanted to thank you for working so well with your mistress. The closer she becomes to the

Emperor, the more favor will be bestowed on us all—"

She raised a hand, and the scent of jasmine drifted to him. "I understand very clearly, Master Zhong. This is my life's work now, to help my mistress rise in rank. Can I count you as an ally?"

Zhong Ye laughed, he was so surprised. "As long as you heed my advice. I think we all want the same thing."

She inclined her head, the silver ornaments pinned to her thick braids catching the morning light. "A peaceful morning, Master Zhong."

It was only after she had disappeared back into the bedchamber that Zhong Ye realized he had been dismissed.

The court had convened for more than two hours, and though protocol dictated that each courtier, adviser, and diplomat stand still in the presence of the Son of Heaven, Zhong Ye heard more shuffling and mumblings as the morning dragged on. Only two months had passed since he had been promoted to adviser, and already his position had shifted from the back of the hall to the middle. The Emperor had been pleased with Mei Gui, and their trysts had continued.

Zhong Ye surveyed the throne hall now. Red columns throughout the massive chamber supported the high wood-beamed ceiling. A crimson carpet shot from the carved dragon doors to the throne, which was raised on a dais. The Emperor sat on his elaborate gold lacquered chair, drumming his fingers on the armrest. An ornate screen, gilded in gold with a clouds-and-lotus motif, towered behind him. Zhong Ye wondered if the Emperor had allowed anyone to hide there that morning, to eavesdrop on the session.

The entire court turned in unison when a latecomer stepped through the massive double doors. A pleasant jingling, like bells, announced his arrival. Taller than most, Zhong Ye was afforded a perfect view of the man, a foreigner, of middle height and thin. His hair was so light it appeared silver. The room began to hum, until the Emperor rapped his fan against the throne.

The silence that followed was immediate. The foreigner strode down the crimson carpet to the Emperor, a delicate chiming punctuating his every step. As he walked past, Zhong Ye saw that the cloth belt tied around his waist was strung with silver objects of various shapes. He wondered if they were solely for decorative purposes. Some of them were shaped like tools or keys.

The foreigner dropped to his knees and pressed his brow to the ground, as was customary. "I am Yokan from the kingdom of Paan, Your Majesty, here to pledge my allegiance and service." His speech was deeply accented but understandable; his voice, reedy.

Paan. It was a wonder he had survived the journey. Zhong Ye knew very little about the frigid kingdom and observed the diplomat with a keen eye.

"Rise." The Emperor waved his hand, and Yokan stood.

"No one sent word that we were to expect you, Yokan from Paan," the Emperor said, his dark eyes heavy lidded. He was reaching his limit of official duty and was ready for food, wine, and his choice of girls, followed by a long afternoon sleep.

"Alas, the ship that was to bring word never made it, Your Majesty." Yokan stood bamboo straight, his pale hands clasped before him. Zhong Ye noticed for the first time the silver rings looped into his ears.

"That's unfortunate. And why have you come? To establish trade between the two kingdoms? To teach us your culture? To spread your gods' words?" The Emperor actually sneered as he rubbed the sharp beard at his chin, something new that boosted his vanity.

Yokan bowed. "I am here as a diplomat to learn as much as I can from your kingdom and its culture, Your Majesty. And in return may be able to offer you—"

The entire court leaned forward. Impressed by the foreigner's theatrics, Zhong Ye lifted a brow.

"—eternal life," he said finally, his accent making the declaration that much more dramatic.

The court erupted as the Emperor sat back in his throne. Yokan remained with his head bowed, his expression impossible to read.

The court dispersed after that, with all of them chattering as they exited the hall. The Emperor had invited Yokan to his study to discuss the matter privately. Only two of his top advisers and the usual array of guards remained. Zhong Ye approached the throne just as the Emperor was rising from his seat.

He dropped to his knees beside the diplomat, who smelled of spiced cologne. "Your Majesty, I humbly offer myself as a guide to Master Yokan while he's staying within the palace."

The Emperor laughed. "And what makes you think such a task would be given to someone as low ranked as you, Zhong?"

Zhong Ye pressed his nose to the floor. "I can prove myself, Your Majesty."

"Indeed, you already have." He could hear the smile in the Emperor's voice.

"It would be good to have a guide," Yokan said. "I'm grateful for Master Zhong's kind offer."

Zhong Ye held still.

"Very well then, your first friend here in Xia, Yokan. Now, let's discuss this incredible claim of yours." The Emperor stepped past Zhong Ye, and Yokan turned to follow. "Make certain you are available to see Yokan to his quarters after our talk," the Emperor said.

Zhong Ye didn't rise. He waited until he could no longer hear the tinkling ornaments on Yokan's sash. But he smiled the entire time.

Two hours later Zhong Ye was still waiting outside the Emperor's private study. The guards didn't move or talk and never bothered to acknowledge his presence. He was used to standing for long intervals and was as motionless as they were. Through the door panels, he could hear low murmurs and, on occasion, a hearty laugh from the Emperor. Zhong Ye wished he could hear the conversation; his mind continued buzzing over Yokan's claim to immortality. Surely the man lied? Zhong Ye reviewed the details, remembering all he could about the diplomat, his dress, the way he carried himself. He didn't doubt that Yokan was an intelligent and powerful man, probably high in rank within his own kingdom's court. Why had he really been sent to Xia?

The dragon panels opened, and Yokan appeared,

his gray wool robes dull and out of place next to the Emperor's richly embroidered tunic. He kept his head bowed.

"Ah, good," said the Emperor. "Zhong is here. He'll show you to your quarters."

Yokan walked briskly and led the way, which amused Zhong Ye, as the foreigner had no inkling where he was going. Although Zhong Ye was taller, he had to quicken his pace to match the man's stride.

"Tell me about yourself, Zhong," Yokan said, his accent thick.

"I was born into a farming family, the fifth child and second son. From the province of Bai He."

"That means nothing to me. Tell me about yourself," the diplomat said again.

Zhong Ye cleared his throat. "I left home at eleven years. I apprenticed with various scholars in different fields. At sixteen years, I gave myself to the Emperor's service as a eunuch."

The man stopped in mid-stride. "You gave up your manhood?" Yokan spoke with such distaste it was obvious what he thought of the practice.

"It was the quickest way to enter the palace and work for the Emperor," Zhong Ye replied.

The foreigner strode forward again, and Zhong Ye

turned down another corridor, forcing Yokan to back-track and follow.

"That is a sacrifice I cannot fathom," said Yokan when he was beside him once more.

"I don't regret it. It's been less than two years, and I'm already part of my Emperor's court." Why was he being so honest with this man? Would Yokan tell the Emperor what they discussed?

They walked through a courtyard filled with song-birds, the sunlight reflecting off their silver cages. He led Yokan to spacious quarters in the outer court. The diplomat was obviously considered important. One always knew by the accommodations.

"Tell me, who is the alchemist at court?" Yokan asked.

Zhong Ye folded his hands behind him. "There are sev-eral, each working feverishly to become the Emperor's best and favorite."

A smile touched Yokan's thin lips. His eyes were so light a blue Zhong Ye was uncertain if blue was their true color. "Will you point them out to me in court tomorrow?"

He bowed his head. "Of course, Master Yokan."

"And you? Have you any skills in alchemy?" the diplo-mat asked, appraising Zhong Ye openly.

"I've studied as much as I could on my own." Zhong Ye

had once been told he was a natural, excelling because of his curiosity and faultless memory. But he didn't think that bragging would be a boon.

"Hear me," Yokan said, waving Zhong Ye toward one of the seats in his grand reception hall. "I need a friend and an ear during my stay. You seem intelligent and . . . ambitious. Willing to learn, yes?"

Zhong Ye was becoming used to his stilted speech and accent. "Yes, master."

"Very good. Perhaps we can help each other in our endeavors?" The foreigner smiled, though it did not reach his deep-set eyes.

"Of course." Zhong Ye wondered what those endeavors were.

CHAPTER FOUR

Chen Yong was still asleep when Ai Ling was woken by heavy footsteps on deck. They had wedged a thin blanket between them. And although she still stared at the dark for quite some time before drifting to sleep, the night had passed. She sat up and stretched, then touched her head. She wasn't used to sleeping with her braid, but she couldn't allow Chen Yong to see her with loose hair either. Only husbands saw their wives' hair unbound. As Zhong Ye had seen hers on their wedding night. The thought came unbidden, and she bit her lip hard to scatter it.

All fifteen crew members were awake. Lao Lu was in a foul mood, and her spirit glided past him. Xiao Hou had helped prepare the morning meal and spilled half the broth on the floor. A mess and a waste! He was not given his portion as a result, and she felt the boy's stomach tighten with hunger, even as hers did.

Leaving Chen Yong in bed, she used the latrine and ran into the galley. She stuffed half a steamed bun into her mouth before clambering onto the deck. Xiao Hou was just beginning his chores and handed her an extra broom. "Make sure you sweep along the edges. Get every nook."

Ai Ling gave him the other half of her steamed bun before taking the broom. "A trade," she said. The boy's round eyes widened; then he grinned. She began sweeping and passed Yam Head, who tipped his hat to her. She circled the ship twice, before helping the crew wash the deck down with seawater and scrubbing the dirt away with a stone.

She was sweating by the time they were done. "Tomorrow you can bring your clothes on deck to wash," Xiao Hou said. An image of all the men scouring their underclothes beneath the sails came to mind, and she chuckled. The boy's eyebrows lifted. "Every three days, miss, we wash our clothes."

Ai Ling inclined her head solemnly. "Thank you for informing me, sir."

"You've been assigned the captain's lot."

She kept a straight face. If Peng wanted her to wash his dirty laundry as punishment, she would.

She retreated to the galley and helped Lao Lu wash the dishes from the morning meal, before finally settling at the table for her lesson. Chen Yong had already begun reading his text and did not greet her. She sat beside him and poured herself some tea.

"How do you keep all the food fresh?" she asked Peng, who had been writing on a thick parchment.

"Giant ice blocks in the cargo," he said. "It takes a lot of planning for such a long journey with a large crew like ours. Everything is rationed carefully."

Peng was dressed in dark blue trousers and a long-sleeved tunic that hugged his lean frame. The tunic was cut at the waist with an opening in the front, showing his gray silk shirt. His black hair was slicked back this morning, the look so unusual he appeared foreign. "As captain I have to account for all possibilities: being swept off course; getting caught in a bad storm . . . even stowaways."

Ai Ling pursed her lips, and Peng laughed. She felt Chen Yong glance at her.

"Do you dress like them?" she asked, taking a sip of tea. "I've never seen such clothes. And your hair . . ."

He smiled as he dipped his quill into the inkpot. "Yes,

it's in the Jiang style. I find it easier for trade when I look a little like them at least." He swept an elegant hand over the thick parchment, where tiny letters were strung together like so many beads on a sleeve edge. "Let's practice what we learned yesterday, then move on to more complicated phrases."

Ai Ling sighed, not looking forward to wrangling her tongue around the strange sounds. She didn't have a knack for language, as Chen Yong obviously did.

After their lesson had ended with a conversation between Peng and Chen Yong that made her head ache, she went up on deck. She pulled a stool to the ship's stern and stared out to sea, holding her sketchbook and charcoal, but became too mesmerized by the diamond-spangled waters to draw. Her chin dipped. The crew's words and thoughts buzzed like distant mosquitoes. She closed herself off, reached for elusive silence . . .

Her head jerked up. The brightness of the day stabbed her eyes, and she winced.

"Miss, you musta fell asleep." Xiao Hou was standing beside her.

"We didn't mean to scare you," Yam Head said. The two boys flanked her like guardian lions.

Ai Ling rubbed her face and smiled. The charcoal clinked to the deck.

"Who's that?" Yam Head pointed to her lap.

Puzzled, she looked down. A detailed portrait of a young woman had been sketched into her book. She didn't remember drawing it but recognized her own hand. Her throat closed, and her fingers flew to her neck. Her pulse fluttered so fast she thought she would faint.

"She's pretty," said Xiao Hou.

"Could you bring me some water, please?" she managed to say in a weak voice.

The two boys scurried off together.

She looked at the portrait again. Piercing wide-set eyes stared back at her from a heart-shaped face. The woman's brows were delicate; the mouth was bow-shaped and full. The ebony hair was pulled up in a style fitting a servant. It was as if she were gazing at a splintered image of herself.

She closed the sketchbook with a trembling hand. Despite the fact that she had never seen her before, Ai Ling knew she had somehow drawn a portrait of Silver Phoenix.

After the midday meal Ai Ling decided to ignore her tight, aching legs and attend Chen Yong's shuen lesson. She needed to clear her mind. The group was larger by two. Peng was dressed in Xian clothing again, the only time he seemed to wear it, and Yen had taken his tunic off, revealing a compact body with powerful muscles. Chen Yong asked everyone to resume the Horse Riding stance after some initial stretching. Her legs quivered in protest, and she had to suppress a cry of pain.

From the expressions on some of the other faces, she was not the only one who suffered. Peng and Yen seemed untouched, however, both sitting deep into the stance. Chen Yong moved down the line with his dreadful bamboo rod, tapping shoulders and legs, correcting form. He passed her without comment.

Again, he demonstrated the Jade Serpent Steals Breath punch. The skies had become overcast, blanketing the world in gray. Yet Chen Yong, dressed in a deep green tunic with gold details, glided like a bold stroke of color across the deck. It was as if he were the only living person and everyone else a pale shade around him. He pushed people lower at the shoulders, twisted hips with his hands to reiterate the power of the punch, pried fingers open and closed them again to form the correct fist.

Ai Ling was at the end of the line once more. She put her heart into every lunge and punch, but a part of her was always aware of Chen Yong. He spoke to the crew in quiet, patient tones, leaned his head close to the boys as they babbled up to him excitedly. Ai Ling thrust her leg and fist out again and again, losing herself in the movement.

Then he was before her, his hands behind his back, so close she had to tilt her head to meet his gaze. "I've been watching you," he said, a hint of something unreadable in his golden eyes. They were the first words he'd spoken to her all day.

He took a large step back, and she almost followed, as if drawn on strings.

"Show me." Chen Yong gave a slight nod.

She lunged forward, punching toward his solar plexus. He circled her, just as he had the previous day. Her nostrils flared; she was determined neither to twitch nor to blush.

"It's perfect," he said.

Ai Ling collapsed out of her stance, almost sputtering. Perfect! She had no inkling what she was doing. If he truly was so angry with her that he wouldn't teach her properly, would just ridicule and ignore her . . .

He cocked an eyebrow, then grinned. It took every fraction of her willpower not to smile back.

Chen Yong ended the lesson by demonstrating a sequence of forms with such fluidity and strength he appeared otherworldly. He twisted and rolled from an imaginary attacker and backflipped twice before spiraling with a series of kicks, floating, suspended in the air for so long it seemed as if he were flying. He had stripped off his tunic, and despite the chill in the air, sweat gleamed at his throat, on his collarbones. But no hint of exertion touched his face, which was intense with focus.

She stared, entranced, admiring the way his muscles tensed and eased as he moved. She realized all at once exactly how powerful Chen Yong was, how lethal and precise. Better than she ever was, could be. He would have made the perfect assassin in the palace.

Ai Ling faltered in mid-thought, bewildered.

Everyone erupted into applause as he landed gracefully and bowed to his small audience. Looking embarrassed and suddenly boyish, he waved his hand to silence them. Several of the sailors crowded around him, speaking simultaneously, and she headed toward the galley for water. She was reminded of the last time she had seen Chen Yong practice his forms, after his sparring session with Li Rong when they had visited Lao Pan's cave. Her heart ached to remember it.

She encountered Peng in the galley, already seated at the table with a cup of water. He didn't look as if he had broken a sweat. "I'll ask Lao Lu to leave a few jugs of water for us on deck tomorrow."

Ai Ling sat beside him and drank in large gulps, spilling on herself as the ship swayed. "Have you practiced shuen before?"

Pensive, Peng swirled his cup. "I did once," he said. "Yes."

They looked at each other for a long moment, and she realized he wasn't going to explain further. The ship lurched as he brought the cup to his mouth for another sip, compensating for the sea's erratic movements without thought. He certainly didn't wash his face by accident while trying to drink.

"Are you not wed?" she blurted.

His black eyes widened; then he laughed. "I'm not. I don't believe a wife would agree with this lifestyle. I would never be there for her or our children." He glanced down at his hands. "It's not something I want."

"How many years are you?" Her curiosity overrode decorum.

Peng laughed again. "You're quite forthright. You'll fit right in in Jiang Dao. If I may ask, how many years are you?"

"I'll be eighteen years in the ninth moon."

"The Jiang consider eighteen years to be a significant year," he said, smiling. "I am twenty-nine years."

Twenty-nine!

"Ah." She cleared her throat. "You don't look—I mean, I didn't think—" She drank another sip of water, managing to keep dry this time.

"Thank you." He smiled with gracious amusement, rose, and rapped his knuckles on the table. "You jested about not having practiced shuen before?"

"What?"

"Your form is excellent," Peng said.

"No . . . my father only taught my brothers."

His dark eyes narrowed a touch as he gauged her. Did he think she was lying?

"The talent must run in your family," he said, then nodded once before leaving the galley.

Ai Ling gazed into her empty water cup, too perplexed to laugh at the irony.

They had sailed two weeks without incident when something jolted Ai Ling from a deep slumber early one morning. She sat up without realizing it, tilting her head to listen to the creak and groan of the wooden ship, the quick scurrying of steps climbing topside. Maybe that was what had woken her. The crew was rising for the day. She lay back and listened to Chen Yong's steady breathing. Just a few moments more . . . Her mind wandered, and her spirit touched the crew, most of whom were still shaking off the heaviness of sleep.

Suddenly she felt something different. She shot up again. Unfamiliar voices. From farther away, but not that far. She cast her spirit beyond the *Gliding Dragon*, felt the tug within her navel, something she hadn't felt in a long while.

The fog hides us. They'll never know what hit them. She heard the man speak, felt his anticipation and greed. Ai Ling shook Chen Yong's shoulder. He was warm with sleep. "What is it?" he asked, his voice hoarse.

"Come on deck with me," she said. "Something's wrong."

"In our sleep clothes?"

"There's no time. Hurry!"

They tried to rise at the same time and tripped over each other. There was a tangle of limbs, before Chen Yong caught her by the waist, set her on her feet, and opened the door. Lantern light filtered in from the passageway. Ai Ling strapped her dagger to her side but didn't bother to pull on her shoes as she followed Chen Yong.

Dense fog so thick she couldn't see beyond arm's length hung over the ship. The air was wet, cold. She shivered. The sun had not yet risen. She walked to the starboard side, with Chen Yong beside her.

"What's wrong?" he asked, peering into the white haze.

"It must be another ship. I heard someone not from our crew speak." She gripped the railing. "Wait, I'll learn more." She looked at Chen Yong. His hair was not yet pulled back, and too worried to appear aloof, as he had these past two weeks, he rubbed his cheek with one hand. She cleared her mind and cast her spirit over the water, searching for the people she could not see but knew were there.

She found them, counted twenty-three men in all. Most were on deck. Eager, filled with the desire to plunder, they carried long wooden tubes and rocked on their heels, waiting for the captain's orders. Their ship had moved closer to the *Gliding Dragon*, but the fog made them impossible to see.

Ai Ling pulled back, gasped when she returned to herself. "We have to find Peng. I think they're pirates, and they're going to attack soon."

Chen Yong ran toward the bridge, and Ai Ling followed, barely able to see in the thick mist. They burst in without knocking. The captain was bent over a large table covered with maps. Yen stood beside him, as they studied one map together.

Peng's head jerked up, and his dark brows lifted.

"A peaceful morning," he said, straightening. "Did you run out of clean clothes to wear?"

She had forgotten about her sleep clothes and wrapped her arms around herself.

"Ai Ling believes a pirate ship will be attacking the *Gliding Dragon* soon," Chen Yong said.

Peng's gaze hardened, the amusement disappearing. "What makes you think this?"

"I can't explain. You must believe me."

"I can vouch for her words," Chen Yong said.

"Where are they?" Peng asked.

"Beyond the starboard side and drawing nearer as we speak," she replied.

"Yen, ready the crew. Prepare for attack."

Yen bowed and retreated with quick steps.

"It's a large ship," she said. "I counted twenty-three men."

"I knew there was something different about you. But this . . ." Peng seemed unable to find the right words.

Chen Yong grasped her shoulder, surprising her. She felt concern and a strong sense of protection before she closed herself to him.

"Go below deck, to your cabin," Peng said. "You'll be safer there."

"No," she replied. "I can help."

He glanced at Chen Yong.

"She can," he said. "And it's no use trying to talk her out of anything."

Ai Ling almost laughed.

Peng shrugged off the dark silver coat he wore. "Put this on at least. It's cold."

She reached for it, the material slippery in her hand. She pulled the coat on, still warm from his body. "Thank you."

He gave a curt nod. "Let's go."

They emerged into the mist. It was as if they were floating in the air, though the ship still swayed with the waves, and she heard them lap against its sides.

"It is beyond, that way?" Peng asked, squinting into the white haze.

"Yes."

"How far?" he asked.

She flung her spirit forward, and there was no tautness in her navel this time. "Soon within shouting distance."

He turned to her, his black eyes unreadable. "Yen!" The pilot emerged like a wraith in the weak morning light.

"Are the fire lances ready?"

"Yes, Captain."

"I'll give the signal," Peng said.

Five men ran to the railing. Ai Ling saw that the closest one carried a tube the length of his arm.

"It's made from bamboo and filled with gunpowder." Chen Yong leaned closer. "It can shoot flame, but not far."

A blast of intense fire burst from the fog toward them.

"The heavens have mercy," Peng said. "They have a flamethrower."

"What's that?" Ai Ling asked, her heart thudding too fast.

"It uses a double-piston bellow to shoot fierce fire oil. The flames can't be doused with water," Peng said in a grim voice. "If it ignites the ship, we're doomed."

They could hear shouting now. And a roar and stench filled the heavy air, as another explosion of fire shot toward the *Gliding Dragon* like a lashing tongue. The fog lifted slightly, and they could see the hulking shape of another ship, heading toward them.

"Extra sails!" Peng bellowed. "Go!"

The crew scrambled to their stations, but it seemed to Ai Ling that the *Gliding Dragon* was stuck in rice glue while the other ship slid on cooking grease. She could see the pirates now, drawing ever closer.

"Put down your weapons! Or we'll set your ship afire!" A voice boomed from the prow of the pirate ship.

A loud hiss and another flare. This time the ball of

fire disappeared into the water just short of the *Gliding Dragon.*

"Curses on the devil's daughter," Peng muttered. "Drop your weapons."

The men obeyed, and their weapons clattered to the deck.

"Very good. I'm sending over fifteen men armed with flame lances. Don't do anything foolish, and no one will get killed." The pirate captain paused. "We want the cargo, that's all. If we meet resistance, we'll burn your ship."

He was lying. The pirates would kill them and take the *Gliding Dragon.* Blood thirst mingled with greed ricocheted among the pirates to her. She flung herself forward, gripping the spirit of every man on the other ship. She held them immobile and focused on the pirate behind the flamethrower, leaped into his being. Excitement coursed though him, and his heart beat hard against his ribs. Heavy sweat rolled down his back.

He was the best with the flamethrower and itched to set the *Gliding Dragon* on fire. But not unless the idiots were dumb enough to fight. He wanted the loot but would almost trade it to ignite the ship. It would burn so gloriously.

Ai Ling was aware of the terrified babbling of the men who had discovered that they couldn't control their limbs. Their terror mounted even as their captain shouted for calm. She folded herself over the pirate behind the flamethrower and took possession of his body. He mewed in surprise. She probed through his mind, understood how the weapon worked, and turned the four-wheel pushcart until its mouth was aimed at the bridge of the pirate ship.

The fire roared across the deck shooting up the masts and igniting the sails.

"Idiot! Are you mad?" the pirate captain bellowed. "We're bedeviled!"

Ai Ling snapped back into her own being with a gasp and collapsed hard against the railing, trying to keep from sliding to the deck. The pirates were screaming. They would burn to death or drown. She didn't know which fate was worse. The *Gliding Dragon's* crew erupted into rowdy cheering, dancing behind her. The mist had cleared, and the sun rose like a blazing god across the sky. Hungry flames fed on the planks of the pirate ship, leaping like angry phantoms.

Suddenly a strong wind blew toward them, carrying the acrid scent of burning flesh and wood with it.

"Hurry, catch the wind and go!" Peng shouted, racing

across the deck. "If one ember so much as touches us!"

Without warning, her knees buckled, and she slumped to the ground. Chen Yong caught her from behind and held her. Horrified shrieks filled the air, and the choking fumes of smoke and fire grew thicker.

Chen Yong picked her up, and only the feel of his strong arms kept Ai Ling conscious, grounded in reality. She clutched his tunic with tight fists, breathing him in: cotton and sweat and the faint scent of lemon. He somehow maneuvered down the steps, holding her still and gently seated her on a stool in the empty galley.

"You did that, didn't you?" he asked in a quiet voice.

Unable to answer him, she rested her head in her arms. She was trembling so hard it was difficult to stay on the stool. He brought her water, and she made herself sip it slowly.

"That entire crew will die," she finally whispered.

"They probably planned the same fate for us." He sat beside her and held her elbow, his concern a dark swelling around them.

"But you weren't the one who sent them to their deaths."

His fingers tightened a fraction. "No. But I would have killed them to stay alive. You did what you had to."

She wiped the heat from her eyes. "I'm tired of it, doing what I have to."

He paused, then said quietly, "Your dream of Li Rong was right. You saved our lives."

She doubled over, hugging herself, unable to look at him.

"Did your necklace glow?" he asked.

Ai Ling snorted, but it came out as a rasp, like a gulp for one last breath. She gripped her clouded pendant and shoved it in his face. "The gods have abandoned me. Abandoned and used me like they did Li Rong." She yanked on the gold chain so hard it snapped, and the pendant fell.

He caught it in one hand, the motion lightning quick.

She wanted to cry. For Li Rong. For herself. But her eyes remained dry. Her face burned. Her neck. Her chest. "Throw it into the sea," she said through gritted teeth.

"Ai Ling." Chen Yong's voice was rough. He closed a cool hand over her open palm, leaned forward, and cupped her cheek.

Peng bounded in, and Chen Yong jerked back.

"Here's our heroine!" Peng proclaimed. "Ai Ling, you warned us about the attack. And the fates blew their own flames back at them. It's a fortuitous sign indeed. The gods smiled down upon us."

Perfect. She wanted to cackle.

"I've asked Lao Lu to sacrifice a chicken. We must give

thanks and celebrate. You'll be the guest of honor."

At that moment her belt slipped from her waist, and her dagger clattered to the floor. Ai Ling stared at it, perplexed.

Chen Yong bent down and retrieved it for her. "Why is the blade black?"

"I don't know," she lied.

Peng drew closer, his brow creased. "Bring it to me. I may be able to clean it." He studied it for a moment longer before stepping back. "I'll see you both at dinner. My gratitude, Ai Ling." He nodded and left.

It took all her strength to hold her head up. She was burning, blazing so hot she was certain that her skin crisped, fell in piles of ash from her bones.

Chen Yong pulled her into his steady coolness, lifted her in his arms, and she rested her head against his shoulder.

She was asleep before he made it to their cabin.

Mei Gui was expecting. Zhong Ye wanted to jump and holler when Silver Phoenix shared the good news. Instead, he grinned widely as if he had drunk too much wine. "Wonderful," he said.

Silver Phoenix lifted her chin. There was not a

fraction of handmaid in her. She was too self-assured, too smart . . . too beautiful.

"That's the first genuine smile I've ever seen from you, Master Zhong."

His eyes widened. "You share good news."

"You should smile more," she said. "You always look so serious."

She smelled of jasmine and spring. Zhong Ye wanted to pluck the pins from her thick hair one by one and bury his face in it. He took a step back. "Being the Emperor's adviser is a serious task."

Silver Phoenix touched her looped braid in one elegant motion, considering him in a way that made him want to shift on his feet. "I'll keep you informed of my mistress's progress. Should I tell anyone else?"

"It's too soon. Let me tell the Emperor when the time is right."

She inclined her head, a hint of a smile on her rouged lips. He exited Mei Gui's quarters, trying very hard to clear his mind.

The oppressive summer months gave way to autumn. Zhong Ye continued to work closely with Yokan, finding ways to ingratiate himself, sharing the gossip at court, telling him about the Emperor's alchemists and their reputations and projects. After his return from summer progress, the Emperor resumed meeting with Yokan alone, elevating the foreign alchemist even higher in the eyes of the court.

Yokan was given his own elaborate study to conduct his research. All four walls were lined with shelves, piled high with books, boxes, and jars, full of compounds the alchemist had gathered from around the world for his studies. Glass lanterns, shining even during the day, were scattered around the square chamber. Yokan had asked the Emperor to make Zhong Ye his official apprentice. Surprised by his good fortune, Zhong Ye spent many hours reading aloud and interpreting texts for the foreigner. Yokan translated what he heard into his own language and transcribed it into bound books with thick pages.

The study never smelled the same on any given day. This morning the faint scent of licorice root permeated the air.

"I've studied Xian for eight years, yet reading the ancient texts still proves difficult for me," Yokan murmured, his head bent over a leather volume.

"I think your command of the language is impressive," Zhong Ye said. They were reading from *The Book of the Divine*, and Yokan had many questions.

"Do you believe in the gods? Of the underworld and its retributions?"

Zhong Ye paused. He had become used to Yokan's personal questions, always direct. "I've never felt the presence of any god in my life."

Yokan glanced up. His eyebrows were so light it appeared he had none. The effect was disconcerting. "I see. And you are not one to believe unless you feel something?"

"Even that is so ambiguous. How can one be sure it's real if it cannot be seen or touched?" Zhong Ye asked.

"What about love?" The foreigner straightened on the stool and smiled thinly.

Zhong Ye tried to contain his surprise. "Love? What of love?"

"Love cannot be seen or touched, but it's real, is it not? Surely, you've been in love before?"

Zhong Ye suddenly felt defensive. Even after four months of working daily with this man, he still knew very little of Yokan, who he was or what he thought. "No. I've had no time for love." He caught himself thinking of Silver Phoenix.

"Interesting." Yokan bent over his book again, his quill raised.

Zhong Ye suppressed his irritation. He couldn't

ingratiate himself by acting abrupt. "And you? Have you ever loved someone?" he asked politely.

Yokan gave a slight shake of his head. "I, too, have had no time for love. It's an unnecessary distraction." He scratched something onto the parchment. "A weakness."

"Is it true that you know the secret to eternal life?" Zhong Ye asked. Yokan had never mentioned it again in conversation, after that first day in court. But there must be some truth to his claim, or why else would the Emperor continue to meet with him alone?

"Have you read from *The Book of the Dead*?" Yokan asked, looking directly at Zhong Ye.

It was as if sharp needles were dancing across his scalp—Zhong Ye would never become used to the pale blue color of the foreigner's eyes. "Only parts, random pages. I've never seen the actual book."

"You will help me translate the entire volume," Yokan said, tapping the tip of his quill against the blackwood table.

Zhong Ye swallowed hard. *The Book of the Dead* was evil. One studied from it only if one were a monk, wanting to combat and understand the enemy. Or if one were devoted to the dark arts. His pulse throbbed fast against his throat, and he nodded. He would do anything to learn Yokan's secrets.

* * *

Zhong Ye walked along the edge of the massive palace square after meeting with a young boy of no more than twelve years, a eunuch and a favorite of the Empress's for his falsetto voice. She was not with child, having been called to the Emperor's bedchamber only once in the past two months. And her relationship with the Emperor's top adviser was souring. Zhong Ye had allowed himself a small smile when he heard the news and had pressed a pouch of coins into the boy's palm. Zhong Ye kept a wide network of spies, each bribed with coins, favors, or threats—whatever combination reaped the best results.

His boots crunched on golden leaves as he walked through the oblong courtyard that connected the outer court to the inner court. Guards saluted him before pulling the massive doors open. The salute was a first, and he wondered what he had done recently or whom he had been seen with that would have garnered this new show of respect.

One of the higher-ranking concubines, surrounded by a retinue of handmaids, was strolling toward him. She was twenty years and had a daughter of two years by the Emperor. Zhong Ye stopped and bowed with a flourish. He did not rise until she nodded at him, smiling. "Master Zhong," she said.

One of her silly handmaids tittered behind a silk sleeve.

"It's been too long since you've visited." She peered up at him coquettishly from beneath lowered lashes. "Not since you've been promoted."

"I'm always at your service, lady."

She pressed an ivory hand to his chest, tipping her head back to capture his gaze. "Yes. I'll remember that, Master Zhong." She had always been too liberal with her touch.

He did not meet her eyes but only bowed lower. She swirled away in a flutter of colorful silks. Her handmaids chattered and giggled, not caring that their voices carried to him.

"Can you believe, only eighteen years . . ."

"So handsome. Those eyes . . ."

"It truly is a pity that . . ." This handmaid had enough decorum to lower her voice.

Zhong Ye felt the blood rush to his face.

"It only means I'll have to be more creative with him." The concubine's words rang out from the other end of the courtyard, and her handmaids erupted in laughter.

He remained with his head inclined and his hands clasped behind his back—clasped so hard he had gouged nail marks into one wrist—until the courtyard was empty. He rubbed his temple when they were gone. Working in the concubines' inner quarters was often like navigating through a chamber of serpents.

Silver Phoenix was waiting for him when he entered Mei Gui's quarters. His mood lifted the moment he saw her. She brushed her fingertips on his arm, the lightest touch, startling him. "I have bad news," she said in a low voice. He closed the panel.

"My mistress began bleeding heavily this morning. She's bedridden."

Zhong Ye punched one fist into a carved chair. "Does anyone know?"

"Did you ever tell the Emperor?" Silver Phoenix's black eyes darted to her mistress's bedchamber.

"Of course not. I would have told you," he said, his mind searching for the best course of action. All thoughts fled when she glided to stand directly in front of him. The top of her head barely reached his chin, but the way she held herself made her appear taller.

"Can we trust each other, Master Zhong?" The scent of her jasmine perfume filled him. "I want the best for my mistress. And you wish to see her rise in status as well?"

As long as she held the Emperor's interest, yes. As long as it benefitted him, he thought. "Was the royal physician told?"

"No. I sent for some willow bark to ease her pain," Silver Phoenix replied. "I said that she had a bad headache."

He could have swept her into his arms, he was so relieved. She was smart. He spontaneously reached for her hand, and she didn't mask her astonishment. "This doesn't change my plans for your mistress. We can still rise together in the Emperor's eyes. If you'll listen to what I say."

"Haven't I always?"

"Yes. It'll be your task to ready her for the Emperor's bedchamber—"

"She just lost her child!" Silver Phoenix met his gaze unabashedly. Two spots of color flared on her cheeks.

"The Emperor enjoys your mistress's company. He has asked for her consistently these past months. It's not a time to disappear."

He released her slender hand, still feeling the warmth of her skin. "There are thousands of other women to choose from. You understand me? And this court runs on ambition alone." He knew she understood perfectly. "Help her heal. Prepare her to be called again by His Majesty."

Silver Phoenix gave a slight shake of her head. "I won't have you hurt her, Zhong Ye."

He swallowed, surprised to hear her speak his full name. "If you wish to see your mistress rise, you'll do this."

"She'll need at least a month. This is no small—"

"We don't have a month. I'll make certain the Emperor is occupied with his usual choices. It's been four days since he saw Mei Gui last. I can give you four more."

She blanched, opened her mouth, then closed it, pressing her full lips into a line. "I understand." She walked back to the bedchamber panel, but before she slid it open, she turned to him. "Know that you need us as much as we need you, Master Zhong."

He inclined his head, hiding a half-smile. There were many concubines to choose from, if the Emperor's interest in Mei Gui waned or if she took too long to become with child again. But no other concubine had Silver Phoenix as her handmaid. Zhong Ye, unsettled by the revelation, straightened when she was gone.

It was well past the thieving hour. Zhong Ye's shoulders and neck ached from crouching over *The Book of the Dead*. Yokan had food brought to them, but Zhong Ye had eaten very little, his appetite robbed by the demons and monsters he read about. The alchemist sat opposite him at the wide blackwood table, rolls of parchment littering its surface so it looked more white than ebony.

Yokan dipped his quill in the inkpot again and nodded,

indicating that he was ready for the next passage. Zhong Ye took a sip of dark tea before speaking. "Between the peaks, where the sun never touches but the moon glows, grows the empress root. Named after the Mother Goddess and shaped like a woman, the empress root burrows deep in wet earth. It grows to the length of a palm and smells of almond fruit when sliced. The empress root's ability to give life is unrivaled."

Zhong Ye paused and cleared his throat. "What does it mean, 'ability to give life'? A fertility herb?"

Yokan continued to write with neat strokes, then finally set his quill down. He pinched the high bridge of his nose, obviously worn by the long day's work as well. "This empress root is what we need to help create the spell for eternal life." His smile was tight, his face made even more pale by the flickering lantern light.

Zhong Ye stretched his arms overhead. He needed fresh air; he needed to practice his shuen forms until he felt the warmth of his own blood pumping. "I've never heard of it. Or seen it in any herbal shop."

"This is the problem and the challenge." Yokan rose from his stool and began pacing the study. "According to the research I did back in Paan, the puzzle always leads me to the empress root, which can be found only somewhere within Xia. But there is bare mention of this root here and no indication of its location. Does any place come to mind from that riddle?"

Zhong Ye reread the paragraph and shook his head.

"More clues. We need more clues to tell us how to find this root," Yokan said. "My immortality spell is useless without it."

"How can you be so certain it will work?"

"Because I used empress root once in Paan, as I lay weak, watching Death trying to clamber through my tower window." Yokan touched the silver hoop in his ear. "It gave me life again. Since then I've put all my effort into creating this new spell, every ingredient precisely calibrated so the empress root's power can be maximized, can be tapped to give a person life on top of life."

"But how did you come across the root in Paan?"

"For years it had been sitting in a jar in the royal laboratory. The last Paan diplomat who traveled to Xia only dabbled in alchemy. A monk showed him the root, told him it was so powerful it could cure any ailment, perhaps potent enough to give ever-lasting life. The diplomat didn't believe him, but he was curious enough to buy it at a rather exorbitant price. He thought he could amuse our court with the tale. Even then the monk shaved off only a few thin slices." Yokan laughed. "In his journal my predecessor wrote that he argued with the monk, saying he wouldn't be swindled and demanding the entire root. The monk insisted that he was offering the shavings at a ridiculously low price. So all I had were two shavings. The diplomat also sketched in detail what the root looked like and mentioned the compelling aroma of almonds when the monk cut into it."

Zhong Ye shook his head, a little unsteady from lack of food and exhaustion. "I don't know if I believe it myself. A half-mad monk and a bewildered foreigner. It's chasing delusions and dreams."

"And what judgment have you passed on my character, after half a year of working at my side?"

Zhong Ye was taken aback, and nothing came readily except the truth. "You are well studied and admirable in your knowledge of alchemy."

Yokan nodded, a hint of a smile on his thin mouth. He swept a hand over his silver charms before waving Zhong Ye away. "We'll solve this riddle together, Zhong, you and I. And reap the rewards. Go sleep. I'll see you tomorrow."

Zhong Ye stumbled on the last step out of Yokan's quarters but caught himself with the base of his palm. The scrape stung, and it helped clear his mind. Was he wasting his time with this old foreigner and his dreams of immortality? He saw his breath in the frigid evening air. Bare branches silhouetted against the moonlight reached like gnarled fingers toward the sky. He shivered. Winter had arrived without his noticing.

Zhong Ye knew the way through the labyrinth of courtyards and elaborate halls and quarters as if the palace were his own, but the day's work and lack of sustenance had dulled his wit. He didn't realize Silver Phoenix had approached him from behind until he smelled jasmine. He stopped to greet her. The handmaid paused at the same moment, like a dancer anticipating her partner's next step.

"I'm sorry to catch you so late, Master Zhong, but I've been waiting to speak with you all day." Her tone was soft and blended into the whispers of the evening. She had a thin coat pulled over her tunic. She deserved to be dressed more resplendently.

The moon was halved, like a slice of melon in the sky. It barely illuminated her features. He wanted to trace the curve of her cheek and almost shook his head: that he could nurse this ridiculous infatuation. Instead, he gave a tired smile. "What is it?"

"You're exhausted," she said. "Follow me." Silver Phoenix turned and began walking toward her mistress's quarters. Zhong Ye hesitated but did as she asked. He hadn't seen her in three days since the last time he had brought Mei Gui to the Emperor's bedchamber. He had missed her.

She led him into a small building tucked behind Mei Gui's quarters. The cramped reception hall was filled with fabrics and embroidering. It was humbly furnished with rough wooden furniture, but Silver Phoenix moved through the chamber like an empress. "Please sit. I had just called for a light meal for my mistress, which she refused." She waved an elegant hand toward a lacquered tray on the small round table.

"Aren't you hungry?" he asked as he seated himself on a stool.

"I've already eaten."

He plucked stewed beef and carrots from a small dish and scooped the cold rice porridge into his mouth with wooden eating sticks. His hands shook slightly. Silver Phoenix poured them both hot tea and settled on a stool across from him. "Don't you eat?"

He laughed. "Working with Yokan can be intense. I find I often forget . . . or don't have an appetite."

"What are you working on?"

Zhong Ye took another bite before answering. "I'm helping him translate ancient text. His knowledge of Xian is not strong."

Silver Phoenix took a sip of tea and regarded him. "Is he a good man?"

"He's a superb scholar and alchemist."

"That's not what I meant." She began unpinning her hair, the braids unwinding until they touched her shoulders.

His heart leaped into his mouth. He cleared his throat before speaking. "That's my judgment. He's intelligent and ambitious."

"I see." She started to unravel the loose braids with slender fingers.

He put down his eating sticks. "Please stop." He gestured at her hair, and her eyes widened.

"Oh. I apologize if I made you uncomfortable. But I thought my being a handmaid and a song girl before that and you, you're—" The color that stained her cheeks made her look even lovelier.

He felt the heat in his own face as he shoved back from the table and stood. "What exactly did you need to speak with me about?" His tone was morning frost.

Silver Phoenix dropped her hands into her lap. "It's my mistress. She's with child again."

CHAPTER FIVE

Ai Ling's eyes flew open. Chen Yong leaned over her, gripping her shoulders. "You were shouting in your sleep," he murmured.

Her next breath hitched into a sob.

"What was it?"

"It was . . . just a dream," she said.

"A nightmare?"

She turned her face to the wall. "I—I can't remember." It was true. But she had a lingering feeling of being violated. Trapped.

"You've slept for two days. I think you should eat something and go up on deck for fresh air."

Ai Ling felt the gentle sway of the ship, a comfort

now, a constant. She let herself be pulled to her unsteady feet.

Only Peng and the cook were in the galley. The captain stood when she entered. "I was beginning to worry." He gestured for Lao Lu to bring food and tea. "But Chen Yong reassured me that sometimes you have these long sleeping spells?"

She gave a weak nod and settled onto a stool. Lao Lu placed a tea-stewed egg in front of her, with rice and pickles. She was starving.

"Your older brother looks after you well," Peng said.

She ducked her head and scooped more rice into her mouth with the eating sticks.

"You missed a great celebratory dinner. But Lao Lu insisted on keeping some chicken meat and broth for you."

She turned to the cook, who was busy chopping carrots and mushrooms behind them. "I'm grateful," she said.

Lao Lu grunted.

"We have a supply of medicines on board. Lao Lu is actually well trained in diagnosing ailments," Peng said. She noticed that his hair had grown a little longer in these past weeks, and it just touched the tops of his ears. "Would you like to consult with him?"

"No. But thank you," she replied. "I was just tired and a little seasick."

Peng nodded. "Come to my quarters when you're finished. I have something for you." He rose from the table and gathered his papers and books, bowing slightly before he exited. "And bring your dagger."

Ai Ling knocked, and Peng opened the door almost immediately. "Ah, good." He waved a hand for her to pass, and she entered his cabin. It was three times bigger than the cabin she shared with Chen Yong, yet still not spacious. A large table strewn with maps dominated the room. Books, dozens of them, were stacked in wooden crates against the wall. She remained standing near the door, her hands clasped in front of her.

Peng nodded to his narrow cot. "I wanted to give you a small gift, for warning us of the pirates."

A silk tunic was arranged on Peng's berth. She ran her hand along the sleeve. It was a deep, rich purple, slippery and cool, with gold designs embroidered on the wide armbands. The silk shimmered like a jewel in the dim light.

"It's lovely," she murmured.

"I'm glad you're pleased with it." Peng smiled. "We sell

a lot of our silks in Jiang, and I often have a few sample outfits made to showcase the fabrics."

He waved to a chair, indicating she should sit. Ai Ling lifted the tunic to her chest and pressed her cheek against the brocade, not caring how foolish she appeared. "My mother is wonderful with needle and thread. She would admire this tunic."

Peng sat down, and she settled in a chair across from him. "And your mother let you run away to chase Chen Yong?"

She tucked her chin in surprise. "He's a responsible brother," she said, after too long a pause.

A smile played at the corners of Peng's mouth. "Come, Ai Ling," he said. "Chen Yong's your brother like I am your brother."

She bunched the tunic in her fist.

"It's so painfully obvious, the way you moon after each other." He chuckled.

"I . . ." She closed her mouth. "He . . ."

Peng tapped his leather boot against the floor and lifted a brow.

"Chen Yong does not moon after me," she said finally, heat burning the tips of her ears.

"He never left your cabin once, the entire two days you were asleep." Peng stretched his long legs in front of him. "We had to deliver his meals."

Her heart expanded, filled. She hadn't known.

He studied her openly. "I've heard of you."

Ai Ling swallowed.

Peng smiled. "Yen and I traveled to the Palace of Fragrant Dreams half a year ago for trade. The gossip in Huang Long centered on the newlywed girl who had killed a much-despised adviser on his wedding night."

She smoothed the tunic in her lap, her palms damp.

"Is it true?" Peng asked. "Did you kill Zhong Ye?"

"What does it matter?"

"You don't seem the vindictive type. Not one to chase power and status. But you're bold."

Flustered and confused, she continued to focus on the beautiful tunic.

"Zhong Ye was powerful in the dark arts," Peng said. "It would have had taken someone very strong to kill him."

"What do you know of the dark arts?" she whispered.

He paused and raised a hand. "No. I never practiced. I studied the dark arts as one studies an enemy's tactics. You cannot fight evil without understanding it."

Ai Ling did not look at him. She shouldn't have come to see Peng alone.

"For example, I can tell that your dagger is tainted."

Why had she even brought her dagger on this trip? True, it was the only weapon she had, but she should have buried it long ago. Cast it into a fathomless lake.

"Do you have it?" Peng's tone was gentle.

She unsheathed it and handed it to him without speaking. She didn't understand why she felt she could trust him. She knew she could never undo what she had done. But perhaps it would help to tell someone, to share her story.

Peng held the dagger by its ivory hilt, the red jewels glinting even in the dim lantern light. "It's been blessed." His black eyes met hers. "Blessed specially for you."

She nodded, thinking of Lao Pan.

"How did it become tainted?"

"I used it—I used it for the Calling Ritual."

Peng sucked in his breath. "To remove a heart. Whose?"

"Li Rong's. Chen Yong's younger brother. He was—" She choked. "He was my friend." She blinked back her tears.

"You've studied *The Book of the Dead*." The teasing amusement had vanished from his voice, and the silence that followed stretched too long. "Do you practice it still?" he finally asked.

"No. I made a rash decision. The wrong choice. I shouldn't have done it. I wasn't thinking. I only wanted to bring him back. He shouldn't have died." She was babbling. "I burned his heart in the end."

Peng was quiet, turning the dagger slowly in his hand. He met her gaze. "Good."

"Chen Yong doesn't know," she whispered. "Please don't tell him."

"Your secret is safe with me." He handed the exquisite weapon back, offering it by the hilt. "But it is one that will only fester."

Ai Ling touched his spirit then and saw that he spoke truly. But what could she do? Chen Yong would never forgive her. "Can you clean the dagger?" she asked.

"No. You'll never be able to restore the color of the blade." Somehow she already knew that deep down. "Thank you for the beautiful tunic, Peng. And for listening." She felt limp when she rose, wrung dry.

"Of course," he said, and opened the door for her.

She walked past him, the tunic draped over her arm.

"Ai Ling?"

She turned.

"I'm always here to help." He inclined his head, his dark eyes serious. "You can trust me."

Two weeks had passed since the pirate attack. They sailed across the Sea of Seven Stars, more vigilantly than before. Peng insisted on increased patrols and double shifts. Chen Yong kept his distance. It hurt Ai Ling more than she would admit, but she would not beg for his friendship.

One evening she strolled the perimeter of the deck to admire the moon—so brilliant it rendered the water into rippling beams. She let the wind fill her lungs, her ears. She had gazed at a full moon just like this one over the curving rooflines of the Emperor's palace, excitement coursing through her. *Wait for the extra moon then dark again.* A riddle solved. She shook her head as if to rid herself of the memory that was hers but not hers. She didn't sense Chen Yong's presence until he was beside her. Her body tingled. And she hated herself for it.

"It's a beautiful night," he said.

She made no reply.

"How have you been?" His features were in shadow.

"You ask now?" She couldn't keep the bitterness from her voice. She felt his regret, and she clutched her spirit tight.

"I'm sorry if I offended you. I didn't expect to see you." He leaned on the railing, cupping his chin. The gesture made him appear young. "Why did you never respond to my letters?" He met her eyes.

Chen Yong had written six letters to her while they were apart. She had replied to only one. "I did respond."

The corner of his mouth slanted upward.

"It wasn't easy to find someone traveling to Gao Tung to deliver them," she hurriedly said. What could she possibly write to him? That she felt alone? How she isolated herself from others as her power grew? That she missed him more than she could say? "Is that why you're angry with me? Because I didn't reply to your letters?"

He laughed under his breath. "I'm not angry with you. Well, perhaps I was when you first appeared on board like a clever cat." Chen Yong turned his gaze back toward the water. "It was a difficult choice to leave home to look for my birth father. My mother wasn't pleased, especially after losing Li Rong." He straightened. "In truth, I'm glad you're here with me. Even if . . ." He shifted, his posture tense. "Ai Ling . . ."

The hesitancy in his voice caught her attention. He was nervous. She tilted her face toward his. His golden eyes slid away from hers before he spoke. "I'm betrothed."

She was certain her heart stopped for a moment, and she dug her nails into her palms, tried to keep her features a smooth mask. "What?"

"My mother arranged it right before I left. I—"

"Why didn't you tell me?" she whispered, her entire being numb.

"I didn't know how to." He met her eyes then, and she was the one who looked away this time. "It's not what I want. I should have said something sooner."

Her lips trembled. She pressed them together hard before replying. "She's right. It's time for you to wed. Our first duty is—"

"To our parents," he interrupted. "You're repeating my own words to you. Don't." His tone was harsh, matching hers.

She wanted to run, to jump into the sea and swim into oblivion. Put an eternity of distance between them. She had no hold over Chen Yong. She'd never had. She pivoted away from the railing.

He grabbed her by the edge of her sleeve. His fingers brushed the back of her hand, trailed to her wrist. His touch was like sparks against her skin. "Please stay."

She closed her eyes and tried to steady herself, too acutely aware of his rough palm encircling her wrist.

"Open your eyes, Ai Ling." His voice was soft.

She did, and he let go of her.

The stars swathed the night in pinpricks of light, and they looked at the moon together in silence for some time. "Doesn't this remind you of our chariot ride across the skies?" he finally asked.

"Yes," she whispered. How could she distance herself from him when she was as drawn to him as the tide to the moon?

* * *

A few days later Ai Ling found Chen Yong peering over the side of the ship with Xiao Hou and Yam Head. The boys were standing on crates to afford a better view. Tien An, Xiao Hou's father, was speaking animatedly, gesturing with his hands.

They had finished their Jiang lesson early that morning. She had spent the past hour sitting high at the stern of the ship, studying on her own. The day was cloudless, and no wind filled the sails. The *Gliding Dragon* drifted over still waters. Yam Head spied her first and grinned. Chen Yong followed his glance and smiled, cocking his head for her to join them.

She saw that they all held thin lines between their fingers.

"We're fishing!" Xiao Hou exclaimed.

"Without rods?" she asked.

"None needed," Tien An replied. "This is how we catch all the fish we eat. Coins to weigh down the line and scraps from the kitchen as bait. We wait for a calm day like this, when the ship is barely moving."

"Want to try?" Chen Yong asked.

She nodded, and he carefully passed the line, then stood beside her.

"Always keep tension in the line," Tien An said. "You never know when they'll bite."

"Have you fished before?" Ai Ling asked Chen Yong. He was dressed in a gray tunic with bronze embroidering along the collar, bringing out the color of his eyes.

"No. We ate plenty of fish in our family, but I never have. How about you?"

"Only once or twice with my father, at the small lake outside our town. But we used a fishing rod."

Something tugged at her line. "I think I've got something!"

"Reel her in!" Tien An mimed the motion.

Ai Ling pulled the thin line hand over hand, feeling the resistance. The boys jumped up and down on their wooden boxes as Chen Yong laughed, and she felt his breath against her ear. Her arms prickled. The line bit into her hands.

"Is it a big one?" Tien An asked.

She kept her eyes on the water. The sea blazed, as if the sun had dived into it. She blinked; the endless sea had changed into a small lake. Ai Ling saw the bank on the far side and a thick grove of trees. She was barefoot, her toes dug into the wet, cold mud. Her arms were sore; her hands, raw. Suddenly her catch erupted from the surface. She swung her arm in one swift motion, just as her sister had taught her. The catfish landed on the bank, flopping in the dirt.

"Great job, Zhong Ye!" His eldest sister patted him on the head. "Not bad for eight years."

His older brother eyed the fish, as it gasped its last breaths. "It won't even feed two of us." He prodded it with a toe.

"Leave it!" Zhong Ye said. He removed the hook from the fish's mouth and placed the fish in the net he had brought. "It's for Mother," he declared proudly, swiping a sticky arm over his forehead.

"Bring her up!" Tien An was shouting.

Ai Ling squinted against the sunlight, stunned and disoriented. Tien An swung his arm in an arc to demonstrate. She stared at him, uncomprehending.

Then Chen Yong was behind her, clasping her hands in his, lifting the fish out of the water with one sweeping motion, guiding her arm with his own. She leaned into him, as fragmented memories rushed through her: her sister gripping her shoulder on the long walk home, her mother frying the catfish in scallions, ginger, and red chili, having to till the field days after with hands cut raw from the line . . . No. Not her memories.

A large sea bass bounced on deck, and the boys leaped from their crates, having wound in their own lines. They danced around the writhing fish like warriors after a bloody hunt. Their whooping and giggling brought a few crew members over to admire the catch.

Tien An unhooked the bass and threw it into the basket Lao Lu had brought. "We'll eat well tonight, friends!"

"It's for Mother," Ai Ling whispered.

Chen Yong glanced at her questioningly. She stepped away from him, clutching herself for warmth, despite the hot sun burning overhead.

They had pored over the same passages for hours, until the characters began to squirm and merge before Zhong Ye's tired eyes. "And you are certain there is no other meaning for this word?" Yokan asked. "Does it sound like any province you know?"

Zhong Ye brought the lantern closer to *The Book of the Dead* and forced himself to focus:

Rising high, path to the moon
Plunging low to catch its glow
Water must glide
Not too heavy or too light
Search for her when dark then bright

Yokan pounded a fist on the blackwood table, and the lantern bounced from the force of it. "It's nonsense! Drivel!"

"This book is a compilation of many things: children's rhymes, stories passed on from the wise monk to travelers, studies and observations conducted by scholars, and from those who pursued the dark arts. There is meaning here; we just need to understand how to extract it." Zhong Ye wondered what time it was. They had eaten a light dinner together hours ago. "A place with hills and valleys obviously. Where it rains. That rules out the deserts and the flatlands," he said.

"We need more clues. There must be enough for us to pinpoint the location. Without it, our task is futile," Yokan said.

Zhong Ye muttered the rest of the children's rhyme:

Only in darkness can she grow
On hands and knees, not far below
Every few years, come take your claim
Wait for the extra moon then dark again

The rhyme seemed to contradict itself. They were more than halfway through the book. Would they ever solve the riddle?

Mei Gui was beginning to flesh out around the hips, and her breasts looked fuller. Zhong Ye studied her with an analytical eye. The concubine emanated a serene contentment as she gazed into the bronzed mirror, one hand over her midriff.

Silver Phoenix sat her mistress down at the dressing table and began braiding her hair and pinning it into loops. "When can we tell the Emperor? It can't be safe, all these . . . visits while my mistress is with child," she said.

He watched her fingers dance in precise movements as she worked on Mei Gui's hair and suppressed a smile. She would be angry if she thought he was amused. "How long since her last monthly letting?"

Silver Phoenix looked toward the ceiling and pursed her lips as she counted in her head. He wanted to kiss her. "Over three months at least," she said.

"A few more weeks then, and I'll tell the Emperor." He ran his hands over his silk robe. "We can't risk others hearing the news so early in the pregnancy. The wrong herb in her tea could ruin everything—"

He didn't miss the sharp glance Silver Phoenix gave him in the mirror, and he stopped talking. Mei Gui's peaceful expression was replaced with a small frown. "I didn't mean to alarm you, lady. You're well protected by me and those who serve me. I only take extreme caution because of the precious gift you carry." He bowed, and the concubine relaxed. Silver Phoenix rubbed her mistress's shoulders with both hands, her dark eyes on him in the mirror. He smiled at her reflection, and she dropped her gaze. "I'll take my leave," he said. The visit had been to confirm the pregnancy with his own eyes.

"Master Zhong." Silver Phoenix turned to him, in a fluid motion that brought to mind the mythical creature she was named for. "Could I speak with you?"

"Of course." He stepped into the reception hall, and she followed, sliding the bedchamber panel closed behind her. She took one small step toward him, and he noticed for the first time a tiny mole beneath her right eye, as if she had accidentally touched the tip of a thin calligraphy brush there. The Xian believed a beauty mark near the eye meant a lifetime of tears; he hoped it wasn't true for her.

"I wanted to apologize for my actions and my words from the other evening." She clasped her hands demurely. "I overstepped my boundaries and broke decorum."

"It's understandable, you having been a song girl and me—"

"That is exactly why I'm asking for your forgiveness." She interrupted. She lifted her heart-shaped face to him, and he drew closer without realizing what he was doing.

"I'll forgive you if you take dinner with me," he said, smiling.

One delicate brow rose. "I tend to my mistress until she retires each night. Only then am I free to dine."

"Tell me when, and I'll be waiting." He pressed a palm to his heart. "Otherwise, I'm uncertain I can accept your apology."

She blushed. Zhong Ye kept his expression as placid as a court mask, although he wondered if his eyes betrayed his amusement and desire.

"On the next full moon then, Master Zhong." She was already returning to her mistress but cast a glance over her shoulder. He saw a hint of a smile on her full lips.

He bowed and then stood motionless in the empty hall until he could no longer smell her fragrance.

The next full moon was three days away. Zhong Ye stalked around his reception hall, punching and kicking the dummies in each corner of the chamber when he passed them. He had had them specially made for shuen practice, as there was no one for him to spar with at the palace.

He would clear his engagements and tasks for the night.

Jab.

And ask the royal chef to prepare him a special meal. The chef thought he owed Zhong Ye his life.

Spin kick.

After the poisoning scheme that was foiled on the Emperor's forty-first-year celebration, the entire kitchen staff was interrogated for hours, and the royal chef had received the brunt of the abusive questioning.

Feint.

Backfist.

Zhong Ye had felt bad for the chef, as he had always been treated well by him, and had stepped in to vouch for his innocence. The chef was so moved by this gesture that he swore to consider him like a brother from then on.

Punch.

He smiled at the irony. Gains could be made in the most unexpected ways. Zhong Ye took a cursory glance at his quarters as he went through his forms. They had become more opulent. He was not one of the Emperor's most trusted advisers yet, less than a year after his promotion, but he was certainly favored.

Flowers! He would fill the chamber with flowers for Silver Phoenix's visit. And a gift, a small expensive token of some kind . . .

Zhong Ye paused in mid-stride. He was acting like a

besotted boy! How could Silver Phoenix ever consider him a romantic possibility?

He stripped off his tunic and spun across the hall with a series of punches and kicks at full force. He welcomed the quickening of his blood, the thundering of his heartbeat. Zhong Ye didn't stop until the sting of his scraped knuckles dulled the aching desire inside him. He stood, breathing hard, sweat trickling down his chest. He'd call off this rendezvous before he made a further fool of himself.

Zhong Ye scooped the last of the scallion flatbread into his mouth, chewing but not tasting. "Listen to this. 'Beware of the Poison Eagle. He has the cry of an infant and guards the life-giving root, on the mountain filled with precious metals.' I think it's referring to the empress root," he said. They had skimmed the passage before but had somehow missed its significance.

Zhong Ye read on. "'Once the root is unearthed, the man-eater will be drawn to the root's scent. It will attack and devour the person carrying the root. It is the reason for the beast's ever-lasting life.' This must be it!" He tapped the book with one finger.

"Does it give any additional clues to the location of the mountain?" Yokan asked.

Zhong Ye scanned the page quickly. "Nothing except

to say that the weather is always mild. Perhaps it's somewhere in the southwest province."

"Yes, I think we're close. Some more details, and we may be able to pinpoint the location." Yokan placed his quill on the stand and flexed his hand. "I'm stiff from so many hours of transcribing. Let's retire early tonight."

"I'll bring the book with me to study," Zhong Ye said as he collected his belongings.

Yokan smiled and headed for the door. "Sometimes a moment to rest the mind can also help," he said. "You've been reading and analyzing all day." The foreigner's every step was punctuated by the tinkling of the charms on his belt.

"Do those charms carry meaning?" Zhong Ye asked.

Yokan glanced down and cradled one with a pale hand. "These are tokens, given by my king for valor or sacrifice. Nothing great can ever be gained without either." He lifted his gaze. "You understand the necessity of sacrifice, don't you?"

Thinking of what he had given up to be within the palace gates, Zhong Ye almost smirked. "I do."

"The time will come when you'll need both valor and sacrifice for what we want to accomplish. I can depend on you?" Yokan's voice dropped as he spoke, his accent almost unnoticeable.

"Yes, master." Zhong Ye bowed as Yokan stepped from the study. When Zhong Ye finally followed Yokan outside and the frigid evening air enveloped them, Zhong Ye couldn't help wondering exactly what Yokan referred to. He still knew very little about the foreigner. Yokan was using him, but Zhong Ye was doing the same; it made for the best of court relations.

He turned the corner, and was startled by the full moon hovering above the sloped roofline. He paused to admire it, something tickling him like a fly on a horse's ear. *Wait for the extra moon and dark again.* An extra moon, an extra full moon within the same month! It happened once every few years. Could this be the meaning of the riddle? Zhong Ye hurried now to his quarters, excitement animating his steps.

He stopped short, alarmed by the lantern light that filtered through the carved panels. His entire hall was lit. He felt for the dagger he kept at his waist, before sliding the door open. Silver Phoenix sat in one of the carved chairs, her hands folded in her lap. She wore a flowing emerald dress, its skirt pooling at her feet. Zhong Ye swallowed the knot of surprise in his throat.

"What are you doing here?" He sounded more brusque than he had intended.

"You asked me to dine with you. I waited for you to

escort me but couldn't wait any longer." Her voice was calm, but he could detect an edge beneath the calmness.

"Didn't you receive the message I sent? I had to retract my invitation." He dumped the large books he carried onto the closest table. "I'm too busy with work."

"No, I didn't receive your message." She stood with fluid grace and raised one hand to touch her coiled braid. She had placed jeweled combs in her hair—for him, he realized. "I see you are not a man to keep your word. I'll bid you a peaceful evening then, Master Zhong."

Suddenly he was no longer tired or interested in study-ing *The Book of the Dead* anymore that night. "Please stay. My apologies. I'll ask the kitchen to send something." A special feast he had wanted, and flowers to adorn the hall, to pin in her hair. Instead, he had nothing except the defiant tilt of her chin. "Sit." He took her gently by the arm and persuaded her to sit back onto the plush brocaded cushion. "Just one moment."

He hurried to the small chamber tucked behind his quarters. It was dark, and he banged the door panel open, eliciting a sharp cry and clatter from the corner. "Xiao Mao!"

The servant boy leaped to his feet. "Master Zhong! I didn't realize you needed me." No older than twelve years, he was going through a growth spurt, and his trousers barely reached past his knees. He was too thin. Zhong Ye would have to ask the kitchen to make sure the boy got his fair share at mealtimes.

"Silver Phoenix is in my reception hall."

The boy's eyes bugged out of his head like a toad's. Zhong Ye almost laughed. "I delivered your message, mas—"

"Never mind. Go to the kitchen and ask for a meal to be prepared for us. Move!"

Xiao Mao returned within a quarter of an hour, bearing a lacquered tray laden with food. Another kitchen boy followed, also weighed down with dishes. Zhong Ye would have to remember to thank the chef tomorrow. The boys set the trays on a round table decorated with enameled orchids and scurried away without a word. Well done, he thought.

Zhong Ye set a ceramic cup in front of Silver Phoenix and filled it with rice wine, then poured some for himself. He raised his cup. "Thank you for staying."

Her full lips curved into a smile, and he didn't look away as she brought the cup to her mouth for a sip. "In truth, I wasn't sure if I would." She began pulling the lids off the dishes. "I considered slipping out when you went to speak with your servant boy."

She picked up silver eating sticks and began filling her plate. He followed suit. "And what made you stay?" he asked.

"I wanted to see you . . . despite your rudeness."

"I was a dolt," he said. "Forgive me?"

"Perhaps I'll let you make it up to me," she replied with a glint in her dark eyes.

Before he came to the palace, Zhong Ye had had affairs with girls who meant nothing to him. Silver Phoenix was different. He needed to know everything he could about her. "How many years are you?" he asked.

"Seventeen." She ate, taking small bites. "I've been on my own since twelve years. Being a song girl forces one to grow up fast."

He leaned back, no longer hungry. He poured himself more wine.

"Twelve years. That's so young." He studied unabashedly the delicate arch of her brows, the curve of her cheek, and the line of her neck.

"No younger than some of the concubines who enter the palace. We're deemed ready when we begin our monthly letting." She met his eyes. "How many years are you?"

"I entered the palace at sixteen years. This is my second year."

"Only eighteen?" she asked. "You act ten years older."

He laughed. "My youth isn't an advantage at the Emperor's court. Better if I appear older than my true age."

"What happened to your hands?" She touched one of his fingers. His knuckles were thick with scabs, and he flinched.

"Nothing." He smiled.

Silver Phoenix considered him as if she could read his thoughts, then finally tapped her wine cup with the tip of her finger. He filled it for her. "Do you miss your family?" she asked.

The question surprised him. It had been seven years since he'd left their small farm. His father, muscular and stoic. His mother, looking older than her years from working day in and out, year round. From rearing five children. She had been the prettiest girl in their village. But Zhong Ye had only glimpsed her beauty fleetingly when she smiled, a rarity. His siblings, with whom he had to fight for food at every meal. "There was no future there." What would be the point of missing them? He could never return.

She nodded. "I tried my best to convince my parents to keep me, did everything I could to be useful, so I could stay. But I was a third daughter."

She didn't need to explain further. Her parents sold her to a brothel when she turned twelve years, and once sold, she might as well have been dead to them. They sat in silence for long moments, as she pushed the food around on her plate.

He leaned across the table and reached for her free hand. "We can be friends to each other? That is almost like family?"

Her lips parted, and she looked at him with shining eyes. Finally, she smiled. And Zhong Ye gazed at her, losing himself, until she squeezed his fingers. Only then did he remember to smile back.

He woke the next morning with a tremendous headache. Swinging his legs to the side of the platform bed, he cursed and covered his face with both hands. They had talked into the early-morning hours, until Silver Phoenix had realized the time. He had walked her back to her small quarters then. He remembered the feel of her hand in his as if he were still holding it. He opened his palm. Had they truly meandered through the silent palace holding hands?

Zhong Ye shook his head at the preposterousness of it, then winced. He'd need a tonic before he went to court. The sun indicated it was at least midday. He cursed again. Court had already assembled, if not dispersed. Xiao Mao was crouched outside his quarters, playing with a cricket in a bamboo cage. He jumped to his feet and bowed.

Zhong Ye blocked the sun with an arm. "The herbal tonic to help ease headaches—"

"From overdrinking, master! Right away."

Zhong Ye cringed at Xiao Mao's loud enthusiasm but couldn't muster the energy to reprimand him. Besides, the boy was halfway to the herbalist by now. He returned to the relative darkness of his reception hall. The table was still stacked with half-eaten dishes from the previous evening. Something on the floor caught his attention: a tortoiseshell comb decorated with plum blossoms. He brought it to his nose, breathed in.

He was startled by the abrupt slam of the door panel. Carrying a small covered bowl, Xiao Mao scrambled in. Zhong Ye tucked the comb into his robe and accepted the drink. He scrunched his face at the bitterness of the brew but felt steadier even as he took the second sip. "Be truthful, did you forget to deliver my message to Silver Phoenix?"

The boy shook his head like a dog ridding itself of fleas. "No, master. I delivered it direct to her, word for word, as you told me. I waited for her reply, and she said, 'I'll pretend I never heard this.'"

Zhong Ye swallowed too fast and choked. He looked at Xiao Mao and knew the boy wasn't lying, then burst into laughter as the rest of the tonic sloshed to the floor.

CHAPTER SIX

Ai Ling was preparing for bed when she heard thumping from above. Curious, she went to investigate. No longer full, the moon looked as if someone had smudged a portion of it away in a sketch. Thin wisps of cloud drifted past. The sea wasn't especially rough, but she still had to do the awkward hip-jutting dance that came so naturally to her now as she moved across the deck. She found most of the crew near the ship's bow, huddled in a circle around a lantern. Yam Head, a wide grin on his face, was banging on a drum. He stopped when he saw her. He was outside the group, with his back turned to the men.

"Ho! Ai Ling's here. Join us," Nine said. Nine was nicknamed thus because he was the ninth of fourteen siblings. He was a hard worker and always friendly and jovial. "We've just convinced Chen Yong to play."

"What are you playing?" she asked.

"Pass the flower. Only we don't have a flower, so we're using the captain's fancy handkerchief." Nine waved a square of silver fabric in the air. She had seen it tucked in Peng's tunic pocket earlier that day.

"I don't drink," she said.

"Come join us anyway." Peng smiled. "You're part of the crew."

Ai Ling sat cross-legged beside him. Yam Head immediately began beating his drum again. Nine passed the silk handkerchief to his right. It circled twice, and when the drum stopped, Chen Yong was left holding it. The men slapped their hands on the deck, laughing and shouting. Lao Lu poured liquor from a cobalt jug, filling a cup to the rim.

"Bottoms up!"

Grinning, Chen Yong swept up his sleeves with a flourish before raising the wine cup. Then he tipped his head back and drank. The crew clapped with approval.

"Give us a song, Chen Yong!"

"No, recite a poem!"

"Let's ask for truth. The man's too closemouthed for his own good!"

This was followed by a grumble of agreement.

She couldn't tear her eyes away from him. Chen Yong spun the wine cup against the deck with one hand, his cheeks flushed. "You'll get no truths from me," he said, smiling.

"Ha!" Nine whacked him on the back. "Is this one even capable of lying?"

"Truth or another drink," Yen said. Even the usually reserved pilot had a glint of mirth in his eyes.

Chen Yong slammed the cup in front of Lao Lu, who filled it again. He drank, and the drumbeats picked up once more. The handkerchief circled the group three times. To her dismay, the drum stopped just as she was ready to toss it to Peng.

The crew roared.

"But I don't drink," she said.

"Just one sip." Peng chuckled.

The cook dribbled a drop of liquor into the same cup that Chen Yong had used. She blushed, raised the cup to her lips, and sipped cautiously. The men banged their palms in unison against the deck. The liquor was clear, different, and much stronger than the rice wine she'd had a few times. It burned her mouth and cut a hot path down her throat. She managed not to choke.

"Truth from Ai Ling?"

"No! A dance from the fair maiden!"

She laughed.

"How about a kiss?" Nine said teasingly.

"No," Chen Yong said. The finality of his tone pierced through the raucous merriment.

"Oh, come now, big brother. Just here." Nine tapped his cheek. "Innocent and harmless."

Chen Yong bowed his head, his face an even deeper red than before.

"Let Ai Ling decide," Peng said. He slanted her a glance, his amusement obvious.

She smacked the cup down in front of Lao Lu.

"Ho! She won't even give you a peck on the cheek, Nine!"

The crew guffawed. Lao Lu dribbled another sip into her cup, and she drank, grimacing.

The game continued on for some rounds. Peng sang a sea ditty for the crew, Lao Lu juggled three potatoes, and Yen recited a beautiful poem about the Moon Goddess, surprising Ai Ling with the rich tenor of his voice.

Dark clouds gathered, and the night deepened. The crew's rowdy teasing faded into the distance. Ai Ling licked her lips. The taste of the liquor stirred a faraway memory.

Suddenly blackness closed in around her. She was

crouched at a small desk littered with scrolls and text. She was so weary she could barely hold her head up. Her hand shook a little as she wrote with her calligraphy brush. Only a few more pages, and she would be done for the night.

Clutching a wine flask shaped like a gourd, her mentor crashed into the tiny study.

"Not surprised you're still up." He fell into the chair beside her, sighing loudly. He reeked of liquor, and the stench seemed to singe her nostrils.

"I've taught you for only two years, and you already know almost everything I do, boy."

He poked her shoulder with one finger. "You'll go far in life, Zhong Ye. You're smart an' ambitious." His words slurred together. "Just don't be stupid; don't become addicted." The scholar waved his wine flask in the air. "Never become a drunk like me!" He shoved it under her nose. "Try it!"

She shook her head. She was barely thirteen years and had never drunk wine. Her mentor pressed it to her lips. "Drink once and never drink again." He tilted the flask, and she was forced to gulp. It was foul, and she gagged.

The drumming reached a crescendo before stopping. Ai Ling, woozy, blinked. The handkerchief was in Chen

Yong's lap again. Disoriented, she jammed her fists into the deck.

"Truth this time! You can't escape it twice!"

"Yah! Do you have a sweetheart at home?"

She felt Chen Yong glance toward her, a glance too quick for her to catch.

"I'm betrothed," he said.

"Betrothed!"

"What's she look like? Do you keep a portrait of her?"

Her stomach cramped. She wondered if someone could become physically ill from jealousy.

"No," Chen Yong said.

"Is she as pretty as your sister here?"

"What kind of stupid question is that?" Da Yun, nicknamed Ox for his size and strength, punched Tien An in the arm.

"No," Chen Yong said without hesitation.

She looked up in surprise, but he was staring into the wine cup. Peng snorted, and the crew burst into laughter.

"At least the man's honest." Nine nudged Chen Yong's shoulder, chortling.

Lightning flashed, electrifying the air. The masts towered like giants, the sails their billowing capes, and the hairs on Ai Ling's arms stood on end.

"I think the festivities are over," Peng said. "A storm's

coming. I can smell it." The captain rose, and his men jumped to their feet.

Peng gave instructions to his crew, then nodded to Ai Ling and Chen Yong. "Return to your cabin. It's going to be a rough night."

They had experienced other storms during their journey, but this was something else altogether. It was as if the Queen Empress of Heaven herself had picked up the *Gliding Dragon* and now shook it with all her might. The winds were violent; the waves, monstrous. Ai Ling managed to prepare for bed, bruising her arms and legs twice before crawling onto the berth. She had rolled the thin blanket against her side when Chen Yong returned from changing.

The ship groaned and rocked across the sea. She and Chen Yong lay side by side like stiff corpses. She imagined the *Gliding Dragon* splitting in half and sinking into the depths. The storm was so loud she couldn't hear herself think. It was impossible to sleep. She had no inkling of how much time passed. Minutes? Hours?

Chen Yong's arm sneaked above the flimsy boundary, brushing against her. He reached for her hand and laced his fingers through hers. Thunder quaked like an angry god, rattling her teeth, and she shot straight up. The ship careened precariously and she flew into Chen Yong. He had barely managed to stay in the berth by flinging a fist against the wall. Now, like a crazy pendulum, the ship was rolling to the other side. Chen Yong threw his arms around her, tightening them across her lower back. "I've got you," he said.

She shouldn't have, couldn't have heard him above the storm. But she did. She shivered when his lips brushed her ear.

In the next instant, the ship pitched again, and they were flipped off the berth. She landed on her back in the narrow wedge between the bed and the wall, with Chen Yong on top, his hands caught beneath her. Her breath was knocked from her. The ship continued to lurch from side to side, but they were pinned securely in the tight space.

She could feel his heart beating wildly against hers. "You've got me?" she tried to shout above the racket.

"Well." He dipped his head to speak into her ear. "I am still here, am I not?"

It was as dark as a tomb, but she could see him as clearly as if they were lying beneath the midday sun. He was grinning, his golden eyes crinkled at the corners. She heard it in his voice. He eased his hands from beneath her and propped himself up by the elbows.

"You're heavy," she said. She couldn't bring herself to ask him to get off. She was light-headed from the fall, from the feeling of the entire length of his body pressed against hers.

He was quiet for a few moments, his breath hot and uneven on the hollow of her neck. "I don't think it's safe in bed."

The wind howled.

Ai Ling snorted, then dissolved into giggles. There was a brief pause before Chen Yong started laughing with her.

A loud pounding at their door made them jump, banging heads. "Ow!" they exclaimed at the same time.

"Chen Yong!" Peng thumped on the door harder. "Ai Ling!"

Chen Yong carefully extricated himself and rose. The door slammed open, and light flooded the cabin. She put her head down and lay still.

"Are you two all right?" Peng asked. She couldn't see him, but his voice sounded tired and tense.

"Mostly," Chen Yong replied, rubbing his head.

"There's a grip set into the wall by the berth. I'd hold on to it and each other for the remainder of the night."

Chen Yong nodded.

"The worst of the storm is over, and the ship survived

well." Peng handed his lantern to Chen Yong. He was soaking wet and dripping onto the floor. She could smell the rain and sea, the musk of wet wood. "Get some sleep."

Ai Ling lurched to her feet as Peng pulled the door closed. Chen Yong raised the lantern, and they saw a carved grip set into her side of the bed. She hadn't noticed it before.

"I'll sleep on your side and hold the grip," Chen Yong said.

"And you've got me?"

He laughed, his eyes glowing in the lantern light. "I've got you."

Ai Ling woke the next morning with his arm wrapped around her shoulder. She was on her side, her face burrowed against his chest, her own arm flung across his waist.

The ship's rocking was once again gentle.

And although fast asleep, Chen Yong was clutching the grip with one tight fist.

Zhong Ye was tired of Yokan's study, tired of *The Book of the Dead*. How much longer before they could unravel the location of the empress root? Remembering something, he reached for the almanac.

Yokan lifted his head from his scroll.

"I think we're due soon for a double moon on the lunar calendar," Zhong Ye said.

"What?"

"When the full moon appears twice within the same month."

"Yes. Wraiths' month, we call it in Paan. When the dead come out to roam. But what does that have to do with anything?"

"'Wait for the extra moon then dark again.' From the riddle we read. A double-moon month." Zhong Ye flipped through the pages of the almanac. "And the next will be in the fourth moon, two months following this one."

"Well done, Zhong! But this means our time is even more limited. 'This heaven-sent root only for a month shall grow, Nurtured in warm climes, by its own soft glow,'" Yokan read back to Zhong Ye what he already knew by heart.

"The Poison Eagle is not listed in *The Book of Bestiary*. Are you certain the empress root grows only somewhere in Xia?" Squinting at the list of common and rare birds in the book already open on the blackwood table, Zhong Ye rubbed his brow with one hand.

"Have you tried searching in the nonavian sections?" His expression caused Yokan to shrug. "It's worth a try."

Zhong Ye flipped through *The Book of Bestiary* and began reading from the beasts section. "By the demons you were right!" he exclaimed. "'Only capable of flight during the month of the extra moon, the Poison Eagle emits the cry of a small infant and will peck the flesh off the bones of man. The creature is tiger-size and is said to devour all, including hair and nails. He dwells on Mount Luwu near the Zegeng River.'" Zhong Ye jumped off his stool and began pacing around the large table. "No mention of the empress root, but I'm certain this is the creature that guards it!"

"Have you heard of Mount Luwu?" Yokan asked.

"The name sounds familiar. I believe he was an ancient god . . ." Zhong Ye ran to one of the shelves and pulled out *The Book of the Divine*. "We'll find the location of Mount Luwu in here, I'd wager on it."

Zhong Ye was early for his meeting with Silver Phoenix. He turned a slow circle in the meadow tucked within the Garden of Tranquility. The plum trees were just beginning to bloom, their delicate scent carried on a soft spring breeze. Zhong Ye lifted his face to the sun and stretched his arms overhead, grinning. He was alone. It had been so long since he'd had time to himself.

He began a meditation exercise to clear his mind and

then limbered up with stretches, before going into some basic techniques of shuen. He flowed from one stance to the next, oblivious of all but his form.

He finally stopped. His breathing came too fast, and his heart thudded hard against his chest. Zhong Ye was about to remove his tunic when a flutter of color caught his eye. Silver Phoenix was leaning against a plum tree, a pink sleeve raised to hide her nose and mouth. But he could tell she was smiling.

"How long have you been there?" he asked.

"For some time," she said, gliding toward him.

He took a deep drink from his water flask. She tilted her head for a kiss, her black eyes like a cat's against the sunlight. He somersaulted, flipped onto his hands, and walked on them, circling her.

Silver Phoenix crossed her arms. "You're just showing off now."

"Yes, I am." He jumped back onto his feet and kissed her on the lips, laughing.

She pursed her mouth, feigning annoyance. But her smile gave her away. "I didn't know you practiced shuen."

"Since I was thirteen years."

She took his hand and pulled him past the plum trees to a small stream. He stopped and splashed water on his face.

"Are you good?" She handed him a cloth.

He laughed into the soft material. It smelled of roses, from Mei Gui's wardrobe. "Not really. Those truly talented in shuen begin learning not long after they start walking."

"You looked so powerful."

Zhong Ye smiled as she laced her fingers through his again. "It helps to clear my mind."

Silver Phoenix led him into the heart of the garden. Yellow, orange, and white lilies fluttered like butterflies at their feet. A brocaded blanket had been spread on the ground, and the air was thick with the peppery scent of wisteria. She sat and carefully adjusted her skirt. He lay down beside her, tucking his arms beneath his head. She set covered lacquered boxes on the blanket.

"Shuen, alchemy, poetry, and politics. Is there anything you can't do?" she asked in a teasing tone.

He grabbed her hand and kissed her fingertips. "I never made a good farm boy." She smiled, but he suddenly couldn't return it. He had meant it in jest, but it was a poor joke. His throat closed, and he glanced away.

"What's wrong?"

"I ran away when I was eleven years. Worked, studied, apprenticed, became a palace eunuch." He waved a hand. "All this. So I could become better than a farmer and give my mother what she deserved in life."

"You're a filial son," she said.

"Am I? Perhaps what they needed more was for me to be there to plow the fields." He tried to picture his mother's face. "I send coin back each month. But no letters. No one can read them." He could remember only his mother's eyes, light brown as a walnut shell. "I just wanted to escape. I haven't seen them in *seven* years."

Silver Phoenix bent over him, cupping his face with a cool hand. "We have each other now."

He reached for her, fingers twining in her hair. She tasted of berries and sunshine. He finally broke away. "I'll be taking a short trip soon," he said.

She had curled against him but straightened up now. "To where?"

"Somewhere close. Just a quick journey, to gather a rare herb for Yokan."

"Why do you have to go?" She plucked at her dress, pouting. "I don't particularly care for that foreigner."

He laughed. "He's high in favor with the Emperor. And my working with him only augments my own status. It's an honor that he chose me for this important task."

"How long will you be gone?" She turned her face away, and the sunlight caught the rubies in her ears, a gift from him. "What herb are you searching for?"

"A week at most. No longer."

"I'll miss you," she murmured against his lips, as the bees droned lazily above them.

Could this goddesslike woman actually care for him? Zhong Ye didn't know if he could allow himself to believe it.

They had agreed that he should take the trip alone; the risk of others' knowing the location of the empress root was too great.

"Can I trust you?" Yokan had asked. "The root can cure many—perhaps all—ailments. But it is useless to gain immortality without my spell."

Zhong Ye had assured Yokan that he would return and bring the root if he were fortunate enough to find it. He was no fool. He wanted immortality, not good health. He only hoped that he was right about Mount Luwu's location. The ancient temple had been built on the mountain now known as Brilliant Tears, not far from the palace. He should be able to journey there on horseback within three days.

He was thankful the weather was mild and he wouldn't be traveling long or far. He strapped a spear to his back, its sharp tip palm length and made from pure gold. The metal was too soft to use as a weapon, but *The Book of*

Bestiary had claimed that gold was the only metal that could slay the Poison Eagle. Zhong Ye touched his belt, where his gold dagger was sheathed.

He had not ridden in a long time, but it returned naturally to him, and he patted the horse's mane as they trotted through the massive city gates. He had decided not to say good-bye to Silver Phoenix that morning. She was already worried for him, despite all his assurances; it was as if she could sense the danger ahead. She had clung to him the last time they had seen each other, every part of her touching him.

He knew he was in love with her. But did she truly care for him? She had given him a silk handkerchief that he carried close to his heart. He would survive this so he could see her again and would return with his satchel filled with empress root.

Zhong Ye climbed the Mountain of Brilliant Tears in the late afternoon after three days of travel. He would search for the stream that started on the peak and flowed into the Zegeng River on the other side of the mountain. It was now called the River of Brilliant Tears.

The air chilled as the sun began to set. His horse snorted and slowed its pace. He reined in the beast and tied it to a dead pine. What had been a lush landscape full of tall trees and foliage had begun to thin as they ascended. Brilliant Tears did not support plant life but was rich with metals and minerals.

Zhong Ye made a fire and huddled close to it, his body tensing each time he heard a noise. Once he heard what sounded like an infant's cry echoing off the side of the mountain. He convinced himself it was his imagination. But his horse nickered nervously and tossed its mane.

He finally fell asleep with his back pressed against a withered pine, the gold-tipped spear across his thighs. His horse's snort startled him awake. The fire had burned to flickering embers, and a sliver moon hung overhead. Zhong Ye winced, his neck and shoulders were stiff. He stood to stretch his arms and legs, then went to pat the horse. The animal was wide awake, agitated.

"We've a long climb tomorrow, friend. We both need sleep."

At that moment a piercing wail shuddered through the night. The horse tried to bolt, straining against its rope.

"Settle down, settle down," Zhong Ye whispered, as much for himself as for the horse. He stoked the fire and wondered how many hours it was before daybreak.

Somehow he managed to doze off again, and it was a misty and gray morning when he woke. The horse was grazing on wild grasses, more brown than green.

Zhong Ye ate some dried beef and mango slices, washed his meal down with water, and fed the horse two fresh apples.

There were no well-worn paths to follow up the Mountain of Brilliant Tears, although the desolate terrain was easy to navigate, the higher one climbed. It was said to be cursed, haunted by vengeful spirits that stole the souls of infants. The mountain was deserted, and he knew of no one who had ever climbed it.

The mist dissipated as they ascended. The smell of ash and burning wood permeated the air, although there was no indication of a fire, ancient or recent. Sunlight filtered through the skeletal limbs of dead trees, and the horse picked its way carefully up the black silt mountainside that was littered with dark rocks.

They reached a plateau just after dusk. Zhong Ye dismounted and investigated the ruins of a stone temple, not much bigger than his own reception hall, built to the god Luwu. Only the foundation remained. He climbed onto the crumbling rock and stepped gingerly toward a rectangular stone altar. It was as long as he was tall and two hand widths across.

He lit his small travel lantern and held it over the surface of the altar. Characters, more like rudimentary drawings than writing, were carved into the stone. The words wrapped around three sides. On the fourth was a carving of the god Luwu himself, a man's head on a tiger's body, standing upright with claws extended. Zhong Ye dropped to his knees and counted nine tails on the god, one so faint he had to trace his fingertip over the shallow groove to be certain.

This was it. Just as *The Book of the Divine* had described. He jumped to his feet, thrilled, until he heard his horse's hesitant whinny. Night was falling. Zhong Ye could hear the soft sounds of moving water in the distance. Was this the river he was searching for?

He fed the horse a few carrots and tied it to a large rock. He stroked its velvet nose, then left the animal snorting contentedly as he picked his way toward the sound of water. He held his spear in one hand and the small lantern in the other. The black silt landscape was disappearing into the darkness of night, and Zhong Ye stumbled into a shallow hole. Cursing, he dusted the dirt from his hands; he was grateful that the lantern hadn't been extinguished when he dropped it. From then on, he navigated even more slowly. He would have plunged to his death if a rush of wind carrying the wet scent of water hadn't hit his face. He knelt, holding his lantern in front of him. Its flame seemed no bigger than a firefly and did nothing to illuminate what was below. It was impossible to gauge how wide or deep the crevice was or in what direction the water flowed. The moon's thin smile from the previous evening had widened to a grimace and still afforded little light.

He would have to investigate again in the morning. He picked his way back toward his horse and exhaled a long sigh when he finally spotted the temple. He should have made a fire but wanted to ration the little bit of firewood he had gathered during the course of the day. Zhong Ye set his lantern on the altar and searched the sky for the mourning star. He'd been gone for almost two hours according to its position on the horizon.

A soft tittering, like a babe's giggle. He spun on his heel, his spear drawn. A cold sweat gathered at his nape in the silence that followed. Was the horse asleep? Zhong Ye grabbed the lantern and vaulted from the temple's foundation to run toward his horse. He skidded short, at first unable to comprehend the scene, faintly illuminated by the wan light. The rope that he had wound around the large rock snaked on the ground toward the horse's skeleton, picked clean to the bones, only its hooves remaining. The monster had done such a thorough job the bones looked as if they had been bleached under a desert sun for weeks. Zhong Ye staggered and almost fell. Another giggle, and he whirled to thrust his spear in the dark. "Come on," he shouted to the night sky. "Come out and fight!"

Something swooped down, unseen wings fanning the scent of fresh kill. Zhong Ye stabbed upward, touching nothing. He turned in a tight circle, every muscle tense, knowing that he was an easy target. He scrambled back to the temple ruin and crouched against the rough altar, straining to hear any small noises. Swallowing the sick taste in his mouth, he stared wide-eyed into the darkness.

He didn't move until daybreak. He hadn't slept, and his lantern had burned out hours ago. The morning shrouded him in mist. He took a sip of water from his flask and forced himself to eat some salted biscuits.

As the weak sunlight began to disperse the fog, he returned to his horse's skeleton. He crouched and scanned the dirt around it. The area was marked with hoofprints. No doubt the horse had tried to run, but he had clinched the poor creature's fate when he tied it to the stone. A different set of prints caught his eye. They resembled tiger prints and appeared only near the skeleton. It became clear to Zhong Ye that the monster had attacked from the air, landing only when it was ready to feed. Perhaps the horse had saved him, satiating the Poison Eagle's appetite. When would it be hungry again?

He began to gather his supplies—firewood, provisions, a jar filled with more lantern oil, a rope. He straightened and dusted off his tunic, his hand grazing over the pocket where he had tucked Silver Phoenix's silk handkerchief. He pulled it out, and the subtle scent of jasmine permeated the air. He brought the fabric to his lips before tying it to the sash at his waist and heading back toward the river.

CHAPTER SEVEN

They were taking the evening meal when a hoarse scream topside startled Ai Ling. Peng and Chen Yong leaped to their feet, and her eating sticks clattered to the table.

Everyone rushed out at once; but Peng stopped short, and Chen Yong paused beside him. She tucked herself behind Chen Yong's back. The sun had just slipped below the horizon, casting the *Gliding Dragon* in an eerie gray. There were four crew members on deck, each transfixed by two naked figures writhing toward them. Both were rail thin; their black hair hung like kelp. Ai Ling could see the sharp edges of shoulder blades as they drew closer to the men, who stood frozen, mouths agape.

Ox took a timid step forward. "Mother? Is it truly you?"

The creature raised a white arm, fingers uncurling. Ox took another step. Ai Ling hissed, and her scalp crawled. There was a thump from the side of the ship, and something pale and wet crashed onto the deck. The thing held itself in fetal position, dark hair covering its face, before rising like a wave to its feet. It was getting too dark to see, but somehow Ai Ling knew who it was. She pushed her way between Peng and Chen Yong, even as Peng shoved her back, and a twinge of annoyance filled her that he should be so rough.

Suddenly, sobbing, Ox had fallen into the creature's embrace.

"No!" Peng rushed forward. "Don't let them touch you!"

Ox began to whimper. He shrank before Ai Ling's eyes, his flesh growing white and puckered. The skin tightened on his face until his eyes bulged. A thin anemic thing, he slid to the deck.

"Sea Shifters! We need fire!" Peng shouted. "Yen!"

She could hear what Peng was saying, but the naked figures captured all her attention. Four of them now. Ashen and slender, some with seaweed clinging to their thighs. Curiously unmoved by Ox's strange fate, she stepped toward them. One figure looked so familiar. If only she could see his eyes. That smile . . .

"Bai Lan? Is there enough to eat at home?" Lao Er, another sailor, stood rigid, staring at the creature that Ox had mistaken for his mother. Now, noiseless, hand outstretched, the creature stepped over Ox. Ai Ling couldn't turn her eyes away. The Sea Shifter spoke words it seemed only Lao Er could hear.

"I'm so sorry." Lao Er opened his arms to welcome her. "I've missed you." Nine, his eyes averted, lunged and grabbed Lao Er hard enough that he fell to the deck with an audible grunt. "Nine, that's my wife!"

"No, it's not!" Peng shouted. "They'll kill you!"

Yen burst from the bridge with two lit torches in hand, their flames so strong that Ai Ling felt the heat. He tossed one to Chen Yong and, brandishing the torch, ran toward the closest creature.

"They fear only fire. Bring more torches. Burn them!" Peng ordered. Yen set fire to the naked woman's dark head. Ear-rending shrieks and the stench of burning flesh and rancid shellfish filled the air.

Ai Ling threw her spirit at the Sea Shifters. She glided over them, but their spirits were slippery, as if encased in flowing water. She could gather nothing from them; there was nothing to latch on to.

"But my daughter—" Tien An protested. Xiao Hou had emerged from nowhere and clutched at his father's trousers, his expression conflicted and uncertain.

Suddenly, the figure that had looked so familiar to Ai Ling moved into the torchlight. Entranced, she reached a hand to him. Although he was so thin that his ribs were defined ridges under almost translucent skin, Li Rong's smile was still the same. He was naked, and embarrassed, she ducked her face for a brief moment. But his eyes compelled her to meet his gaze.

"Li Rong . . . I'm so sorry," she whispered.

Chen Yong made a choking noise beside her.

"Burn them!" Peng shouted. "Drive them back to the sea!" The bewildered crew moved in slow motion but dutifully raised their torches.

Li Rong was so close now that his entire face was lit by Chen Yong's torch. She took a step toward him without realizing that she did so. He opened both arms to her, and she stumbled into him. "Forgive me." She tasted the hot salt of her own tears.

"Of course, Ai Ling."

She heard him say it, even though his lips never moved. His hand brushed her wet cheek. She gasped as coldness convulsed through her. "I forgive you." His words were ice against her ear. He wrapped damp fingers around her neck, and it was as if her spirit were plunged into a frigid sea.

A strong arm wound around her waist. Chen Yong pulled her against his chest, and she stifled a cry. He brandished the torch, a guttural sound escaping his lips, and she screamed. The Sea Shifter cowered, its unnatural shriek piercing the air.

"Go below deck." Chen Yong shoved her toward the hatch. His amber eyes were wild with something she couldn't identify.

"But—"

"Go!" he roared. Chen Yong raised his hand to push her again but froze at the last moment. As if he couldn't bear to touch her.

Ai Ling fell back and pulled open the hatch. She staggered below, her throat full of tears, the scent of burned flesh and seaweed smothering her.

The screaming and shouting seemed to go on forever. Ai Ling lay on the hard berth, her knees drawn to her chest. Unable to stop shaking, she buried her face in her blanket and recited the mantra for protection first soundlessly and then aloud, stringing the words together like a silk cocoon.

Finally, unable to endure it any longer, she climbed the

steps and tried to push the hatch open. But it was locked from above. She pounded against it, the sound muted by the commotion on deck.

She returned to the berth and didn't know how much time had passed when an eerie silence descended on the ship. The lantern had burned low. A scraping, and the door opened. Chen Yong, his face drawn, his eyes haunted, stood in the doorway.

Ai Ling sat up. "You're not hurt?" She reached for him.

He entered the small cabin, filling the space, and sat down beside her. "We forced them all back to the sea." He dropped his face into his hands and rubbed hard. "I can still hear the screaming in my head. Smell their burning flesh."

"Goddess. It was awful," she whispered, and touched his shoulder. Chen Yong flinched, and she snatched her hand back.

He raised his head and tried to smile. "We were fortunate Peng was familiar with sea lore. Sea Shifters I know nothing about."

"Did he tell you more?"

"Yes. After they all were driven back, we met on the bridge." He pressed his fists over his eyes. "We lost Da Yun."

Da Yun. The large man they had fondly called Ox.

They had not spoken many words to each other, but he had always been kind to her.

"Peng said the Sea Shifters seek warmth from living humans. And they"—Chen Yong's brow creased—"they take on the image of loved ones."

She picked at her blanket with trembling fingers.

"You saw Li Rong?" Chen Yong's voice was a hoarse whisper.

"I did." She blinked away the tears.

He brushed the back of her hand. "He's at peace now, Ai Ling."

Was he? Or was Li Rong trapped in the underworld? Had she burned his heart in time?

She nodded, wiping her eyes. "Whom did you see?"

But he would not look at her and simply shook his head.

They buried Da Yun at sea the next morning. Peng and Da Yun's closest friend, Lao Er, wrapped his pale and shrunken corpse in sky blue cloth as Yen recited prayers from *The Book of the Divine*. Ai Ling shuddered when the body slipped into the water. She imagined the Sea Shifters clutching at him now with spindly arms, triumphant, claiming him as their own.

The day was gray and cold, and remained so. The

crew took their midday meal in silence. She didn't have an appetite, couldn't forget the sight of Da Yun's body sinking into the waves, of Li Rong wrapped in sky blue cloth on his funeral pyre.

"You should eat something," Peng said. "You look exhausted."

Her throat closed. Chen Yong touched her knee beneath the table. She looked at him in surprise, but he had already pulled his hand back.

"Are the Sea Shifters something you've encountered before?" she asked Peng.

The captain fiddled with a gold button on his shirt. He hadn't shaved, and there were dark shadows beneath his eyes. "No. It's a tale we shared while drinking to try to spook one another." Yen poured him more tea, and Peng thanked him by tapping a finger against the table. "I wasn't even certain the fire would work. It was a risk to our ship, but the Sea Shifters were far more dangerous." He gave a slight shake of his head. "Da Yun was the first crew member I've ever lost."

"Chen Yong said they take on the image of a loved one," Ai Ling said. She swallowed the lump in her throat.

"According to lore. Yes." Peng studied her, and she tucked her spirit close. "A loved one, living or dead.

They prey on guilt, on unspoken emotions, or the unre-
solved. . . ."

They sat at the table without speaking for long
moments, each lost in thought.

Everyone dispersed after the meal, and much of Lao
Lu's delicious food was left in the pot.

Ai Ling went up on deck. Several of the crew nodded
somberly as she strolled the perimeter of the ship. The
dampness seeped through her, and she drew in the salt
air. The *Gliding Dragon* flew over the waters.

She stepped over Yam Head and Xiao Hou, who were
sprawled on the deck, playing war with wooden sticks.
"Wanna fish with us again when the winds drop, miss?"
Yam Head asked.

She ruffled his hair. "We'll see," she said, although a
chill crept down her spine. They were so vivid, these
memories that were not hers, it felt as if she had lived
them. Had she made them up? At the stern she wandered up the two flights of stairs to the top deck without
thinking. It was her favorite place on the ship because of
the quiet.

She almost turned around when she saw Chen Yong
hunched on a stool, facing the sea, his head bowed over a
book. Instead, she stood and watched him. She realized
he was sketching and smiled. She knew that he studied

art as she did but had never seen any of his work. She took stealthy steps toward him, hoping to peek.

He turned when she was only a few paces away and closed the book, his mouth twitching into a half grin. Dark shadows curved beneath his eyes. He hadn't been sleeping well either. "I was drawing," he said.

"And I was trying to steal a glimpse."

He smiled. "You've never shown me your sketchbook."

"No." She leaned against the railing, facing him. "I didn't even know you had one."

"I remembered our last journey together and you always sketching in yours. I packed one for this trip."

"So—" She held out a hand.

Chen Yong gave her his sketchbook. "This means I'll get to look through yours?"

"No promises," she said. The book was bound in soft brown calfskin, luxurious to the touch. She ran her fingers over the cover before opening it. The *Gliding Dragon*'s masts, bridge, and stern were rendered in strong strokes. There was the same boldness in his drawings as in his calligraphy. Portraits of the crew, including an exact likeness of Yam Head, grinning mischievously from the page. She came across a profile of herself, chin tucked in one hand. She was drawn in delicate, careful lines, a dreamy look in her eyes.

"It's me." She glanced up, amazed.

"Oh." Chen Yong stood. "I think you were looking out to sea." He took the sketchbook and closed it.

"You're very good," she said.

"It's only a hobby." He fumbled, finally clasping the book behind his back. "Are you all right?"

She remembered the slow-rising terror; the shrieking and jumbled emotions pulsing across the massive ship. "I hadn't seen the like since . . . our last journey together."

"I know," he said in a low voice.

"I couldn't do anything to stop them. I tried." At least until she was seduced by the image of Li Rong.

"I'm sorry for locking you below. I was worried. I—" He was studying her intently, as if she had changed somehow. As if he didn't recognize her. "You always act with courage, Ai Ling."

She remembered the frantic look in his eyes, the way his voice had reached through to her. She hadn't felt courageous; she had felt lost. "You were the one who saved me."

He blushed and dropped his gaze.

They climbed down the steps to the main deck together, without speaking. Awkward as wooden puppets.

Zhong Ye hiked back toward the sound of flowing water. His trip seemed shorter in the daylight. Still, when he came upon the edge of the deep gorge, it was a surprise. He dropped to his knees and leaned over, feeling a small gust of air from below. The crevice was no wider than the length of two men, and from what he could see, it both narrowed and widened as it wound its way down the mountain. The drop could kill him; he would have to climb down. He stood and scanned the skies, tilted his head to listen for any other sound besides the river below.

He decided to hike along the edge of the gorge and stopped when he saw the waterfall. A sheer rock face prevented him from climbing higher. The sun was directly overhead; the silt below glittered with gold and coppery flecks. The bottom of the gorge was much closer now but still not close enough to jump. And there was nothing to tie a rope to.

He ran his hand over the sharp black crystal of the crevice walls. The rocks were uneven, and he could find handholds; but one mistake, and he'd fall, an easy meal for the Poison Eagle. He left everything at the top, except for the spear that he strapped to his back, the lantern, newly filled with oil, his flask, and a few slices of dried beef. He secured the gold dagger at his waist.

Zhong Ye had done many things as a farm boy, but he had never climbed down the face of a rock wall. He prayed as he concentrated on finding one sturdy foothold after another and carefully navigated his way down the jagged wall. His arms began to burn, and his palms became slick. After what seemed like hours, he finally jumped and landed gracefully on his feet.

He went to the stream and drank deeply, then flung himself down on the damp dirt. In the next moment, when he opened his eyes, the day had darkened: he had fallen asleep. He cursed himself for his stupidity, then stood quickly and looked around. He could see or hear nothing except the waterfall.

Hidden beside the falling water was a fissure wide enough to slip through. He pulled his spear from his back and cautiously stepped through the opening. The ground squelched beneath his feet. It was a small cavern, and he glanced up to catch a circular view of the sky. Water trickled down one wall and collected in a shallow pool. He crouched and examined it; it was not more than two hands deep.

Zhong Ye left the cavern and climbed to higher ground. He would wait for night, search for her when dark then bright. He settled against the rough wall of the gorge, feeling safer with it pressed against his back, and chewed on a piece of dried beef. It was already dusk, and he lit his small lantern in anticipation of evening.

The darkness gathered in degrees, until all he could see was the small beacon from his lantern. Alert, he strained his eyes in the darkness. Nothing. He squeezed through the fissure again and approached the pool. The lantern light reflected in the shallow water.

He extinguished the flame. A glow seemed to emanate from the pool, so indistinct that he blinked several times, wondering if he imagined it. As the moments passed, the glow grew brighter. Faint circles the size of his fist bloomed. He rolled up his sleeves, then plunged his hand into the water. He began to scoop out cold mud in handfuls and was elbow deep when he finally touched something smooth and firm.

Zhong Ye's fingers were numb by the time he was finally able to pry the object free. He lit his lantern again with a long pinewood match, and the flame guttered and danced. Almost the size of his palm, the empress root was ebony colored and shaped like a peanut, which could be described as a woman, he supposed. He cut off a thin slice with his dagger. A subtle scent like almonds wafted through the air. After placing the root carefully in the satchel slung across his shoulder, he turned back toward the shallow pool.

He snuffed the lantern and closed his eyes, his heart racing. When he opened them again, he counted the number of glowing circles. Eight. He noticed that a faint glow still hovered above the spot where he had found the first root. He spent the next hours digging in the dark. He was shivering and exhausted by the time he had all eight empress roots secured in his satchel.

He was lighting the lantern when the wail of an infant echoed through the small cavern, and he cursed, dropping the match. There was a soft titter by his ear. He lunged for the cave opening, and something massive swept overhead, then thumped him from behind, gouging holes in his back. He sprawled to the ground, teeth clacking. He could hear mad giggling through his pain.

Zhong Ye crawled on his hands and knees, fumbling for his spear in the dark. Where was it? There was a loud wail, and he rolled away, felt the flap of wings as sharp claws tore into the arm he had thrown across his face. Warm blood dribbled across his skin. Zhong Ye shouted in anger and pain and drew his dagger. If he were to die in this cavern, he would die fighting.

A sudden swish of wings, and he thrust the dagger through the air and connected with something leathery and yielding. The monster screeched and swooped away. Grinning, he spun to follow the noise. "It's pure gold—if you'd like another taste!"

The abrupt silence was eerie, and the dimming phosphorescence from the shallow pool did nothing to illuminate the cavern. He stalked toward the opening of the fissure, gripping his dagger, too furious to notice his injuries.

Zhong Ye stepped out into the gorge and was just able to catch a breath before he saw a blur of motion, a shadow in the starlight. Two brilliant yellow eyes stared at him. The monster was pacing. It was the size of a tiger, the color and print of its fur impossible to make out in the darkness. But he saw the shape of the beak and a long tail swishing, and as it came at him, its huge wings unfurled.

He pressed himself against the rock wall, heard the waterfall splashing into the stream beside him, felt a soft spray and the stick of blood on his arms and face. The monster sat back on its haunches, the same stance the palace cats took before leaping upon their prey. Zhong Ye crouched, dagger drawn, as it pounced.

Claws dug into his shoulders, almost a hug, as the Poison Eagle stabbed him with its beak. If it pierced his throat, he would die. Zhong Ye tucked his chin and drove his dagger up. It slid between the beast's ribs. The

Poison Eagle wailed, sounding exactly like a hurt babe, and fell back. Zhong Ye lunged after it, slicing through one of its wings.

The monster whipped around, spitting poison, and swiped at Zhong Ye with its huge paw. If only he had his spear. The Poison Eagle stalked toward him, tail thrashing. Zhong Ye was beginning to feel faint. It sprang again. He twisted as the horn slashed across his midriff before puncturing his side. He fell to his knees, and the beast followed, its beak slicing into his scalp. He slammed the dagger into the creature's throat. It gurgled, then collapsed to the ground, shuddering. Pain erupted in an explosion of light, and he forced himself to rise, clutching his side with one hand, blood running between his fingers. He drove his dagger into one golden eye and looked away as the beast's body twitched, then stilled.

After a few moments Zhong Ye pulled the blade out, gagging at the thick scent of blood. He limped back into the dark cavern, head spinning, and crashed unconscious to the ground.

When Zhong Ye woke, he wished he hadn't. Every bone in his body ached; every muscle screamed in agony. It hurt to breathe, and he couldn't abide the thought of moving. Had he actually lived? He tried to flex his fingers but couldn't feel them. He began to shake and groaned as he struggled to rise to a sitting position. Light shone from above, but he had no way of knowing what time it was—or even what day. He glanced down at the dagger, surprised that he still clutched it.

The dampness of the earth had soaked through him, and his teeth chattered from the cold. He slowly rotated onto his hands and knees and, still holding the dagger, crawled to the cavern entrance. Dagger hand. Other hand. Scrape. One knee. Other knee. Shudder.

Somehow he made his way outside, where the daylight drove a spike of agony into his throbbing head. The Poison Eagle's corpse sprawled in front of him, and he swayed away from it toward the stream, where he fell onto his stomach to drink from the edge like some wild animal. He kept drinking until he felt sick, then submerged his face in the water. He managed to pull back and lay his cheek on the bank, before losing consciousness again.

Perhaps it was the warmth of the sun that stirred him awake. Zhong Ye opened his eyes to find himself staring at the Poison Eagle's corpse. Like a leopard, the creature had a golden coat with black spots. But its head was that of an eagle, with a sharp beak and a horn the length of his index finger on its head. Its claws were lethal.

Zhong Ye staggered to his feet. His tunic was crusted with dried blood, and he gingerly pulled it over his head, biting back a cry of pain. A deep, jagged gash stretched from his navel to his waist. He bundled his tunic and pressed it against the wound. A tight burning radiated from his shoulders across his upper back. He wouldn't be able to climb up that rock wall. He searched for the last piece of dried beef in his pocket and forced himself to eat. Even his jaw ached. He hadn't thought to pack any medicinal herbs. He had expected either to succeed unscathed or to die, not to be injured and barely alive.

His eyes fell on his satchel by the water. He limped to it and withdrew one of the empress roots. What a fool he was! According to the ancient text, he had the best healing herb in the world right here. He rummaged for the thin slice he had cut from the first root and pinched it between his fingertips. The subtle scent of almonds perfumed the air, and he drew his next breath without shuddering. The flesh of the root was ivory. Cautiously, he licked it—a little sweet—then popped it in his mouth. It crunched like a water chestnut, although drier in consistency. Instantly he felt stronger, the pain lifting from him.

But how much should he eat? He glanced at his midriff. The gash closed and healed even as he stared at it in amazement, forming a thick scab that snaked across his waist. He watched, transfixed, as the deep hole in his side knitted itself together. He threw his arms over his head, flexed his shoulders, and felt nothing. Zhong Ye stripped off his trousers and walked into the water until he was waist deep, then stood underneath the waterfall and scrubbed the dried blood and dirt from his body. The empress root pulsed through him, exhilarating and potent.

His clothes were ruined, and he only donned his trousers for the climb back up. He tied Silver Phoenix's handkerchief at his waist. With one finger he traced his wounds, now lines of soft pink skin, and shook his head in awe. He jogged back into the cavern to retrieve his spear and lantern. The spear was resting flush along the far edge of the cave; the shallow pool gave no clue of what it had carried.

Zhong Ye left the cave and crouched beside the Poison Eagle's carcass, wishing he had brought paper and charcoal so he could sketch the beast for Yokan. Instead, he hacked off one sharp claw with his golden dagger; the dagger had been poisonous to the beast and had saved Zhong Ye's life. He wondered if the monster had eaten enough of the empress root somehow to resurrect itself; would it rise to live again, growing back the claw that he had taken? After committing every detail of the creature to memory, he packed up his belongings and started up the side of the gorge. He did it without thinking, like a spider on its own web. When he reached the top, his heartbeat had barely quickened; he had never felt this invincible.

He changed into fresh clothes, secured his provisions, and jogged down the path, resting only once before reaching the base of the Mountain of Brilliant Tears.

When Zhong Ye returned to the palace, he went straight to Mei Gui's quarters. Silver Phoenix rushed into the reception hall and barely closed the panel to the bedchamber behind her before he swept her into his arms and lifted her off the ground to spin them both in dizzying circles.

She gasped and laughed. The sound sent a surge of love, then desire through him. He set her down with care and kissed her. She gasped again, a different sound this time, and pretended to push him away. "I've been so worried over you," she whispered. Her face was flushed, her parted lips, a deeper color.

Zhong Ye glanced toward the bedchamber and stepped back decorously. "How is Mei Gui? How is the babe?"

"She's beginning to thicken at the waist. She glows."

He caressed her cheek. "How beautiful you would be, with child." In his exuberance, he did not think before he spoke, and time stopped, the words hanging between them like jagged ice. An overwhelming sorrow filled him. He could never give her a child, this woman he adored. Zhong Ye swallowed hard, wished he could swallow his words. Silver Phoenix reached for his hand and drew it to her lips.

"I'm so glad you're home." She smiled, her dark eyes bright.

Home. He would make one for her someday. One where she was the mistress with dozens of handmaids to serve her. "I'll give the Emperor the good news. I'm certain Mei Gui carries a boy."

"Will I see you again soon?" she asked.

"Never soon enough, love," he said as he stepped from the quarters.

He went next to Yokan's study. The foreigner jumped off his stool to greet him. "You were delayed. I began to worry," he said.

Zhong Ye retrieved the empress roots from his satchel and felt a twinge of regret as he placed them on the blackwood table. Yokan let out a long whistle as he picked one up, turning it in his hand. "Are you certain this is it?"

"I would be dead if it wasn't."

Yokan's brows lifted, and he gestured to a stool. "Tell me everything."

Yokan listened to Zhong Ye's story, interrupting with a question here or there, shaking his head in wonderment all the while. When Zhong Ye was finished, Yokan directed his servant to fetch them a hot meal. He rubbed his hands together, a faint smile on his thin mouth.

"You have succeeded beyond my expectations. I would not have wagered that you would live through this."

Zhong Ye couldn't help laughing. "Yet you sent me anyway?"

"You welcomed the opportunity, did you not? Someone had to pursue this myth. And I couldn't risk going with you. What if we both died?" Yokan played with the charms at his sash, causing a melodic jangle.

"I appreciate your honesty." Zhong Ye smiled wryly. "Now I'd like my split of the prize."

Yokan arched a pale brow. "How do I know this is all you found?"

"Other than the slice that healed me, I brought everything back to you. You'll have to take my word."

"Very well. Four empress roots as your reward. But you

may be interested in trading them in order to try my immortality spell?"

Zhong Ye clamped his mouth shut. He knew that Yokan had used him, but he was using the foreigner in return. "How do you know that this spell of yours works?" Zhong Ye asked as he pocketed his roots.

"I'll learn soon enough," Yokan said.

A servant boy delivered a tray with two bowls of broth and noodles. Zhong Ye hadn't realized how hungry he was until he smelled the minced pork and scallions. Yokan whispered to the boy as Zhong Ye attacked his meal, the mouthwatering scent rising to his face.

Shortly after they were finished, Yokan stood and began pulling various boxes and jars from the endless shelves in the study. "I'll need you to leave now," he said, barely acknowledging Zhong Ye, his pale eyebrows drawn together in concentration.

Zhong Ye left without another word. As he crossed the courtyard, he saw two palace guards hauling a man toward Yokan's study, a prisoner to gauge from the filth of him. He was weak, and he stumbled. A chill rippled through Zhong Ye. He wondered what the alchemist was up to and whether his spell would work . . . and would Yokan really share it with him?

* * *

Later Zhong Ye decided to use the secret passageways to deliver a message to one of the Emperor's concubines. As he passed by Mei Gui's quarters, he paused at one of the peepholes. He rarely eavesdropped on Mei Gui, as Silver Phoenix reported everything to him. She proved to be an excellent spy, with a faultless memory, able to relay entire conversations to him nearly verbatim.

But he had been away for more than a week.

The women were seated across from each other in the reception hall, playing cards. He knew from playing with Silver Phoenix that she hated to lose. He drank in the sight of her and was turning to leave when Mei Gui spoke.

"Master Zhong has returned?"

He peered again through the peephole.

His love looked surprised. "Yes, this morning. Did you see him?"

Mei Gui laughed. "Oh, no. I never see Master Zhong unless you see him. I could just tell." She drew another card and giggled. "You were glowing all day. Like a festival lantern."

Silver Phoenix blushed and pursed her lovely lips. "Don't tease."

"Are you in love with him?" Mei Gui put down her cards and appraised her handmaid with a smile.

Silver Phoenix lowered her gaze, shifted in her seat. "Mistress . . ."

Zhong Ye realized his pulse was racing much too fast, and he leaned into the wall, both palms pressed against the rough wood.

"He's certainly handsome but so . . . intimidating," Mei Gui said. "And serious. And determined. Not to mention—" She gave Silver Phoenix a look and glanced down meaningfully between her thighs.

He squeezed his eyes shut, his heart thudding so hard he was certain the women could hear it. He really should go; he shouldn't be spying on the woman he loved. Despite all that he had faced this past week, every challenge he had met in life, Zhong Ye was certain he was not prepared for this conversation.

He opened his eyes and saw that Silver Phoenix's heart-shaped face had flushed to an alluring pink. "Mistress, I do care for him. He is intelligent and ambitious. And I think he's very handsome, yes." She tilted her chin in that way of hers, and he wanted to crash through the wall and obliterate the vast space between them. "Besides"—and her voice dropped lower—"love isn't all about sex."

Zhong Ye tried to swallow, but his mouth had gone dry. He took one step back as Mei Gui uttered an uncharacteristic yelp. "My darling Phoenix is in love," she said in a singsong chant.

He didn't hear anything else, as he floated through the secret passageways, completely forgetting his original task.

CHAPTER EIGHT

The next afternoon the crew gathered to resume their shuen lessons, which had been canceled the previous day. The weather remained overcast, and thick clouds robbed the sea of color. Ai Ling had donned a pink tunic, blanched so pale from the sun she felt as if she could fade into her surroundings. She was encrusted in salt; there was a thin film on her skin, in her hair, and covering all her clothing. She had been looking forward to the lesson, looking forward to clearing her mind.

After more than eight weeks of practice, it was apparent that Peng was the strongest among them. Chen Yong continued to stroll the line of students holding his bamboo rod. He worked with each person on technique and form but rarely spoke to Ai Ling. Today they stretched and cycled through some basic forms to limber up. Chen Yong then waved her to the front of the class.

She was so taken aback she didn't move. "Could you please join me for a demonstration, Ai Ling?" he asked, suppressing a grin.

All eyes turned to her, so she marched forward, chin up. She stopped in front of him. He was dressed in beige today, the edges of his sleeves chased with silver embroidery. He appeared leaner and more muscular than when their journey had begun. She had seen him eager to learn, helping with the sails, moving large cargo boxes, and winding ropes as thick as her wrist. His face had tanned, so his eyes appeared even more golden. They met hers now as he pressed a fist into his palm and bowed.

She mirrored him.

"We've just begun to learn some simple sparring routines." He nodded to her. "Let's review."

Chen Yong shot a fist toward her chin, and she swept it aside. A straight palm like a knife's edge to her temple. She ducked and whirled. Punch to the solar plexus, kick to the knee, and a hard jab to the abdomen. Ai Ling blocked each parry, light on her feet, as they circled each other. She took the offensive stance, mimicking

Chen Yong's attacks, allowing him to display the defensive techniques to the others.

After throwing the last punch in the routine, she drew her feet together to bow. But Chen Yong glided into a roundhouse kick to her head, which she barely sidestepped. She stared at him wide-eyed. He hadn't taught beyond what they just demonstrated. What was he doing?

His intense gaze never left hers, and he gave an imperceptible nod, as if in encouragement. She copied his roundhouse kick and almost connected. Taken by surprise, he jumped back just in time. But now he was a streak of motion, of punches and kicks that came too fast. They weren't full strength, but solid attacks that would bruise if they made contact.

She blocked Chen Yong's every move instinctively, drawing on some distant memory of sparring in fragrant meadows and empty courtyards. Ambition and anger burned deep within her, expanded. She hated to lose. And she wanted it all.

She attacked now, each thrust of the fist, snap of the foot thrilling yet terrifying. Chen Yong rolled, twisted, and dodged. His eyes narrowed; his astonishment was evident. Suddenly he grabbed her wrist, swept her legs from under her with one foot, and threw a strike that didn't quite touch her throat.

Ai Ling lay on her back stunned, her heart pounding in her ears. Someone gave a low whistle. Chen Yong still held her wrist, his touch cool against her skin. He helped her to her feet. "That was impressive," he said. He bowed, and the class burst into applause and began speaking all at once.

But she didn't return the bow. The exhilaration from the fight dwindled, replaced by a growing sense of horror. Flashes of memories pushed against her mind, like swollen fruit about to burst. She grabbed her head and ran.

Tripping below deck, she crashed into the cramped cabin and slammed the door. She fell onto the berth, clasping her knees to her chest. Her heart would not slow. Her breath would not slow. She was burning from the inside out.

"Ai Ling?"

She hadn't heard Chen Yong enter. Why was he here? He towered over her, and she wished he'd go away.

"I didn't mean to make you angry," he said. "You seem such a natural I only wanted to gauge your abilities." He touched her arm, and she jerked away from him, curling tighter. "You've been practicing on your own?"

She laughed. The sound was harsh in her ears. Mad. "No."

He crouched down, so their faces were level. "Was it your power?"

"Shuen is not my power. It's yours."

Chen Yong flinched. His concern was warmth against her skin. "Tell me what's wrong," he said in a soft voice.

Her head sagged. "I don't know." It felt as if she were being watched. Or perhaps as if she were watching someone. Somewhere else. Her mind cluttered. Crowded.

Chen Yong brushed the back of his cool hand against her cheek. "You're feverish. I'll ask Lao Lu to prepare a tonic." He drew a blanket over her before slipping from the cabin.

Ai Ling stared at the flickering lantern in the corner until she forgot where she was, forgot who she was.

The fever lasted for two days. Chen Yong helped nurse her back to health with Lao Lu's tonics. She stayed below deck during the day because the glaring sun reflecting off the endless sea hurt her head. On the third day she felt completely herself again.

It was difficult to believe that they'd been on the *Gliding Dragon* for more than two months. She had become used to life at sea and the company. Now when she made her way topside, the crew was bustling with more energy than usual. They chattered in loud voices about their impending arrival in Jiang Dao. Most had traveled there before, but it was new territory for a few. Yam Head and Xiao Hou bobbed at Ai Ling in greeting. "Today's the day, miss!" Xiao Hou exclaimed. "Couldn't ask for better sailing conditions either."

She smiled. She had grown fond of the two boys, regarded them as the little brothers that she'd never had. It was a beautiful day, not a cloud in the sky. The wind blew strong, filling the sails, and she lifted her face into it.

Yam Head pointed at a flock of seabirds flying overhead. "They're coming from land."

"And what will you do once we dock?" she asked.

"The captain said he could make use of me. As errand boy and such. I'll be given an allowance and a place to sleep!" He grinned wide, the exuberance gleaming in his eyes.

"And my father is taking me traveling through the kingdom," Xiao Hou added, tugging his queue with excitement.

She left them to their tasks and joined Chen Yong, who was chatting with Peng at the ship's bow. The captain turned as she approached and smiled. "I'm glad you won't miss our landing. No matter how many times I've arrived in Jiang Dao, the excitement doesn't lessen."

"Peng believes he can take us to my father," Chen Yong said.

"When Chen Yong told me his father's Xian name, I didn't recognize it. But when he mentioned that he had been a diplomat at the Emperor's court, one man instantly came to mind."

"That's wonderful! But how can we know it's truly him?" she asked.

"We can't," Chen Yong replied, gazing out to sea. "We won't know for certain until we meet him."

Ai Ling wanted to reach for him, reassure him but fisted her hands instead.

"Master Deen lives in one of the large estates in the valleys of the southern province." Peng turned to Ai Ling. "I know of one other man who has traveled to Xia as a diplomat, but this is a good place to start."

Yam Head was the first to shout and point to the horizon. Nearly everyone converged on deck, moving to the bow. Before too long, blue-tinged cliffs emerged in the distance, thrusting high over the churning black sea. Ai Ling's arms prickled at the sight. The sea gods favored their arrival, and the sails billowed, pushing them with great speed toward the kingdom of Jiang Dao.

Yen gave one shout, and the excited crew dispersed, to take their positions and return to the task of bringing the *Gliding Dragon* safely to shore.

"They've built a harbor, but there are a lot of rocks

beneath the water, hidden dangers," Peng said. "It takes careful maneuvering."

Ai Ling's eyes widened as the jagged mountains loomed before them.

Peng smiled. "Don't worry. Yen has done this many times before and makes it look easy."

"Is the entire kingdom like this?" Chen Yong nodded to the slate blue cliffs, the corners of his eyes crinkled against the sunshine and the sea's reflection.

"No. It's very green with gentle slopes and valleys. But Jiang Dao is enveloped by these cliffs, a wonderful natural defense. Once we travel beyond them, you'll see how the land lies."

Ai Ling brushed stray wisps of hair from her face. "How does it feel?" she asked Chen Yong.

"It feels a little like coming home," he said. "Almost as if I've seen these mountains before."

She stared at the majestic cliffs. Would Chen Yong choose to remain here if he did find his birth father?

He grinned widely, his face softening. "I feel hopeful. And nervous—" He broke off, suddenly serious. "What will happen if I actually find him? Will he even accept me?"

"Of course he will." She wanted to say more, but his expression stopped her.

He gave a slight shake of his head. "He left Xia

immediately after I was born. He never tried to look for me."

She touched his shoulder then. "You don't know that."

The ship hurtled over the water, and she was amazed it did not smash to pieces with the force of the swells. She and Chen Yong gripped the railing as the ship soared toward the coast. She gasped, and he laughed beside her. There was one final push as if from the Queen Empress of Heaven herself, and the ship glided like a whisper through a narrow channel and into the sheltered harbor.

The entire crew burst into applause.

There were only a few other large ships docked at the wharf. No grand city, just a small fishing village, filled with mud-colored huts, square and squat, greeted them.

Ai Ling stood on her tiptoes and stared down at the people. Was this what Chen Yong's father looked like? The men were tall, with pale yellow and light brown hair. Their brows were high; their noses, narrow and pointed. They dressed simply, in form-fitting tunics and trousers in muted earth tones. The men shouted at one another as they secured the *Gliding Dragon* to a giant post driven into rock. She couldn't make out many words, they spoke so rapidly.

"Can you understand what they're saying?" she asked

Chen Yong, who had joined her again after speaking with Peng on the bridge.

"Only snippets," he said. "The foreigners have arrived; that much I caught."

She studied his face. "You don't look anything like them."

"I don't look anything like anyone." He gave her a wry smile.

Wasn't that the truth? she thought. His features had become so familiar she'd forgotten how different from everyone else he appeared.

Peng strode across the deck. "It's too late to set out today for the journey to the inner parts of the kingdom. We'll be spending all afternoon unloading our cargo. Feel free to go onshore, and look around if you'd like."

"Without you?" she asked.

Peng smiled. "Chen Yong knows the language well enough to get by."

"But what will people think? I haven't seen any women yet. Do they travel unchaperoned?"

Peng laughed. "Ai Ling, in Jiang Dao the women behave however they please."

She glanced toward the small village and could not fathom what he meant.

* * *

They disembarked with Jiang money in their pockets, gold and silver coins similar to their own, but with different marks on them. Peng had given them the coins, explaining that it made for easier trading, especially since they had foreign faces. She was unsteady when she finally stepped onto shore, still feeling the lurch of the sea despite the solid ground beneath her.

It smelled entirely different. Like the earth, like moss and flowers. She drew a deep breath, wide-eyed. Chen Yong glanced at her, and she saw that he smelled it, too.

"It smells like . . . land," he said.

"Like wet earth and—"

"Life," he interjected.

"And the colors . . ." No longer did her world consist solely of varying shades of blue or gray. Or the brown masts and bleached planks of the ship. She marveled at the potted daisies blooming in bursts of magenta and gold, the deep greens of the hedges manicured into square columns outside a storefront.

They walked on wobbling legs toward the little village nestled beneath the cliffs. "What is *that* smell?" She raised her nose and sniffed. It smelled like burned honey, and her stomach grumbled.

Chen Yong chuckled and covered the pouch at his

waist. "You will not rob me to clean the whole village out of its food."

She made a face at him but laughed as she rushed on to find the source of the delicious scent. A woman who was her mother's age stood in front of a cozy hut. There was a giant stone hearth tucked in the back, and the ground was strewn with baskets, all stuffed with objects of various shapes—long ovals, square and round. They didn't look like anything one could eat, but the aroma!

The woman greeted them with a hello, or literally, good meeting, as Peng had once translated for her. Chen Yong spoke, surprising Ai Ling again with his ease at speaking the language. The Jiang woman replied too quickly for Ai Ling to understand. Her wheat-colored hair was in two braids, draped over her ample bosom. Her face was ruddy, and her round eyes were a clear light blue. She wore a loose dark green dress with a white tunic tied over it.

The woman cast a curious glance her way, and Ai Ling looked down, embarrassed that she had been gawking.

"It's bread. She bakes the loaves in the hearth. Some are filled with nuts or dried fruit."

"Which one smells of burned honey?"

Chen Yong chuckled. "Hmm. I'm not certain I know how to say 'burned' in Jiang." He turned to the woman and spoke again, this time in a more hesitant tone. She nodded at a tray on a low table, and Ai Ling was beside it before Chen Yong could translate.

"Fresh from the hearth, she said. Filled with dried grapes and covered in sugar."

Ai Ling leaned over the round lumps and inhaled. "Can we have four, please?"

His eyes widened; then he laughed. "Four, if you can," he said in Jiang. Which was the closest they had to "please."

The woman pointed at one of the baskets and asked if they had one. Chen Yong said no. She pulled a small basket from a shelf behind her. It was oval and deep, with a single braided handle. She placed four of the sweet buns (as this is what Ai Ling was calling them in her mind) into the basket for them.

"Thank you," Ai Ling said, haltingly in Jiang.

The woman smiled, surprise flitting across her face, and nodded. Chen Yong handed her a silver coin, and she tucked it into the front pocket of her tunic.

Ai Ling poked at one of the buns with her finger. "They're still warm," she exclaimed. "Let's try one now!"

They sat on a rough bench near the dock and watched the crew of the *Gliding Dragon* unload the cargo. The buns were sticky, and she licked her fingers. "I think it's the best thing I've ever tasted," she said, closing her eyes.

Chen Yong took a large bite out of his bun, nodding. "It's really good," he said, his voice muffled.

The sun was beginning to sink, and the sky blazed with swirls of orange. She sighed and glanced at the other two buns in the basket.

He caught her. "You can't possibly eat another!"

"I'll save it. But I'm certain they taste best when warm."

He laughed. "I want some tea now."

She did as well. "Do you think they drink tea here?"

"I know that Peng has brought many crates of it. I don't know if they have their own version."

They sat in silence then, listening to the soft roar of the sea.

"Will you wed her?" Ai Ling asked softly. Her entire insides seemed to sour, to curdle.

He tensed, but he did not look at her. "I owe my mother that much." It sounded as though he were trying to convince himself.

She turned and studied the massive cliffs behind them. They were like a living entity, while her own heart was cold. Stone heavy. Chen Yong felt very far from her in that moment, as the sun slipped beneath the sea.

Two weeks had passed since Zhong Ye had returned with the empress roots. He continued to work on translating texts for Yokan, although the alchemist often sent him away early these days. It was the fifth moon, and the air was fragrant with peonies in bloom; the courtyards and imperial gardens were wreathed in the colors of spring. Zhong Ye visited Mei Gui's quarters after the evening meal. He entered the bedchamber without announcing himself, as he did on purpose every so often.

Mei Gui stood in front of the bronzed mirror, and Silver Phoenix hovered near her, both hands pressed to her mistress's lower abdomen. Their chatter and laughter stopped abruptly. His love dropped her arms and stepped away from Mei Gui, almost as if she had been caught in an illicit act.

He was adept at reading people, and Silver Phoenix, although an enigma in the beginning, was opening herself up to him. He knew what he had seen in her expression: joy and longing. Her eyes were downcast now. *Too late.* He cleared his throat, heart heavy, wishing he had knocked.

"Lady." Zhong Ye dropped to his knee by the concubine, and her eyes widened. She was growing plumper in the face, and it made her more fetching. Her black hair flowed down her back in thick waves. "I spoke to the Emperor regarding your news. He is much pleased and gives you this." He drew a slim gold ring from his pocket.

Mei Gui's hand flew to her mouth. Zhong Ye nodded, and she extended the other so he could slip the ring on her finger. It was a powerful symbol, for it announced to the court that she was pregnant with the Emperor's child.

"Thank you, Master Zhong, for choosing me," Mei Gui said, twisting the ring nervously.

He stood and smiled. Silver Phoenix was by far the more beautiful, the more intriguing. Thank the gods she could never be a royal concubine. "I only brought you to him. The rest was from diligent work on your part," he said. Mei Gui ducked her head, and he gestured toward Silver Phoenix.

"Be sure you are even more aware of all that goes on around your mistress. Now that the pregnancy is public, we'll gain enemies."

"Yes, Master Zhong," Silver Phoenix said as she followed him back to the reception hall.

He drew her to him for a brief moment, long enough to whisper, "Can you come to me tonight?"

She smiled and nodded. Zhong Ye left the quarters without a glance back, almost afraid that she'd change her mind if he lingered.

* * *

They lay tangled in silk sheets, and Zhong Ye ached with a desire he would never be able to satisfy. Silver Phoenix rested with her head tucked against his shoulder, her hair fanned out, tickling his face. She touched the faint scar on his torso. "How did you get this?"

He was grateful she had never seen him without his tunic before. "I was whipped only once in my life, when I was thirteen years."

Her mouth formed a small circle, and he fought hard not to smile.

She shifted onto her side so she could see his face. The lanterns burned low, and her black eyes were liquid. "What did you do?"

"I stole . . ." He caressed her bare back, attempted to gather her thick hair into one hand, then nuzzled her throat.

"What did you steal?" She pulled back and stared at him so intently, his mouth twitched.

"Someone's wife."

"At thirteen years!"

He couldn't contain his laughter, and she tried to smack his chest with an open palm. But he was too quick and twisted out of reach. He caught her wrist when she tried to hit him a second time.

"Tell me!" she said.

"It was from a tree branch. I was climbing after a swim and fell." He composed his features and tried to look earnest.

"When you were thirteen years?"

"When I was thirteen years," he said.

She leaned over and kissed the scar, sending a shiver through him. "You have yet to tell me about your journey."

Zhong Ye closed his eyes as he started the story, giving her a milder version of his adventure, in which the Poison Eagle was just a hungry wildcat, and he did not nearly die killing it. He told her he had been searching for a root that could cure the ache of swollen joints, and it probably could. Silver Phoenix listened quietly, tracing his scar with her fingertips until it felt as if she were an extension of him.

It wasn't until the sixth moon that Yokan shared his news. The alchemist looked different when Zhong Ye saw him that morning. He couldn't stop grinning and paced the large study with a spring in his step. "I've made my spell work!" Yokan exclaimed. "It truly is the empress root, and my potion can extend your life!"

Zhong Ye kept his face smooth. "You tried it?"

"I did." He waved his hands frenetically. "I feel ten years younger!"

"How can you be certain? It could just be the healing effects of the root."

"No. Your body can feel it. Your soul can feel it. I am replenished. Renewed." He gripped Zhong Ye's arm in a surprisingly tight clasp. "Do you understand what this means?"

"You can live forever?" Zhong Ye didn't flinch from the foreigner's pale gaze, wondering if it could be true. Or if he were mad. Healing he could believe, had experienced. But immortality?

"Give me your share of the roots, and I'll show you," Yokan said. His eyes almost glowed. Zhong Ye didn't respond, and Yokan went on. "It takes almost one-third of the root for the ritual to work. You can experience it for yourself."

"I want to know the ingredients for the spell."

Yokan's eyes widened; then he laughed. A nasal hitching sound. "Perhaps you should try it once before you bargain with me?"

What could be the risk? Because certainly, immortality would be worth it.

Zhong Ye, curious yet wary, sat down and rested his arms on the blackwood table. "Remember these charms given to me by my king?" Yokan swept one finger across the silver pieces at his waist. "For valor and sacrifice."

What was the man's point?

"Nothing great can ever be achieved without either." He smiled.

Zhong Ye could swear there were fewer lines in his face, that they were less deeply etched around his mouth, all but gone from the corners of his eyes. Was he imagining it?

"But to have something as wondrous as immortality, it takes even greater valor and sacrifice, you see."

"I'm willing," Zhong Ye said.

Yokan pursed his lips, ran a hand through his short hair, which appeared a deeper and more lustrous shade of yellow this morning. "You are willing to do anything to achieve immortality?"

Zhong Ye was certain of it.

"Because it requires that you take someone else's life," Yokan said.

"What?" Zhong Ye jerked back, accidentally sweeping sheets of parchment to the floor and knocking over a jar of ink. It stained several pages before he set it upright again with an unsteady hand.

"Something as great as immortality: it can't be easily achieved. You need someone else's life for it to work.

Another's soul." Yokan steepled his fingers and leaned forward.

"Someone's soul?" The sick feeling in Zhong Ye's gut spread to his chest. "Is that what you did?"

"It was."

He remembered the disheveled prisoner who had been dragged into Yokan's quarters. Was he the victim of the alchemist's dark arts? "It can't be. It's not right."

Yokan laughed. "There is no right or wrong in this quest, Zhong. It's a tremendous opportunity. Can you do this or not?"

He wished for some rice wine. Or for Silver Phoenix to talk to—not that he could ever speak to her about any of this. "I need to think about it."

"Maybe if you observed me once?" Yokan scrutinized him with narrowed eyes.

Zhong Ye nodded slowly. "You'll take another prisoner?"

The alchemist shrugged. "They would be killed anyway, in a much crueler fashion. I'm doing them a favor."

As Zhong Ye headed to the alchemist's quarters the following morning, a dark mood clamped down on him like a death vise. He arrived at Yokan's study all too soon.

The alchemist was weaving around the chamber, gathering jars and boxes. "Ah, Zhong. Are you ready for today?"

Zhong Ye unpacked his materials and began to grind ink.

"Be certain it's dark. You'll want to write very clear instructions for yourself."

Yokan tapped his thin lips with one finger. He whirled toward Zhong Ye. "Did you bring your empress roots?"

Zhong Ye hesitated, then took them out of his satchel and placed them on the table. Yokan reached for the one that had already been sliced and brought it to his nose. "It's a heady scent. Even the smell revives me."

Zhong Ye finished grinding his ink and pulled up his sleeve before dipping his brush in the ink slate. He looked at Yokan expectantly.

The alchemist clapped his hands together. "Right. These are all ingredients that can be obtained in your kingdom, but most are seasonal. Fortunately, they don't need to be fresh for the spell to work." The alchemist began rattling off various medicinal ingredients, each time showing Zhong Ye the component, before adding it to a bronze bowl. Zhong Ye was familiar with most of the ingredients, but some, such as the ground molar of a giant bear cat, were used less often. That particular animal dwelled in the remote mountainous regions of Xia. He had never seen the creature with his own eyes, only in sketches rendered by traveling scholars.

After Yokan had explained the preparation of all the ingredients for the spell, he indicated how much empress root was needed. "The spell is useless without it. Ingest the empress root; then begin the ritual by lighting the potion." He waved a hand at the bronze bowl. "I've already eaten the root slices."

Zhong Ye remembered the surge of energy and life he had felt when he ate that one thin slice. What was Yokan feeling now?

"Then you must utter the incantation I've written, a calling and honoring of the gods."

"What gods?" Zhong Ye asked.

Someone rapped on the door panel. "Good. The prisoner is here. Enter!" Yokan called.

The panel slammed open, and Zhong Ye glimpsed the guards outside. A broad-shouldered guard pushed a thin man toward them, and the prisoner fell to his knees, slouching forward. Tears and saliva dribbled onto the stone floor. What was this poor wretch's offense?

"This is the traitor?" Yokan wrinkled his nose.

"Yes, master," the guard said.

"Pull him up."

The guard kicked the man in the rear. He scrambled on all fours until he reached the edge of Yokan's robe. "Please, master. Show mercy!"

"I am. Stand."

The man swayed to his feet. His face was gaunt and filthy. How many months had he spent in the prison? Zhong Ye took a step back. The traitor reeked of feces and urine. Of vomit.

"It's your lucky day. Instead of hacking your limbs off and feeding you to the hunting dogs, we'll give you a quiet death. Here," Yokan said.

The prisoner's dark eyes bulged. "No. Please! Spare my life!" He sank to his knees again.

"Pull his head back," Yokan told the guard.

The guard yanked the prisoner's stringy hair, and his face jerked. Yokan drew a vial from his robe. He poured the green concoction down the prisoner's throat. The man thrashed his head from side to side, and tears streamed down his face. Zhong Ye's stomach turned, and he backed away until he hit the blackwood table.

"Leave us," Yokan said to the guard. He stared at the prisoner. "Did you think your act would go unpunished? Planning the assassination of your emperor?" He turned and struck a match, then ignited the concoction in the bronze bowl; the oil he had poured over the ingredients brought it ablaze instantly. Incense had already been lit, to counter the dreadful odor that began to rise from the burning potion.

The prisoner was fading, the life seeping from him. Zhong Ye dug his fingers into his own arms, trying to keep still, to contain his horror. The traitor had hunched forward, as if bowing to the gods. Yokan crouched down, put one hand on either side of the prisoner's head, and began chanting aloud. He entreated the demons of greed and desire, lunacy and compulsion. His voice grew louder, more commanding while the prisoner started to twitch until they both shuddered together. The prisoner stopped moving. Yokan remained crouched, his eyes slits, his head thrown back.

The silence in the chamber terrified Zhong Ye. He couldn't hear anything but the frantic pounding of his own heart. His back was damp with sweat. Was Yokan alive? He didn't move to help him.

After a long silence, Yokan groaned and stretched. He jumped to his feet, thumping his hand against his chest. "This one was strong!"

Zhong Ye forced himself to nod. "Yes," he replied.

"Go tell the guards to take the body away," said Yokan, dousing the burning potion in the bronze bowl with water.

Zhong Ye somehow managed to walk into the

courtyard. He motioned with his chin toward the study door and was grateful one of the guards understood. He then stumbled into the garden and retched beneath a peach tree. He was still coughing up bile when two guards dragged the corpse away.

Zhong Ye fought the urge to run. Instead, he swiped a sleeve across his mouth and returned to Yokan's study. The alchemist was seated at the table, scribbling frantically on thick parchment. He didn't glance up when Zhong Ye sat across from him.

"What does it feel like?" Zhong Ye asked, his voice harsh.

"Indescribable."

"And that man, the prisoner . . ."

Yokan raised his head. He looked younger, energized. "What of him?"

"Couldn't the potion have worked without him?"

Yokan snorted a laugh. "Don't be naive. We're talking about immortality. Nothing that immense can be achieved without sacrifice."

"You used his soul . . . to prolong your own life?"

"I'm not certain. It's why I had hoped you would consider studying this with me. I'm taking as many notes as I can, but the effects are difficult to quantify."

"Does the Emperor know?" Zhong Ye asked.

Yokan grimaced, pulled himself straighter on his stool. "I haven't told him everything. He's been funding my research generously for almost a year. I'll have to show him something. Soon."

"You're not going to tell him about the ritual?"

"It was never our intent to extend your emperor's life." Yokan squinted at him, then cocked his head. "But it's an opportunity you can seize."

"Why me?"

"Why not you? You're intelligent, ambitious, capable. I need someone to help me study the effects of this process, but not some royal drunkard who will demand immediate immortality." Yokan tapped his quill against the table, his sharp gaze never straying from Zhong Ye.

He couldn't think clearly. There was too much to consider.

"I can offer you the chance to be whole again," Yokan said after a long pause.

"What?" Zhong Ye was stunned.

"Not permanently. What's done is done. But I came across something from *The Book of the Dead*. You could be made whole for when you need to be." He raised one eyebrow, and Zhong Ye looked down at his clenched fists.

The bastard. What did he know about his need to be

whole? Had Yokan's spies rooted out everything about his relationship with Silver Phoenix? "I've read *The Book of the Dead* in its entirety. There was no mention of such a possibility," he said.

"You've read *your* version in its entirety," Yokan replied. The foreigner smiled, his face too youthful, too serene.

How many souls had he stolen? And where were those souls now?

"The Emperor has the most comprehensive collection in his private study. I transcribed the passage, as I thought it might interest you. Of course you understand that I can't give you the ingredients for the spell just yet." Yokan pulled a page from his sheaf of papers and held it toward him. "Help me, and I can help you."

"What happened to their souls?" Zhong Ye dug his knuckles into the edge of the table, fighting hope, anger. Horror. He didn't take the parchment.

The alchemist shrugged, flicked a hand as if swatting a gnat. "What does it matter? They were thieves, traitors. What could their souls possibly be worth?"

Zhong Ye shook his head. "No. I can't." He didn't raise his face to see Yokan's reaction, but the foreigner's hard silence spoke volumes.

CHAPTER NINE

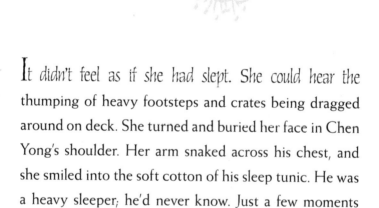

It didn't feel as if she had slept. She could hear the thumping of heavy footsteps and crates being dragged around on deck. She turned and buried her face in Chen Yong's shoulder. Her arm snaked across his chest, and she smiled into the soft cotton of his sleep tunic. He was a heavy sleeper; he'd never know. Just a few moments more . . . They would never be this close again.

When she next awoke, Chen Yong was already gone. Embarrassed to have drifted back to sleep curled against him, she dressed quickly. Ai Ling made it topside and found the crew lined up against the railing, standing at attention as Peng spoke to them. Yen stood beside him. Peng turned after the men had dispersed, saw her, and smiled. The sun had just emerged. "Good. I was afraid I'd have to dig you out of bed. The carriage is ready for us."

Yen and Yam Head helped load crates onto one of the horse-drawn wagons. There were four others stacked with cargo and one covered carriage for them to ride in. She stared at the horses, all milk white in color, with dark brown or black markings. Chen Yong opened the carriage door, and Peng held out his hand to help her in. She thought she sensed a prickle of jealousy from Chen Yong and turned, but his head was bowed. He took the seat beside her, and she wondered if she'd imagined it. Peng and Yen sat next to each other. Yen was so broad he seemed to fill half the carriage.

"Hiya!" The horse driver shouted, and their carriage rumbled off.

Peng stared out the window with a faraway look in his dark eyes. "It's good to be back," he said.

Ai Ling, too, gazed out the glass window. She'd never seen glass used in a carriage before. "How long will it take for us to reach the manor?"

"It's at least a five-day journey," Peng said. "We'll stop at the usual inns."

The wagons and carriage each had six horses. She finally understood why when they began climbing upward between the sheer cliffs. The road was steep and rocky. She bounced against Chen Yong, practicing Jiang phrases in her mind all the while.

Chen Yong had drifted to sleep, his body pressed against hers. He was warm, and she didn't move. They had emerged on the other side of the mountains and were now descending. Jiang Dao stretched as far as she could see, with pockets of towns nestled between green hilltops.

"It's a beautiful kingdom," Peng said in a quiet voice.

Ai Ling studied the captain, then glanced nervously toward Yen.

"There's nothing you can say to me that you can't say in front of Yen."

Peng, perceptive as always. Her mouth was dry when she finally spoke. "You said you had studied the black arts. Did you work directly—"

Chen Yong stirred, opened his eyes, and Ai Ling stopped in mid-sentence. He wore the drowsy expression that she loved. He straightened, looking embarrassed that he had fallen asleep.

"We'll be at the first inn before nightfall," Peng said in a casual tone, as if continuing their conversation.

Relieved by his quickness, she touched Peng's spirit. He was curious yet thoughtful. Could she truly trust him?

She had her own chamber at the inn. She missed Chen Yong, but the privacy gave her the opportunity to seek Peng out. She climbed the light wooden steps, trailing her fingers against the gray stone walls. At each landing was a rectangular glass window composed of mosaics, their colors muted at night. Peng's room was on the fourth floor, the top floor.

Aware of her racing heart, she steadied herself before knocking.

"Come in," Peng said.

She entered and closed the door behind her. It was two hours after the evening meal, and she knew that most of the guests had retired. They would set off again at daybreak.

"Ai Ling. I was hoping you would visit me. I asked the innkeeper to bring some tea."

He indicated the chair on the other side of the round table. His chamber was identical to hers, with a single bed strewn with cushions and flowered curtains framing the windows. A leaping fire crackled in the large hearth. She sat, inhaling the jasmine fragrance. "Do they drink tea here?" she asked, sipping slowly, letting the warmth wind through her.

"A variation of it. But not the kind we drink. Although those who have tried our tea leaves love the taste. I've brought many crates to sell."

She took another sip and threw her spirit toward his; she encountered curiosity and calm. This man was rarely rattled or anxious. Even during the pirate attack, he had been in control.

"You said I could trust you." She set the ceramic cup on the table. "Can I truly?"

"Have I given you reason not to?"

"I don't know you."

"Not well yet, no." He leaned back. "But yes, you can trust me."

Their eyes met, and he held hers. She finally looked away and cleared her throat. "I did send Zhong Ye to the underworld. It was a task given to me."

"By whom?"

"By a goddess."

He was startled, and she almost laughed. It sounded so ridiculous to say it aloud. Had it been real? If Chen Yong hadn't been with her, she would have believed herself mad.

Peng shifted to the edge of his chair. "And she helped you kill him?"

Ai Ling sighed and stared into her teacup. "In a way. But I killed him with my own power. I have a gift . . . of sensing others' feelings, hearing their thoughts." Of possessing their minds and bodies.

"Incredible!" Peng said, shaking his head.

They sat silent for a long moment. She thought she could feel the sway of the waves again. It was strange to be back on land.

"What am I thinking now?" he asked.

"That you hope Chen Yong will find his birth father. That you will do your best to help me, too," she answered without pause, not missing the glint of surprise in Peng's dark eyes.

There was a knock at the door, and the innkeeper's daughter entered with a silver tray. She set it on the table, smiled shyly, and left.

"These are Jiang cakes," Peng said, helping himself to a piece. "And they go very well with tea."

Ai Ling couldn't help grinning as she took a bite. The cake was light and airy. It was covered in a brown paste that was both sweet and nutty. She finished it and emptied her teacup. Peng poured her more.

"That was delicious," she said.

"Have another." He nodded at the plate.

She did and felt content. "You're trying to buy my trust with sweets."

Peng laughed. "Is it working?"

It was.

"I think I've been having visions. Of Zhong Ye. I was hoping perhaps . . . you could help—"

"What kinds of visions?" he asked.

She shrugged, and a tremor ran through her. "I think they're memories from his life. I feel like I'm losing my mind, losing my self."

Peng, pensive, stared into the fire. "I don't recall coming across anything such as this during my studies at the monastery."

"You were a monk?"

"For ten years. I studied many of the texts, but I was formally trained in the lore for healing. I was young. And my heart was wild; I craved adventure. It wasn't what the monastery could offer. I continued to study on my own after leaving. When I heard the rumor Zhong Ye's new bride had finally killed him, I was intrigued."

"Did you know him?" Her pulse quickened. She didn't like to think of that night, to think of him.

"We met once. He made quite an impression. Powerful, smart, cunning. Rumors swirled around him. That he was immortal. Or that he was an Immortal, put on earth to spy on us, to judge us for our deeds." He slanted his head, his black eyes intense. "Tell me, how exactly does your power work?"

"I cast my spirit into others. That's how I can hear their thoughts and understand their feelings." It felt good to speak of it. Almost as if it were normal. "And I can also take control over their bodies; it's how I forced the pirate to set fire to his own ship."

"You did that?" Peng jumped out of his chair and began pacing the small chamber. "Unbelievable! And to kill Zhong Ye, you touched his spirit as well?"

Ai Ling closed her eyes. She felt it again: their spirits intertwined and the hundreds of trapped souls thrusting her into the air as they slashed through her bare skin. She shuddered. "Yes."

"And his body was burned, sent to the underworld?"

She could see the roaring flames in her mind. She had focused on the cloth wrapped around Li Rong's heart, never letting her eyes stray to Zhong Ye's emaciated corpse. She had stayed until the air was too scorching to take another breath. "Yes."

"It's been almost a year since his death. Zhong Ye should be reincarnated—as a toad or mule, whatever the gods saw fitting."

The blood drained from her face. "He was a eunuch."

"What?" Peng was stunned but drew the conclusion much faster than she had. "And you burned everything? *All* of him?"

"No. I didn't even think of it. I wasn't thinking." She put her face in her hands.

"He's trapped in the underworld then. A fitting punishment for his deeds."

"But how is he haunting me?" she asked. "How can I make him stop?"

Peng sat back down. "Your spirits touched when you sent him into the underworld. Perhaps that bound you somehow."

She wrapped her arms around herself, cold despite the warmth from the hearth.

"Let me research it. I'll tell you if I discover anything." Peng's expression was grim. He was worried for her.

She agreed to accept his help and returned to her bed-chamber. But it was a long time before she finally drifted to sleep that night.

Ai Ling woke with her face wet from tears. She dressed quickly, wondering what she had dreamed. There was a knock on the door, and she yanked it open. Chen Yong smiled at her. "I was worried you hadn't risen yet."

He studied her face. "You look tired."

She almost told him everything, but something stopped her. He would never understand what she had had to do to kill Zhong Ye. She could never speak of that night with him—even if he had been there, imprisoned because of her.

"I'm still getting used to being on land again," she said, lying.

They walked down to the dining hall together, and she smelled the delicious fresh-baked bread from the stairway. Long wooden tables and benches were arranged around a hearth with a roaring fire. She watched Peng and Yen eat their eggs with some salt and pepper and tried it herself. But her stomach didn't like the strong taste of boiled egg alone. Ai Ling was used to eggs stewed in tea or soy sauce. She loved the sweet bread, however, stuffed with nuts and dried fruit. She helped herself to three thick slices accompanied by two cups of warm goat's milk.

They set off again before the sun had risen, rumbling toward the green glades of the valley. She stared out the carriage window at the brightening sky. What would the new day bring?

Lemon blossoms perfumed the air. The landscape was lush and hilly, and the groves of fruit trees were plentiful. Each vista was new and breathtaking. Yen had chosen to sit with the coachman this morning. It always seemed to Ai Ling that the carriage's interior caged him in.

"How long do you usually stay at Master—" She fumbled for his name.

"Deen's," Peng said, and smiled. "Usually a week or two. Deen is kind enough to accommodate us as we trade in the nearby cities. He was my first and remains my most loyal client."

"What does he buy?" Chen Yong asked.

"Everything. Teas, biscuits, spices, and silks. He also makes special requests for books, ink sticks, rice paper, and calligraphy brushes. Even incense. I think he misses our kingdom greatly."

"Can you tell me more about him?" Chen Yong asked.

Peng considered before he spoke. "He owns one of the largest manors in the province. He is from a well-respected and wealthy family. They are master craftsmen of stained glass."

"Of what?" Ai Ling asked.

"Windows made from fragments of colored glass. They are like paintings."

"I saw them on some of the houses and inns," Chen Yong said.

"Yes. But those were small. Poor examples compared with the masterpieces the Deen family makes. You'll see."

The scenery unfurled below them as the carriage descended. Ai Ling had seen black and white sheep dotting the hillsides, and the neat rows of crops etched into the hills reminded her of the rice terraces of home.

"Master Deen never married and has no child of his own to call heir," Peng said after a brief silence, his expression thoughtful.

She looked toward Chen Yong, but he had bowed his head and was staring at his hands. What would it mean if Master Deen was his birth father? He finally met her eyes and, as if reading her thoughts said, "It's pointless to speculate."

"True. But I believe what you tell me, Chen Yong. And Deen is a good man." Peng leaned forward. "As the current patriarch of the family he has the responsibility to choose an heir. And I believe he favors his sister's daughter."

"Daughter!" Ai Ling exclaimed.

Peng laughed. "It's not unusual. The women have as much power and rights as the men in this kingdom. This is what was hinted at when last I visited. He believes she is a better fit than her twin brother."

Bypassing a male heir in favor of a girl? Ai Ling was stunned. "How old is she?"

"Eighteen years," Peng replied.

"Do you believe she is suited for the job?" Chen Yong asked.

"I do believe so. She's sharp." Peng paused. "Also very beautiful."

Ai Ling crossed her arms and sat back on the carriage seat. Of course.

"Thank you for sharing what you know," Chen Yong said.

Peng inclined his head. "I'll be glad to help as much as I can when we arrive. It is a rather delicate situation."

Chen Yong turned to gaze out the window. She did the same, catching glimpses of her reflection as the green countryside swept past them.

In the days following, Yokan acted as if nothing had happened, and relieved, Zhong Ye never mentioned the immortality spell again. He didn't even ask for the return of his portion of the empress roots. One afternoon at week's end, Yokan dismissed him early, and he wandered through the palace grounds deep in thought. Finally, he headed toward Mei Gui's quarters. The flutter of color between the buildings caught his eye before he saw the two women in the courtyard.

They both were wearing trousers instead of their customary dresses. Silver Phoenix had a long green silk ribbon, wide as a scarf, draped across her shoulders. It was at least three times her height. She held the ribbon as she danced, twirling the material in intricate patterns above her head, then dipping so it swirled just above the cobblestones. Her body swayed to music that only she could hear, her face raised to the sunlight, her smile exuberant. The ribbon was alive, an extension of her. It never touched the ground.

Zhong Ye felt as though his breath had been knocked from him.

Mei Gui tried to imitate her handmaid, giggling as she did, her own pink ribbon dragging across the stones. She glanced up and saw him. "Master Zhong," she said, stopping abruptly.

Silver Phoenix flicked her wrists so the long ribbon ends snapped neatly into her arms. She whispered to her mistress, and Mei Gui nodded, before retreating to her quarters. "Sit," Silver Phoenix said, smiling coyly. She nodded at a bench nestled among rosebushes.

"As you wish," he said, and obeyed. The red and yellow roses were flowering, their fragrance scenting the air.

She tucked a leg behind her and bowed so low he

found he was looking down at the top of her head. "I'll dance for you," she said. She rose and unfurled the ribbons, weaving them again through the air.

"But what if I want to dance *with* you?" he asked.

She laughed and looked at him from beneath lowered lashes. "You're not allowed to dance. You can only watch."

Zhong Ye made a show of sitting on his hands, stilled like a statue.

Silver Phoenix nodded in approval, then backed away, her ribbons fluttering all the while. She bent forward, folding herself down like a swan, then arched her spine in a graceful line, until her head nearly touched the stones. She stretched her arms up, and the ribbons twirled above her like butterflies. She held the impossible position, painting the air with elegant strokes.

"You're just showing off now." Zhong Ye's voice sounded thick to his own ears.

She flashed him a smile before rising in one fluid motion and springing across the courtyard, spinning in circles in midair, snapping her arms so her ribbon ends looped back toward his face each time, a caress.

Unable to sit any longer, Zhong Ye jumped up and vaulted in the air with her, mirroring the way she twisted, weightless. Her delighted laughter echoed off the pavilions as she led him on a chase. He leaped with her for a full circle, before she stopped, flicking the ribbon so the ends glided onto his shoulders. Then she reeled him in.

They stared at each other, their chests rising and falling in rhythm, until Zhong Ye embraced her, crushing his mouth to hers. She clutched his arms, tucking herself against him, and the ribbon fell from his shoulders.

"You're incredible," he whispered.

She smiled, her eyes luminous. She led them back up the steps to Mei Gui's quarters, but something on the ground caught her eye, and she bent to retrieve it. Cradling it in one palm, she examined it. "How curious," she said.

"What is it?" he asked.

"A silver charm of some kind."

It was the length of his thumb, curved like a scythe. He recognized it as one that had dangled from Yokan's belt, and the blood drained from his face. "Give it to me!" His voice had gone hoarse.

"What is it?" She handed him the charm, fear flitting across her face.

It was impossible. With the exception of eunuchs, no men were allowed within the inner court. Yokan could not visit the concubines' quarters. Zhong Ye turned away and ran.

* * *

Zhong Ye crashed into Yokan's study and slammed the charm down on the table in front of him. "What is the meaning of this?" His question erupted as a growl.

Yokan straightened, unfazed. "My charm. I thought it was gone for good." He picked it up and held it between bony fingers. "Where did you find it?"

"In front of Mei Gui's quarters." Zhong Ye's insides had twisted into something ugly and unrecognizable.

"The concubine with child?" Yokan clipped the charm to his belt and smiled innocuously. "What's her handmaid's name again? The stunning one?"

Zhong Ye had the alchemist by the throat in an instant, nearly lifting him off the stool.

Yokan laid a finger on Zhong Ye's wrist and tutted. "This is bad form, Zhong." Yokan's hand was icy, and Zhong Ye let go, stumbling back. He doubled over, sick to his stomach.

The alchemist adjusted his collar. "You've only shown me exactly how much you care for her," he said.

Zhong Ye raised his eyes to meet those pale blue ones. What a stupid fool he'd been. Every action in his life had been deliberate, calculated. And he'd lost control when it mattered the most.

"You'll try the immortality spell now, yes?" The

foreigner's smile looked more like a grimace. He handed him a single piece of parchment. "You help me, and I'll help you."

Zhong Ye snatched the paper from him, his own face a smooth mask once more.

"Very good. We have an understanding." Yokan wiggled his fingers, as if shooing a dog away. "Go. We'll continue this tomorrow morning."

Zhong Ye left Yokan's study, closing the door quietly behind him. He had a vague impression of passing others—of eunuchs and concubines murmuring uncertain greetings—as he stormed through the palace.

He burst into his reception hall. Xiao Mao was cleaning, but one look at his master's face, and the boy scuttled away without a word. Zhong Ye wanted to throttle someone, but the only person who deserved a thrashing was himself. He tore off his robe and attacked the dummies near the back of the chamber, beating them with his fists and feet until they crashed, broken, to the ground.

He stalked across the hall, bathed in sweat, his mind spinning and almost slipped on the parchment, the parchment Yokan had handed him. Zhong Ye fell into a chair and unrolled it. "Drawing the Jade Stem" was written in the alchemist's spidery calligraphy across the top. Nine ingredients were required, as well as some blood from the supplicant and something from the body of the proposed lover, a snippet of hair or nail clipping. Yokan had omitted the actual names of the ingredients, as well as the incantation itself. Instead, he'd included this: "A slice of empress root must be ingested for this spell to work. The effect will not last longer than a day, but it will be true. The supplicant will be whole during this time of enchantment, and all is possible. Give thanks and offerings to the Demons of Loss and the Guardians of Envy."

All is possible.

Could he make a child with Silver Phoenix? Zhong Ye clutched his head. She hadn't been part of his plans. Ingratiating himself to the Emperor, to the alchemist who held the Son of Heaven's favor and knew the secret to eternal life: those endeavors made sense. Supporting and bringing honor to his family: these things made sense. But his love for her was as unexpected as pearls falling from the skies, yet so real and tangible, he felt as if he could cradle it in his hands.

The sheen of perspiration had dried, cooling against his skin, and he felt his muscles grow taut. He stood and stretched, shouting to Xiao Mao for a hot bath. Tomorrow morning would come soon enough. He just wanted to get it over with.

CHAPTER TEN

Chen Yong was anxious. She could tell by the set of his jaw and the tension in his shoulders. It was obvious even without using her power. She wished she could make this easier for him somehow. He turned to her as the carriage rolled past sheep, orange trees, and gentle hills. "I'm grateful you're with me," he said. She touched his arm for the briefest moment and smiled. She was glad as well.

After three more days of travel, she finally caught a glimpse of their destination when the carriage rounded a bend. Chen Yong slid to her side, and they looked out the window together. She had never seen anything like it. The Deen manor was built of white and gray stone with a massive arch over the main entrance. Above the arch was an enormous circular window, a sunburst in jeweled tones of red, indigo, and yellow. Stained glass. It was stunning.

"Mother of the heavens," she murmured.

They drove through the lush gardens that surrounded the estate. She caught glimpses of roses in colors she had never imagined—oranges and deep pinks. There were unfamiliar flowers, too, and she was glad of her sketchbook so she could draw them. She was suddenly aware of Chen Yong, his shoulder pressed against her back, his excitement and nervousness. Laughing, she drew her spirit tight to herself and nudged him back. "You're pushing me out the window," she said, her voice unnaturally high in her ears.

Chen Yong scooted back and chuckled. "Sorry."

Their caravan rumbled to a halt, and Yam Head hopped off the first wagon to help Yen direct the unloading of merchandise. She stepped from the carriage when Peng offered her a hand. They were in a courtyard with a cobbled floor. She glanced up, and the sunburst pattern was even more beautiful up close. The dark wooden door leading into the manor was also arched, mimicking the design of the front entranceway.

It opened, and several manservants stepped out,

dressed in black and white. A young man followed. He was as tall as Chen Yong, with light brown hair that reflected hints of gold in the sunshine. It was cut close to the head, like Peng's. He approached the captain and grasped his hand. They spoke in Jiang, and Ai Ling understood only snippets—about travel, weather, and food. Toward the end of the conversation, the young man glanced their way. His eyes lingered on her, and she stared down at the ground, feeling foolish. Peng strolled over to introduce them.

"This is Nik, the nephew of Master Deen," he said.

Nik extended his hand to Chen Yong, and she saw that his eyes were light green, the color of shallow seas. He studied Chen Yong with interest. "You're here to meet my uncle?" he asked. That much she could understand.

Chen Yong nodded. "I believe he may have known me once."

"My uncle was a diplomat in Xia for many years. But he returned before I was born. I doubt you could have known him?"

"Perhaps not," Chen Yong replied. "But I would like to meet him still."

"Of course. Any friend of Peng's is a friend of ours," Nik said. But there was a wariness in his tone as he assessed Chen Yong.

Chen Yong met his gaze, unconsciously squaring his shoulders, and they gauged each other for a long moment until Peng stepped forward and cleared his throat. Reminded of the task at hand, Nik nodded to the manservants, who proceeded to haul the various crates and chests through the massive doors. "We'll look at the merchandise and settle costs later?"

Peng agreed.

They spoke frighteningly fast, but Ai Ling was able to understand some of what was said. She assumed the introductions were over until Nik turned to her and caught her hand, pressing his lips to her fingers. Her face flushed so hot she thought her hair would catch fire.

"Who is this beautiful woman?" he asked.

She snatched her hand away, then realized how rude she must appear. "My name is Ai Ling," she said in Jiang, just as she'd been taught and had practiced so many times.

Nik broke into an easy smile. "She speaks the language! Wonderful."

"Ai Ling is my sister," Chen Yong said. "She wanted to travel with me, explore."

"Ah Na will be delighted to meet you both." Nik bowed to Ai Ling. He offered his arm, and there seemed to be no choice but for Ai Ling to rest her hand on it as he guided them inside the manor. She wasn't being vigilant, and his interest in her flared when she touched him. She snapped back, feeling the heat rise to her face again. Who was Ah Na? she wondered, to distract herself.

They followed Nik into a reception hall with a domed ceiling. Scenic views were painted directly on its curved surface: maidens frolicking in meadows filled with flowers and streams with majestic peacocks meandering on the banks. The stained glass threw a kaleidoscope of color onto the stone floors, and Ai Ling was transfixed by the glittering light until she heard a deep-throated laugh.

A young woman glided down the winding staircase. She was wearing a dress Ai Ling could never have imagined. It was tight-fitting and a luminous green on top, with a full skirt in a deeper forest green that must have been created from many layers. The sleeves hugged her arms to the elbow, but ended in cascades of cream lace. Her eyes held Ai Ling's for a brief moment.

"You've brought guests this time, Peng?" She reached the bottom of the stairs and held out her hand. "Can we keep them if we like them?"

Peng kissed her fingers, chuckling as he straightened. "I don't dabble in that type of trade, Miss Ah Na."

So this was Ah Na.

"Where is Yen?" she asked. "Are things well?"

"They are." Peng smiled. "He's checking the merchandise. He sends his regards, of course."

Ah Na turned to Chen Yong and extended her arm, a smile playing at the corners of her rouged lips. He bowed awkwardly and took her hand. Jealousy so strong that her stomach cramped swept through Ai Ling. Ah Na wore her honey-colored hair loose, and it fell in waves over her shoulders, perfectly framing her ivory face. Her eyes were a light green, like Nik's.

"And you are?" she asked.

"Li Chen Yong." He straightened but still held her hand. Ai Ling saw that Ah Na clasped his with her fingertips.

"My name is Wen Ai Ling," she said.

Ah Na released Chen Yong. "Such long names you have. You are wed?" She flicked her catlike eyes from Ai Ling to Chen Yong.

"She's his sister," Nik said with a grin.

"Oh." Ah Na brought her hands to her hips. The scent of lavender rose in the air. "You look nothing alike."

"I am"—Chen Yong fumbled for the right word—"adopted."

Ah Na's shapely eyebrows lifted. "You've certainly brought an interesting lot to our manor, Peng."

Peng laughed and offered her his arm, which she took. "Chen Yong is a friend. I thought your uncle might like to meet him."

"I see," Ah Na said. She bit her lower lip with small, perfect teeth. Ai Ling could almost hear her mind at work, whirring. "He's taking his afternoon break in the reception room." She led Peng down the grand hall, her heels clicking against the stone floor.

Nik offered his arm again, and Ai Ling wondered if she could go anywhere without being led like a donkey. She took it, so as not to appear rude, but not before discreetly making a face at Chen Yong, to show him what she thought about the entire matter. He looked distracted and was fidgeting with his collar. She felt her own palms dampen.

They followed Ah Na to a set of double doors. A manservant opened them for her, and she glided in with Peng. Chen Yong followed, while Nik escorted Ai Ling. The chamber was more intimate but still had a high ceiling, this one carved with a flower and leaf motif. Tall rectangular windows lined the opposite wall. These were accented with colorful geometric glass borders in cobalt, gold, and red. Bookshelves in a dark wood covered the entire wall at the far end of the chamber. A man sat in a high-backed plush chair near a fire blazing in the grand stone hearth.

Something about Master Deen's profile seemed familiar. He was the same age as her father, perhaps a few years older. His silver hair was cut close to his head, and he had a tall nose and a boldness in his features, even at his older age. "You've returned, Peng. With more beautiful things from Xia. You've brought tea for me? And date biscuits?"

Peng stepped forward as Master Deen rose, and they clasped hands. "All your favorites, my friend."

Master Deen turned to them, his high brow furrowing in puzzlement for a moment. "And you've brought guests? Please sit. Be welcomed."

Ai Ling sat next to Chen Yong on a long cushioned bench upholstered in a rose brocade, while Nik and Ah Na settled in high-backed chairs. Peng remained standing.

"Yes, I've brought two travelers from Xia. The young man believes he may . . . know you?" Peng nodded at Chen Yong.

Master Deen's ease disappeared in an instant. She realized then that he was nearly blind. "Who?" His gaze was urgent, gliding over their faces, as if he could see them clearly. "An old friend? From Xia?"

"Not an old friend, Master Deen," Chen Yong said,

his voice low and steady. "But perhaps someone you left behind?"

Master Deen rose from his chair, his full attention turned toward Chen Yong. "What is your name?"

"My mother named me Chen Yong."

"Impossible." Master Deen slumped back against the cushions as if he'd been punched. "It's not possible," he murmured.

Ah Na reached over to grasp her uncle's hand. "What's going on here?" Her tone was as cutting as the look she gave them. "Peng, what is the meaning of this?"

"Hush, Ah Na." Master Deen patted his niece's arm, his head lowered. As tightly as Ah Na gripped her uncle's hand, it still shook visibly. "I never told anyone. The gods forgive me. But I left a son back in Xia."

"What?" Ah Na and Nik exclaimed at the same time.

Chen Yong sat perfectly still. How Ai Ling wanted to touch him, to grab his hand in reassurance! Even with her spirit wound tight, she could sense emotions so strong and jumbled in that chamber it was as if someone had splattered buckets of colors across her mind. But it was Chen Yong's hope and fear that she felt the most sharply.

"And this is he?" Ah Na asked.

"How can you be certain?" Nik demanded. "His name could be as common as Nik or Ah Na in Xia."

"But only one was born in the Emperor's palace," Master Deen said. "By an imperial concubine."

The color drained from Chen Yong's face. Deen's niece and nephew gaped at their uncle, speechless.

"Who raised you, Chen Yong?" Deen asked.

"I was adopted by the Li family." His words were stilted now.

Deen swiped a palm across his cheek, rubbed his eyes. "And did you know you were born in the palace? Then smuggled out?"

"Yes."

"By my old friend at court, an adviser to the Emperor."

Ai Ling's eyes stung, as she thought of her father and how much she missed him. She did squeeze Chen Yong's arm then, and he clutched her hand for an instant, before dropping it. "I met Master Wen last autumn, and he told me his story."

"Your story, Chen Yong." Master Deen's eyes were bright. "Did he tell you your father's name?"

Chen Yong nodded. "You say it." The request came in a choked whisper.

"Wai Sen," Deen said. "It was the Xian name given to me by the Emperor."

Chen Yong doubled over, covering his face with his hands.

"Chen Yong. My son. Forgive me. I should have returned for you." Deen's voice was soft. "I wrote to Master Wen many times but never heard back. I assumed the worst."

Chen Yong did not lift his head, and although she could not see his face, she knew that he was fighting back tears.

Deen rose and approached them, stumbling once. Ah Na and Nik sprang to their feet, but Deen waved them away. He knelt before his son and touched his shoulder. "Your mother was beautiful," he said in Xian. "I loved her."

Chen Yong finally looked at his father. "My birth mother died, Master Deen."

Poisoned by Zhong Ye.

It was a moment before Deen was able to compose himself. "It may be too much to ask for you to call me Father, but please call me just Deen at least." He clasped Chen Yong's shoulder. "Tell me." Master Deen half turned. "What does he look like, Ah Na?"

The young woman considered Chen Yong, and Ai Ling felt his shock. He hadn't realized his father was nearly blind. "He's very handsome, Uncle. With a wide brow and a strong jaw—like yours." She tilted her head and pursed her lips. Ai Ling knew she liked what she saw. "But he looks . . . different as well."

"His hair is dark," Master Deen said with certainty in his voice.

"Almost raven."

"Your mother—" Deen choked and couldn't continue.

Chen Yong rose and took him by the elbow, guiding him back to his chair by the fire.

Master Deen smiled up at him, through his tears. "If you could show our guests to their chambers, Ah Na. "

Ah Na rose elegantly, spreading her full skirt and lowering herself in a formal bow before him. "Of course, Uncle."

"Chen Yong. Please stay. You must have as many questions as I do." He nodded at the chair beside him, the one that Ah Na had occupied.

Chen Yong sat down, and his eyes found Ai Ling's as she stood to leave. She simply nodded, her heart full, and smiled.

Somehow he returned it, the faintest curve of his mouth.

忠業

The sun was barely visible above the horizon when Zhong Ye made his way to Yokan's study. The closer he got, the heavier his footsteps became. The summer morning was still cool and crisp. Despite this, his palms were clammy, and he felt dampness beneath his arms by the time he arrived. The alchemist never seemed to sleep these days, and he knew he wouldn't be too early.

He entered without knocking, as they had forgone that formality a long time past. Yokan sat at the black-wood table, grinding something with an ebony mortar and pestle. The study smelled of ginger, both sweet and bitter. "You're early," Yokan said.

"I could come back." Zhong Ye hadn't even stepped across the threshold.

"No, no. Sit."

Zhong Ye placed his books and journals on the table, then rubbed his palms against his robe.

"Do you have any questions before we start?" Yokan asked. When Zhong Ye shook his head, the alchemist went on. "I'd like you to prepare the concoction today." He stood and scooped the herb he had been grinding into a glass jar.

Zhong Ye turned to his notes and began gathering the ingredients for the spell from all over the chamber. Yokan placed the large bronze bowl on the table for him. "You can ingest the empress root at any time before the ritual—as long as it's within an hour." He cut a third of a root into thin slices, the subtle almond fragrance filling the air.

Zhong Ye felt as if he were moving through mud. He mixed the ingredients and lit incense. Yokan pulled a single page from his sheaf of papers. "You'll need to recite this aloud. Just repeat after me, understand?"

How had the foreigner written an incantation in Xian without his help?

"Light the concoction," Yokan said.

He did what he was told, and it burst into sudden flames, emitting a thick, sickening odor. He then ate the sliced empress root. His reaction was different from the last time, as there were no wounds to heal. Within seconds his senses were heightened, the colors vibrant, the sounds more crisp. The root's power reverberated through him, and his heart thumped like a drum.

"Guards!" Yokan shouted.

The panel slammed open, and Zhong Ye experienced a potent sense of déjà vu, the details were so similar: the emaciated, groveling prisoner; the oafish guard who shoved him to the floor; the other guards snickering in the doorway.

The prisoner shrank from Yokan, then turned pleading eyes to Zhong Ye. "Master! Spare my life, please! I only stole to feed my starving family. Just one bag of rice was all!" He banged his forehead against the ground.

"Enough!" Yokan proffered the small vial filled with green

liquid. The prisoner's eyes bulged, and Zhong Ye couldn't take it.

Yokan snorted. "Don't be soft, Zhong." The guard yanked the prisoner's head back. Yokan uncorked the vial and gripped the prisoner's face with one hand, while he poured the liquid down his throat. "This won't hurt a bit," he cooed, then nodded to Zhong Ye. "Do it. Remember our agreement."

Zhong Ye sank to his knees and pressed his fingers to each side of the man's temples as he lay prone, writhing. Yokan began chanting, and Zhong Ye repeated the words, his throat parched, his voice croaking.

It started as warmth on his fingertips, quickly tightened and rose, until he had drawn the man's dying spirit from his body. Sinuous and silver, it hovered in the air. Beautiful. He threw his head back and stared up at it, the words he repeated growing louder now, coming faster.

The man's soul whirled, coalesced into a streak, and shot between Zhong Ye's lips, slamming down his throat. He gasped. Heat erupted from his solar plexus, gathered, spreading in waves through his heart, emanating past his groin. He collapsed to the floor, convulsing with pleasure, the corpse cold and still beside him.

* * *

When Zhong Ye opened his eyes, he felt the essence of life surging through him. Suffused with energy, frantic with terror, he jumped to his feet.

Yokan sat at his usual place, staring at him. "How do you feel?"

"I ate his spirit!" Zhong Ye shouted, not realizing he had until the words pummeled from his mouth.

"Did you?" The alchemist smiled, then turned to write in his journal. "Explain."

Zhong Ye resisted the urge to leap across the chamber and hit him. Instead, he took a step back and glanced down at the body. The prisoner had died curled up in the fetal position. Zhong Ye tried to look away but couldn't.

"It was part of our bargain." Yokan spoke in coaxing tones, as if he were addressing a child. "You will share your experience for study." He sighed, then called for the guards. They came and dragged the corpse away.

"You didn't tell me you ate their souls," Zhong Ye said, his voice cracking.

Yokan scribbled another note. "I couldn't influence your perception. What I experienced may not be what you experience."

"I ate his soul." Zhong Ye slumped down onto his stool.

"Tell me," Yokan said.

Zhong Ye described all that he could remember, and

Yokan kept writing for a long time after he was finished.

"And how do you feel now?" Yokan asked.

"Different." He felt so potent and strong he could defeat an entire army bare-handed. "More alive."

"The effects are undeniable. And cumulative." Yokan closed his journal. "Be prepared to do this again soon."

Zhong Ye jerked his head up. "No!"

"You say no now. Besides, it would be the perfect time to use that other spell I gave you." The alchemist smiled and handed him a piece of parchment. "Here it is transcribed in its entirety. You won't even need another slice of empress root for it to take." He ran a palm across his silver charms and after a pause said, "It would please her, no?"

Zhong Ye's scalp crawled. He would kill the alchemist if he ever spoke Silver Phoenix's name aloud. "You never said I had to do this more than once." But even as the words left his mouth, he was imagining feeling that incredible rush again. Craving it. He shook his head until it hurt, trying to obliterate the desire, the need.

"Don't be foolish. Recording our experiences is a boon for posterity. The study is much more worthwhile from two perspectives," Yokan said.

What had he gotten himself into? What frightened Zhong Ye more was the part of him that ached to try it again.

* * *

Silver Phoenix lay on his bed, her thick hair fanned like a peacock's tail. "I don't understand. How is it possible?"

Zhong Ye couldn't believe it himself. "It was a spell from . . . *The Book of Making.*"

She furrowed her brow, her heart-shaped face still flushed. "I don't know it. And I've studied it well."

"You must have missed the appendix section on eunuchs," he said, propping himself onto one elbow so he could see her better. The lanterns had burned low in the chamber, adding to the dreamlike quality.

She laughed. "That's terrible!"

"My lovemaking?" He smiled down at her, filled with love, stirred once again by physical desire. He had almost forgotten it. "I'm wounded." He drew slow circles around her navel with a finger.

But Silver Phoenix's face grew serious. "You know I would love you the same? Without this."

An unfamiliar lump rose to his throat, and he swallowed hard, as she ran her fingertips along the planes of his face, sweeping his cheekbones. "We could wed. Have children," he said. Her full lips curved into the hint of a smile, and he rushed on. "I'm serious!"

Was it something she didn't believe could happen? Or something she didn't want? It felt as if his heart would hammer out of his chest until she laid a hand over it. "It would be an honor to be your wife, Zhong Ye."

He grinned, couldn't find the right words to say to her. But it didn't matter, as she turned to him, pressing closer for a kiss.

CHAPTER ELEVEN

Dinner had consisted of creamy squash and potato soup, braised lamb, and stewed plums drizzled in honey and cream. Ai Ling felt overwhelmed and exhausted as she returned to her bedchamber. She wanted to be alone.

But Nik trailed after her up the wide staircase. "The days are longer now that it's summer. It's my favorite season."

She slowed her step. "Does it become hot?" she asked in broken Jiang.

He smiled. "I like the way you speak our language. It sounds different, more melodic."

She delved into him to understand what he said. She hated feeling as if she were both deaf and mute, hated being unable to express herself. He was amused and hoped she would invite him into her bedchamber. She snapped back, flustered.

"Thank you," she said.

"It can get quite warm. We often swim in the lake on the really hot days." He stopped outside her wide bed-chamber door. She stood with her back against it.

"Where do you sleep?" She spoke without thinking and grimaced.

Nik laughed. He was dressed in a sleeveless dark gray tunic that he wore over a cream shirt with wide sleeves. His gray trousers were tight, tapered to his legs, and she could tell that the clothing was of fine craftsman-ship. She sneaked brief glances at his face. His eyes were large and deep-set, his nose pointed and sharp; he was peculiar and foreign. She blushed when she noticed him studying her back with interest. "My bedchamber is on the third floor, where Ah Na's is. And my mother's, too, when she deems us worthy of a visit."

"It is a beautiful manor."

"I'm glad you think so." He unbuttoned the silver pearl at his neck, loosening his collar. "What is your brother's business with my uncle?"

She was shocked by his boldness. "That is not for me to say."

They stood for a few moments in silence. She wondered when he would be gracious enough to go. "I'm tired," she finally said. "I want to rest."

Disappointment flitted across his face. "Of course. Perhaps I can show you our gardens in the morning? Do you like flowers?"

She used her power again to understand his questions and felt his eagerness. "Yes. I like flowers," she said with reluctance.

"Wonderful. After breakfast then." He bowed, and she averted her face, then retreated into her bedchamber. She leaned against the back of the door for some time before her heart stopped racing.

Ai Ling found a ceramic tub in the bath chamber filled with hot water and thanked whoever had had the foresight to do this. She undressed after locking the doors and slipped into the smooth tub, sighing loudly. She scrubbed the feel and taste of the sea salt from her skin with a sponge, washed her hair in soap fragranced with sweet pea. When she finally climbed into bed limp and wrinkled from her long bath, Chen Yong had still not returned to the bedchamber adjoining hers. Master Deen had invited him to his study after dinner. She had hoped to see him, speak with him, but she finally fell asleep filled with regret.

* * *

Not even a morning meal of fresh bread slathered in preserved fruit and honey could lift Ai Ling's spirits. She was told that Chen Yong had risen at dawn and was touring the manor grounds with Master Deen. She was ready to crawl back into bed when Nik grabbed her by the elbow in the domed entranceway to the reception hall.

"Are you ready for a tour of the gardens?"

She had forgotten her promise and could think of no excuse to decline. He grinned and offered his arm, which she had to take. They made their way across the manor, through the immense kitchen and toward the back garden. When they stepped outside, she was glad that she had come. The fresh air and sunshine revived her and cleared her mind.

The sky was cloudless and a pale blue. A light breeze carried the scent of roses. They meandered past hedges that towered over them and followed a graveled path that curved across sloping lawns.

"Do you keep gardens in Xia?" He strolled at a leisurely pace, and she sensed his contentment.

"We have courtyards. Not as much land as you have. There is so much"—she struggled for the right word—"place."

Nik smiled. "We do have a lot of land. My family is fortunate."

She used her power to understand him. Was it so wrong? She pulled back before she could hear a true innermost thought.

"Your family is small?" she asked.

"It is. Just my sister and mother. We had another uncle, but he died rather unexpectedly."

"I am sorry."

"Yes, that was difficult for my family. We are close. It sent my mother into the arms of a new lover and travel."

"Your father?" she asked.

He seemed confused for a moment, then laughed. "No. My father and mother are not together. I haven't seen him in three years. My mother took a new lover, a much younger lover."

Ai Ling tried to wipe the shock from her face. A woman choosing a younger lover? Free of her husband? "Your ways are very different here," she said.

He extended his long legs in front of him and rested the heels of his hands on the bench they had settled on. "Oh? How so? Tell me about Xia. Uncle has talked about it a few times, but not much. Now I understand why not."

"I cannot say it well in Jiang." She blushed.

"You're speaking very well."

"Women in Xia cannot choose lovers. They have one husband, and they stay with that husband."

His light green eyes danced with amusement. "Really? That *is* different. So the man may choose his wife?"

"It is usually . . . done by the parents. But when men are older, they can choose other wives."

He looked taken aback. "More than one wife?"

Ai Ling laughed at his stunned expression. "Yes."

He stood and dusted off his trousers, then offered her a hand. She took it but let it drop once she stood. "You'll have to tell me more," he said.

"After you say more about Jiang customs," she replied.

"All right."

The rest of their stroll through the vast gardens was pleasant. Ai Ling paused by many unfamiliar flowers and asked Nik to name them: queen's heart, angel breath, lover's sorrow. She regretted not bringing her sketchbook. "Next time I will draw the flowers," she said.

"You're an artist?"

"A student. Learning."

"I'd be happy to accompany you again tomorrow morning," Nik said. "I draw as well."

She pretended to be engrossed in studying a delicate purplish blue blossom that she had never seen before. "I think I can find them again."

"And if I said I would like to come with you?"

She felt his gaze and straightened. They certainly were forward in this kingdom. "Maybe another time," she said.

He nodded and offered his arm. She took it to be polite, and they walked back toward the white and gray stone manor.

Master Deen invited Ai Ling and Chen Yong on a two-hour journey to the city center of Seta a few days later. Peng joined them. Yen and Yam Head followed in a separate wagon loaded with merchandise. The plush carriage rolled over gentle slopes, past a small town tucked among them, through woods thick with trees. They clattered through another town with a massive temple built of bluish gray stone, similar in color to the cliffs that surrounded Jiang Dao.

Peng shouted a word to the driver, who stopped the carriage in the square, across from the temple. Peng pointed upward. "These stained glass windows are Deen masterpieces."

The topmost facade of the temple was almost all glass and composed of four rectangular domed windows. They had arrived at the perfect time. The morning sunlight slanted over the jeweled panes, each depicting two figures.

"Who are they?" she asked.

"The major gods we worship," Master Deen replied. "Sun and Harvest. Moon and Fertility. Love and Health. Faith and Piety."

"Each major god is formed from two separate entities." Peng held up two fingers, pressed together. "It's why they are so powerful. The lesser gods are singular. Mateless."

"Are they male and female pairings?" Chen Yong asked.

Peng smiled. "No. Sun and Harvest are male, Moon and Fertility, female. The other two are a mix."

Ai Ling gazed at the gigantic windows, and they seemed to glimmer with magic. She was especially drawn to Moon and Fertility, who were rendered in circular and oval panels of pale lavender, silver, and pearl. The Moon Goddess bore a wreath of gold stars across her brow. Her hair fell in cobalt waves. The Fertility Goddess's silver hair was cropped, and her hand was clasped around a swelling belly. Ai Ling couldn't distinguish where one goddess ended and the other began.

"They are magnificent, Master Deen," she said, unable to look away.

"Who is your favorite?"

"Moon and Fertility."

Master Deen nodded and closed his eyes. "I can still see her so clearly. And you, Chen Yong?"

They were crushed together near the carriage window again, for the view. She realized that her hand was on Chen Yong's shoulder and that she was peering around him. Their faces were almost touching. She felt the warmth radiating from him, the slide of his muscles beneath her fingertips as he turned to his father.

"Love and Health," Chen Yong said.

Master Deen chuckled. "A romantic. I worked long hours to achieve the exact deep shade of crimson for that piece." He opened his eyes. "The technique to capture that color is now used by other craftsmen. I named it desire."

Peng rapped on the carriage roof then, and they continued on their journey.

Master Deen leaned back, and Ai Ling thought he had fallen asleep. She almost jumped when he spoke again after a long silence. "The most difficult part of the process now is designing the pieces. I can't see well enough to draw."

"But you still design?" Chen Yong asked.

Deen smiled, a smile so like Chen Yong's. "I can. Nik draws what I see in my mind's eye. The glass panes of the piece are fitted between lead rods to create the picture.

Nik glues a thick thread to his sketch, following where these rods would lie in the piece. I'm able to see it with my hands to judge if he's captured the image right." He twisted the carved ivory handle of the cane he was never without. "It's worked so far. I'm afraid I won't be creating any new colors, however."

"Who taught you the craft?" Ai Ling asked.

"My father. Your grandfather, Chen Yong. And his mother taught him before that. The Deen family has created stained glass for centuries."

"You're the best master craftsmen in the kingdom for good reason," Peng said.

They arrived in the city center of Seta before midday. Peng hopped down from their carriage and joined Yen and Yam Head for their meetings with merchants interested in their imports. When Yam Head saw Ai Ling, he pulled a face with his hands, waggling his tongue at her. She laughed and made her own face before their carriage rolled away.

"It's been sometime since I've visited Seta. Ah Na deals with most of our business contacts and negotiations these days," Deen said. "What would you like to see?"

Her stomach was beginning to growl for a meal, but she didn't want to appear demanding. Or piggish. As if reading her mind, Chen Yong said, "Perhaps we should stop for something to eat before we explore?"

She beamed and nodded at him. He laughed under his breath.

"Yes, let's," Deen said.

Ai Ling continued to stare out the carriage window as they jounced over the cobblestones. She saw elegant women shopping along the main street, trailed by servants carrying bags and boxes. The women's dresses were trimmed in furs and velvet and were as revealing and luxurious as Ah Na's. They wore elaborate hats, oval or triangular, decorated with colorful flouncing feathers and jewels. That morning Ai Ling had finally put on the deep purple tunic Peng had given her back on the ship. Grateful that she was dressed in something so beautiful for her first city outing, she glided her hand over one silk sleeve.

The grand city of Seta had more than just one main street, and Deen's carriage traveled from one to the next. Shop windows were filled with familiar items, like bedding and fabric, but in colors and patterns completely foreign to Ai Ling. There were shops that displayed boots dyed in all colors, some which reached above the knees, a few with incredibly high heels. She gazed at it all in wonder.

The carriage pulled into a massive square, filled with

merchants manning stalls, sitting at tables, or squatting over rugs thrown on the ground. She glimpsed carved Jiang gods, woven baskets, and boxes decorated with seashells. The delicious aroma of roasted meats, fresh baked breads, and other enticing sweet, spicy scents drifted toward the carriage. "Can we stop here?" Ai Ling asked.

Deen tilted his head. "You want to stop at the market?"

"Could we? They have food."

Deen laughed. "Of course. I was going to take you to my favorite inn, but this will do nicely."

The coachman halted their carriage near one of the large four-story buildings flanking the square. The buildings leaned against one another, their roofs triangular, their facades painted in pastel lavender, yellow, blue, and green. Chen Yong took her hand and helped her from the carriage. His palm was warm and rough. There was nothing she wanted more than to stroll through the market with her hand clasped in his.

He let go and grinned. "So like the markets in Xia but so different, too."

Deen climbed down from the carriage and tapped his cane on the ground. Chen Yong reached for his other arm to help guide him. "Where to first?" Deen asked.

"Let's follow Ai Ling's nose," Chen Yong said. Both

men chuckled, but she had already trotted away, chasing the mouthwatering aromas.

They passed a woman with hair like mahogany. She had threaded ribbons of every color through her tresses, and she carried a basket spilling over with them.

"Let me buy you some," Chen Yong said.

Embarrassed, Ai Ling shook her head. She had never woven ribbons through her braid before.

"I promised you a gift from Jiang Dao, didn't I?" He smiled and began choosing ribbons from the basket.

She laughed as he contemplated a variety of colors, tilting his head and looking very serious. He finally settled on six, in different jewel tones and widths, then presented them to her.

They stopped at a stand where a short man with a bristling beard was cooking almonds in sugar. He stirred the nuts with a wooden stick, and the sugary scent was divine. Deen bought them each a portion, poured into a cone twisted from paper. She chomped on the almonds as she followed her nose toward the aroma of roasting meats.

They finally found the stand where two men and one woman were grilling sausages and roasting whole chickens and pigs. The woman, her wavy hair pulled back in a turquoise scarf, was slathering a dark sauce onto the sizzling meats. Ai Ling could smell the spice and garlic, and her mouth watered.

"What would you like?" Chen Yong asked.

"Anything." She gasped. "Everything."

Chen Yong laughed and spoke to one of the men and pointed at the grill. The man wore a red scarf tied around his forehead, and his cheeks were smudged with ash. He threw slices of meat on a thick slab of bread and dolloped grilled onions and peppers over them before putting another slice of bread on top. He cut everything in half, then wrapped it in paper.

Chen Yong paid and juggled the various packages, already beginning to stain with grease. "I bought enough so you can try everything." He grinned at Ai Ling, and she wanted to kiss him.

They wandered into a tent. A puppet show was taking place, with a white wooden horse and a maiden in a puffy pink dress bobbing across a small painted stage. Children, transfixed by the action, clustered near the front. They sat on benches at the back of the tent and ate their stacks, as Master Deen called them, and washed everything down with an iced drink of lemon and elderflower.

Ai Ling sighed contentedly after the meal, wiping her fingers on the paper the stacks had been wrapped in. They then strolled through the market for another hour before Deen took them on a tour of the rest of the city. They stopped at two other temples that featured the Deen family's magnificent stained glass. Deen explained that rich nobles also commissioned his work, but their estates were set back behind elaborate iron fences, hidden from public view.

"Your windows are so inspiring," she said as they headed back into the countryside toward the Deen manor. "The color combinations are breathtaking."

"It makes me think of brush painting," Chen Yong said. "And how we utilize colors in our art."

Master Deen's face lit up. "You're an artist?"

"I draw a little. But mainly paint," Chen Yong replied.

"So you sketch and work with color?" Master Deen asked.

"Yes."

"I would love to teach you my craft, son. To pass this skill on to you so that you can continue the family business."

"Father . . ."

Deen reached across the carriage to grasp Chen Yong's hand. Ai Ling's throat tightened. Is this what Chen Yong wished for?

"I've never considered it," Chen Yong said. "You're offering me too much."

Master Deen shook his head, his face thoughtful. He did not drop his son's hand. "It's your right, Chen Yong. It can all be yours if you want it."

The rest of the carriage ride was a quiet one. Ai Ling glanced at Chen Yong several times, but he stared out the window, lost in thought.

She turned away and peered out her own window. The sun was slanting low in the horizon. A movement caught her eye: a lone crow spiraled in the distance. As the carriage thundered forward, the bird seemed to follow them, dropping lower and gliding on the wind. Its wing feathers were white. Her chest tightened, and she pressed her face against the window. Perhaps it was a reflection of the light. The crow swerved closer and flew parallel to the carriage. There was no mistaking it: a white-winged crow.

An omen of death.

Her skin prickled, tingling to her fingertips, and she turned to Chen Yong, but the words caught in her throat. She ached to know where his thoughts ran but held her spirit to herself. When she glanced back out her window, the crow was gone.

Ah Na greeted them at the door to say dinner was ready in the dining hall. She slid a curious look at Chen Yong. "How was your visit to Seta?" she asked, waiting for Chen Yong to offer his arm. He did, and she sashayed down the marbled hallway, her full peach skirt swishing behind her.

Unable to shake her unease, Ai Ling followed.

Peng fell in step with her after dinner. "We haven't had a chance to talk," he said.

Ai Ling glanced behind her. Nik and Ah Na were walking together and speaking conspiratorially. Chen Yong had disappeared after the meal.

Peng paused when they arrived at her bedchamber. "I've been reading up on your plight as best as I can." He shot a glance up and down the hallway and lowered his voice. "There isn't much information in the books I have. And what there is, is rather cryptic. But I'm researching and hope to find a solution for you."

She knew he was honest, earnest. "Thank you."

"I do need your help," he said. "Will you tell me everything that happened? On your wedding night?"

She shuddered, then forced herself still. "Would it be useful to you?"

"Tremendously," he said.

She dropped her chin. Ai Ling did not want to remember that night, tried her best never to think of it. But it was like a seed deeply rooted within her mind, it was always with her. "I'll tell you everything I can."

Peng followed her into the bedchamber, lit now by gilded lanterns.

Mei Gui had her baby in the tenth moon, a chubby boy with a healthy cry. The Emperor visited personally, after Zhong Ye brought him the good news. Mei Gui's trysts with the Son of Heaven had stopped months before, but Zhong Ye had never let her or the baby slip from the Emperor's mind. All this hard work and diligent attention had resulted in the perfect outcome, a baby boy who had a high chance of becoming Emperor one day.

The Emperor cradled the bundle swathed in imperial yellow to his chest and peered down at the babe, his face beaming with pride. "He has his beautiful mother's eyes," he said, smiling.

"But your nose and mouth, Your Majesty," Mei Gui murmured from her bed.

The Emperor passed his son to the nursemaid and leaned over to kiss Mei Gui on the lips. "You're to be promoted in rank, my rose. I'll give you gifts the next time we meet. Alone."

Zhong Ye looked at Silver Phoenix. They would

celebrate Mei Gui's rise in stature as well. The Emperor waved for Zhong Ye to accompany him back to his private study.

"Congratulations on your son, Your Majesty," he said, matching the Emperor's stride. Eight guards trailed them, their footsteps beating in sync against the cobblestones.

"You did well to bring Mei Gui to me, Zhong. I like the girl." He rubbed the short beard on his chin. "If I don't have enough sons, I risk their dying young, leaving my kingdom without an heir. I have too many, and I risk their killing one another." He barked a loud laugh. Zhong Ye kept his face expressionless and stepped ahead to open the door panel for the Emperor.

The guards remained outside as the Son of Heaven made himself comfortable in his study, which was filled with books and paintings by famous artists, living and gone. A handmaid of no more than fifteen years stepped from a hidden alcove and poured them rice wine. "Tell me, how is the research on immortality progressing with Yokan?" The Emperor leaned back in his chair and regarded Zhong Ye with heavy-lidded eyes.

"We're making progress on the spell, Your Majesty." His emperor was shrewd, when he wasn't distracted and chose to be. Zhong Ye knew Yokan had been giving the Emperor a fake potion, laced with minimal amounts of the empress root. It was powerful enough so he'd feel the effects, but it was nothing life-altering.

"He tells me you slew a horrible monster, a beast, to harvest this root?"

Taken aback, Zhong Ye paused before replying, "Yes, Your Majesty." He didn't know that Yokan and the Emperor had been talking about him or what had been said. Had the alchemist been truthful?

"Well done. And the next harvest?"

"Not until the eighth moon next year. According to the royal astrologer."

The Emperor drummed his fingers against a gilded desk. "And you will be the one to retrieve them again?"

"I'm not certain, Your Majesty."

"Will there be another beast protecting the roots?"

"I don't know, Your Majesty."

"You'll go. And you'll bring the entire batch back to me," said the Emperor. "I don't trust that foreigner. But I need to keep him content as he works on his spell."

Zhong Ye nodded, trying to hide his thoughts with another sip of wine.

"Make it happen." The Emperor pounded on his desk.

"Yes, Your Majesty."

The Emperor stood, and Zhong Ye jumped to his feet. The Emperor came around to clasp Zhong Ye on the shoulder with a firm hand, startling him. The Son of Heaven had never touched him before. "You're also to be rewarded, Zhong, for your hard work."

Zhong Ye bowed low. "I do have one request, Your Majesty."

The Emperor crooked his fingers, indicating that Zhong Ye straighten. "Do you?" There was a mixture of curiosity and amusement in his narrow eyes.

"It is in regard to Silver Phoenix. . . ."

Zhong Ye and Silver Phoenix had eaten the light meal quickly, feeding each other fresh slices of pineapple and giggling like children. They dipped their hands into the pond to rinse off the fruit's sticky juice. A white swan, as regal as any empress, glided toward them. Silver Phoenix made a soft, clucking sound and extended her hand toward it. "This one's female."

"How can you tell?" he asked.

"She's smaller." The swan made an elegant arc in the water and swam back to her partner.

"They mate for life," Silver Phoenix said, her head tilting a little as she watched the pair swim side by side.

"So do people."

She laughed. "People! People are as fickle as the cravings of a woman with child. As changing as the tide in—" She stopped in mid-sentence when she caught the expression on his face.

"I'm not fickle or ever-changing," he said in a quiet voice.

"My love." She wound her arms around his waist. "I never had a reason to believe in anything otherwise until I met you."

His heart seemed to expand within him until it was difficult to breathe. "I've spoken with the Emperor; he's given his blessing for our betrothal."

She stepped back and stared at him, her lips parted. "You jest."

Zhong Ye laughed and caught her hand. "I wouldn't. Not about this. You know it's what I've wanted all along." Too afraid to look at her, he cleared his throat. "You haven't changed your mind, have you?"

She squeezed his fingers and smiled. "Of course not."

Two kingfishers with emerald throats chased each other across the pond before disappearing. Silver Phoenix and Zhong Ye meandered through the tall grasses and vivid wildflowers. She stopped to pick some, humming as she made a fragrant bouquet, then tucked a purple blossom behind her ear and fixed one of deep green behind his. He laughed, indulging her. She rewarded him with a kiss.

They entered the Lovers' Garden, named for the secret alcoves tucked throughout for romantic trysts. He drew her into one. The heart's blossom was in bloom, winding its way up an arch above them, and he pulled a flower down, admiring the periwinkle petals. Silver Phoenix would look beautiful in a tunic of this color, he thought. She wore a flowing dress of pale blue today, and her hair was braided and coiled close to her head. She pushed him playfully onto the bench and sat beside him.

"I need to speak with you on an important matter," he said.

Her expression grew serious, and she brushed his silk sleeve. "What could be more important than our betrothal?" she asked.

It was hard for him to meet her eyes. "I believe I've discovered a way to extend my life. To extend yours."

She stiffened and leaned away. "It's that alchemist. He's put strange ideas in your head."

"Not strange, love. Think of the possibilities. The Emperor is a drunkard, a slave to his libido. He couldn't make the right choice for a banquet menu if he had to."

Silver Phoenix didn't speak, would not look at him.

Zhong Ye smelled the subtle jasmine of her hair and skin and the sweet scent of the heart's blossom. "I can help guide the Emperor in his mandates, as I rise higher in rank. I can become his most trusted adviser."

She lifted her face then to meet his eyes, and his heart dropped, to see her love and worry. He reached for her hand, but she brushed it aside.

"I know you'll be able to accomplish all these things. You have a lifetime before you." She swept her arm in a grand gesture, as if anything were possible. "They'll dedicate poems to you, sing of all your good deeds, your wisdom. Isn't that enough?"

It wasn't. Not after what he had seen, had experienced.

"But we could have more. Don't you want the chance to live forever?" he asked. "We've discovered the spell for immortality. It works."

She shifted farther away from him on the bench. "You've tried it?"

Five times already. It had become a need, a compulsion. And he had learned not to think of the prisoners as people, but rather as another component of the spell. He lied. "Only once. To know that it works." His scalp tingled as he wrenched his gaze away from her. She'd never understand, *couldn't* understand until she tried it herself.

"Please don't do it again, Zhong," she whispered. "It's wrong, unnatural."

He suddenly felt defensive, angry. What did she know? He was the scholar, the one to solve the riddle, the one to kill the Poison Eagle and harvest the precious empress root. She didn't understand enough to appreciate fully what he offered, all that he had risked to share this gift with her.

Her body was tense, although she tried to hide it. He could tell by the stiff arch of her neck, the way her hands lay rigid in her lap. They were silent for a long time, sitting side by side, barely touching.

Zhong Ye wondered what he could do to change her mind.

Returning to him late that evening, she slipped into his bedchamber ethereal as a goddess, her green gown luminous in the moonlight. She climbed onto the tall platform bed, and he said nothing as she pulled each comb and hairpin from her head, until her black hair fell down her back.

She folded herself against him, draped an arm across his chest, and whispered about her day: how Mei Gui's baby, Tang Er, was progressing, what visitors had come to see him, the jade ring carved with roses sent by the Emperor. . . . Soon after, she was asleep, her quiet breathing warm against his neck. He kept replaying their argument from earlier in the day. She stirred against him; he kissed her shoulder. She smiled, murmured something without waking, and he buried his face in her hair.

Was it truly so wrong to want it all?

CHAPTER TWELVE

Master Deen had invited Chen Yong and Ai Ling to his studio. It was a twenty-minute walk from the manor. Deen led the way, using his ebony cane, refusing his son's assistance. "I've walked this path countless times," he said.

Chen Yong, grinning, offered her his arm. They followed Deen down a gravel path lined with giant oak trees. The pungent scent of hyacinths perfumed the air. As they came around a bend, she glimpsed a meadow filled with them: explosions of fuchsia and violet.

She paused, awed by the colors, seduced by the heady scent.

Deen stopped as well. "The hyacinth is part of our family crest." He smiled at Chen Yong. "It symbolizes serenity and beauty. What we hope to convey with our glasswork."

"What else is on the family crest?" Chen Yong asked. His hand, warm and reassuring, was covering hers. She closed her eyes for a moment, trying to memorize the feeling. If only she could press it like a blossom between the pages of her sketchbook and keep it forever.

"You'll see." Master Deen smiled.

They soon arrived at a massive building, hewn from the same white and gray stone as the manor. There was a giant diamond-shaped stained glass above the wide double oak doors. Master Deen swept his arm overhead. "The Deen family crest," he said.

Chen Yong tilted his head back, his eyes narrowed slightly against the morning sunshine. "The oak tree for strength?" he asked.

Deen clasped Chen Yong's shoulder; his face lifted up, as if he could see it as well. "And longevity. The pomegranate symbolizes abundance, prosperity."

The backdrop of the crest was a deep golden orange, offsetting the rich hues of the hyacinth, oak tree, and pomegranate perfectly. "The pomegranate's color is incredible," said Ai Ling.

"Come inside, and you'll see how it's done." Deen pushed open the door for them.

Both Chen Yong and Ai Ling stopped dead at the entrance of the studio. The rectangular building was gigantic, one large chamber with a high-pitched roof. Stained glass windows of all sizes and shapes lined the walls, throwing a rainbow of kaleidoscopic color below. More framed pieces of stained glass hung from the ceilings. The room was filled with dozens of enormous wooden worktables. People bustled around them. The studio smelled of wet pottery, fire, metals, and other scents that Ai Ling couldn't place.

She spotted Nik, bent over a table studying something intently. He was speaking to a man and woman beside him.

"Let's join Nik," Deen said, certain that his nephew was there. "Could you lead us, son?"

Chen Yong took his father by the arm, and Ai Ling felt his rush of conflicted feelings: pleasure and pride, caution and uncertainty.

She followed the two men, both striding in similar fashion, shoulders squared and heads held high. She smiled. Ah Na had sent her personal tailor to Chen Yong and had Jiang clothing made for him. His gray trousers fitted perfectly and were tapered to the ankles, making him appear taller. He wore a deep blue shirt with a sleeveless silver tunic. Would he cut his hair short next? she wondered.

Nik greeted his uncle and cousin politely but beamed when he saw her behind them. "Ai Ling! What a surprise. Welcome."

She nodded shyly at him.

"Tell us about this piece, Nik," Deen said.

Glass panels were set in a huge wooden frame on the table.

"This window was commissioned by the Arra family. The Lady Arra wanted a flower motif," Nik said.

"We decided on lilies and irises," Deen interjected.

"The glass has been cut; it's all laid out. Now we're finalizing colors."

"We create the colors with metal oxides, then fire them in the kiln," Deen said. "It takes a lot of skill and experimentation. If the heat of the kiln is off by a few degrees, the colors might be something entirely unexpected."

Nik nodded. "It's the most difficult part of the entire process. We're mixing colors now."

A man approached their table with a white ceramic bowl, stirring its contents with a spoon.

"This is a combination of copper oxide and vinegar. We'll paint directly onto the glass. . . ."

Ai Ling, mesmerized, stared at the bowl. The white ceramic began to gleam, turning bronze as Nik's voice droned on in the distance.

A rank odor rose from the bronze bowl, and she almost gagged. The giant studio swirled around her, and steady chanting filled her ears. She realized that she was the one speaking in archaic Xian in Zhong Ye's rich voice, her fingertips pressed to the temples of a man sprawled in front of her. He was on the brink of death, and she tried to cry out.

Her voice grew hoarse. She flung her head up, her eyes rolled back, and when the dead man's spirit rushed down her throat, it suffused her being with an intense wave of pleasure. The man's life essence filled her, exploded through her veins, trickled from every pore.

She shuddered and crashed against the side of a wooden table, tears streaming from her eyes. Jeweled glass glittered and flashed above her.

"Ai Ling!" Chen Yong sounded very far away.

She had no voice to answer him.

Master Deen had called the family physician. Ai Ling had lied to him. It had been too warm in the studio, the smells overwhelming. She had simply fainted. She stayed in bed all day, with the windows flung open so she could enjoy the garden breeze. Both Chen Yong and Nik had visited her, separately.

She gazed now into the gilded mirror hanging above

the washbasin and barely recognized herself. Her coloring was sallow, and dark rings curved beneath her eyes. She splashed water on her face. Her head was heavy; her mind, compressed and robbed of space. She felt as if she couldn't take a full breath or form a full thought.

She tried to speak with Chen Yong at the morning meal, but he refused to meet her eyes. He left the dining hall without speaking a word to her, as if she hadn't existed. She almost chased after him, but an inexplicable feeling of dread stopped her. Unsettled and hurt, she escaped to wander through the back gardens. Finding a bench beneath an orange tree, its blossoms scenting the warm summer air, she sat and hoped for birds to come near. If only she had brought some bread to share with them. She sketched a flower called firefly's spiral, trying to clear her mind.

She felt their presence like a tickle in her ear: Ah Na strolling arm in arm with Nik. They were far from her, beyond the rows of towering hedges, and Ai Ling instinctively threw her spirit toward them.

"Uncle hasn't mentioned anything to me yet. I don't think Chen Yong has decided. But I'm certain he's been offered the business, the manor. Everything," Ah Na said. Ai Ling felt her annoyance, her disappointment.

"That isn't right. We are Uncle's family. How can we

even be sure Chen Yong is who he claims to be? For all we know, he's an impostor after our fortune." Anger and jealousy from Nik. He kicked at a rock along the garden path.

"I don't think Chen Yong is lying. Look at him. He's too easy to read. And what impostor travels with an adopted sister?" Ah Na laughed, amused, feeling superior and a little mean.

Ai Ling twitched, knowing she shouldn't be intruding, but she didn't pull herself back. They were talking about her, about Chen Yong. . . .

"Ai Ling's nice," Nik said.

"Don't think I haven't noticed you trailing after her with your tail wagging and your tongue hanging out."

Nik laughed this time. "I wonder if she'll take me as a lover?"

Ah Na's amusement was so strong it was a burst of light in Ai Ling's mind. "Dear brother, she's a virgin." Ah Na shook her head, laughing. "I'm certain of it."

"A virgin!"

Ai Ling cringed. Why were they discussing this? How could— She stopped sputtering and kept listening.

"Did you not guess it? Wearing that chaste braid every day and those tunics that cover her from the earlobes down." Ah Na chortled. "Isn't it obvious?"

"She explained a little about Xia culture, but no," Nik

said. "I thought she was just stringing me along, to amuse herself."

"You're such a catch. Why waste your efforts on a strange foreign girl? Plenty of women would be happy to take you as a lover."

"I like Ai Ling," Nik replied.

"She looks like a milkmaid."

Ai Ling ground her fists against the stone bench. They were meandering away, toward a small pond. She rose and followed them, guided by the faint pull at her navel.

"She's beautiful. I like that she's different. She'll bed me soon enough."

Ai Ling paused in mid-step, hating the hotness she felt, the way it spread to her ears and down her neck.

"Would you wager on it?" Ah Na asked.

"I would. I wager I'll have Ai Ling before you ensnare Chen Yong."

Ah Na stopped walking and faced her brother.

"You take me for a fool? I've been watching you, too," Nik said. "What are you conniving now?"

Ah Na cleared her throat and resumed walking, her full skirt swaying at her ankles. "If I can't be the heir to the family estate, I can at least be wed to the man who owns it."

It was Nik who stopped this time. "You jest. You would marry him?"

Ah Na shrugged. "What's wrong with the idea? Our fortune would stay within our family. Uncle would be pleased; he's hinted as much to me."

"I thought you never wanted to wed, after seeing what happened to our own parents?"

"It's only a formality. A small sacrifice. It's not as if I'd be bound to him. I can still take lovers if I chose and hold title of mistress to the estate." Ah Na fussed with her hair. "Besides, he's nice to look at."

Nik snorted. "Is Chen Yong interested?"

Her laughter was throaty, sensuous. "Does he stand a chance?"

"Probably not."

Ai Ling halted in her tracks again, her stomach cramping. She closed her eyes. The world had grown blurry around the edges. She'd known Ah Na was interested in Chen Yong but had had no inkling she planned to wed him. With Deen's blessing? She sank to the ground and pressed her hot face into her thighs. Her world had spun upside down, and she didn't know how to make it right again.

She stayed there, curled up, until she was certain that Ah Na and Nik had returned to the manor. Her legs were numb when she rose. She stumbled a little as she wandered, not caring where she went. The sun was hot on her back. She entered a grove of trees. The branches were thick with leaves and blocked out the sunlight. A caw shook Ai Ling from her stupor.

Her head snapped back. She didn't see the crow until it spread its wings to pick at white feathers with its beak. The bird considered her with gleaming eyes and cawed again. She fell to her knees, hands scrambling for a rock. Her fingers clutched one, and she cast it into the tree, but it fell short. The crow hopped a little farther up the branch, its call sounding like harsh laughter.

She ran, racing deep into the garden, between trees with dark, gnarled trunks. The branches turned into skeletal fingers, snatching at her braid, her tunic. She tripped and staggered forward, the twigs scraping her cheeks. Too winded to scream, she crashed into a clearing filled with tall stone sculptures and almost collided with two bloody figures. One was decapitated, snaking on the ground, grappling futilely for his lost head. The other appeared to have had the skin peeled from her face and her hair burned to wisps. She keened ceaselessly. The two figures morphed to four, then to eight.

Zhong Ye appeared suddenly on one of the stones. He was naked, his entrails spilling from a wide slit in his abdomen. His head hung low, lanky hair obscuring his features. He lifted his chin, and his eyes met hers. But it wasn't Zhong Ye. Ai Ling stared into her own face, and her choke turned into a sob.

She opened her mouth, but no sound came.

Zhong Ye's entire life, his entire consciousness flooded her. Filled her. Brilliant. Potent. Vibrant. She fell to the ground, screaming. The tortured men and women who made up his spirit, his essence, and his memory crushed against her, through her, stealing her voice, her breath. She was deluged with the smell and taste of their blood, her blood, their burned flesh, and her flesh. . . .

It was almost dusk when Ai Ling woke, her cheek pressed against the damp grass. She sat up. She was in a small meadow, dotted with wildflowers. A tall hedge, the border of the garden, was to her left. No trees were in sight. She heard hurried footsteps on gravel, saw Nik enter the meadow from a gap in the hedge. He ran to her.

"Ai Ling!" His relief was plain. "Where have you been? We've been scouring the entire grounds for you."

She rose unsteadily to her feet, and he caught her in his arms.

"Are you all right?" He bent closer to look at her face.

She tried to pull away but was too weak. He embraced her, and she punched him in the chest—in poor shuen form and without strength. He stepped back, unhurt, but surprised. A hot rage filled her. "I am not some girl to be bedded and wagered on!"

"No," he said, his green eyes wide.

But she saw the guilty flush in his cheeks. She seized his spirit and forced him back across the meadow, moving so quickly that he stumbled. Her anger spread until it consumed her.

Nik slapped his own face, and Ai Ling laughed. She forced him to hit his other cheek again and again. Hard enough to leave angry welts. His shock was turning to terror. Fear rolled from him, sharp and sour, was a dark knot in the pit of his stomach. She had never felt so powerful. She jerked his legs like a puppeteer until he was crushed against the tall hedge.

"Ai Ling!" Chen Yong ran into the meadow. "Stop!"

She released Nik's spirit, and he collapsed to the ground.

"Sorceress!" Nik scrambled to his feet and raced from the meadow before Chen Yong could reply.

He glanced after his cousin, then turned toward her. Her mouth went dry when she saw his face. "What happened?" he asked.

"I—I don't know." She stuttered.

"We've been looking for you for more than an hour."

His jaw muscles flexed. He hadn't shaved, and the new growth on his cheeks made him look older. Harsher. "Why did you possess him?"

"I had to." But the anger had seeped from her like ink from a cracked jar.

"You had to make him hit himself?"

She had no reply.

"What did he do to deserve that? What's happening to you, Ai Ling?"

She clutched her arms around herself, trying to keep from trembling.

"What have you been keeping from me?"

"Nothing," she said, barely above a whisper.

He scrutinized her, and his glance was accusing. "I had a dream last night."

"No." She wanted to run, to cover her ears, but stood frozen, as if spellbound.

"It was—" He faltered. "It showed you removing his heart. Li Rong's heart. When—when he died. And your blessed dagger turned black."

She felt faint and swayed on her feet. "It's Zhong Ye! He's everywhere! He's trying to—" She knew she wasn't making sense.

"Is it true? Is that how the blade turned black?"

His anguish brought tears to her eyes. She dropped

her gaze, nausea cramping her stomach.

He lifted her chin with one hand. "Is it true?" The words came slower now, deliberate, each like a blow to her chest. "What did you do?"

"I only wanted to bring him back. I know it was a mistake. I burned—" She felt his fury as if lightning had struck all around her, as if she were standing in the center of a tornado.

"Bring him back how?"

"Wi-with the Calling Ritual."

He shook his head, uncomprehending and impatient. Of course he wouldn't know it. He had never read *The Book of the Dead*.

"Were you using the dark arts?" he asked. Her lack of response was confirmation enough. "How could you? You risked his chance on reincarnation. You made his body unwhole!" His voice cracked. "I trusted you."

She reached for him, and he jumped back. "Chen Yong, let me explain—"

But he had already whipped around and was walking away. He disappeared through the hedge, leaving behind his anger and grief, so palpable she could taste the bitterness in her mouth.

Yokan was astounded when Zhong Ye told him about his betrothal. "Congratulations, good man! And you've the Emperor's blessing, too?"

"He indulged me. I think it amused him." He would have been insulted if he hadn't been so pleased. The Emperor had promised him an extravagant wedding and banquet, in exchange for all of the empress root from the next harvest.

"You did find time for love then, despite our pursuits." Yokan chuckled.

Zhong Ye didn't respond. He was flipping through the lunar calendars. He had both his star chart and Silver Phoenix's in front of him. He had gone directly to the Emperor's astrologer and had them drawn up in order to determine the most fortuitous day to wed. He found the date and shuffled back and forth between the charts.

"Is something wrong?" Yokan asked.

"The best date is in the eighth moon next year, the same month that the empress roots will be growing."

"A wraiths' month so soon again?"

Zhong Ye glanced up briefly. "It's true, the double-moon month usually occurs every two to three years. This is rare, but it has happened before." He paused to read the royal astrologer's notes. "According to this, the double full moons will be only seen in the Eastern Hemisphere next year."

"How unusual," Yokan murmured. "And fortunate for us. It shouldn't be an issue. I was thinking we would harvest at the end of the month this time, so the roots may grow to their full size." The alchemist squinted at him, as if he were studying a live beetle pinned to a board.

"It makes sense," Zhong Ye said, his own expression bland. Was Yokan planning to come with him? If so, how could he talk him out of it?

"Do you think there will be another Poison Eagle guarding the harvest?" Yokan replaced a book onto the shelf.

"Or perhaps the same one." Zhong Ye didn't know for certain. But the danger might deter the alchemist.

Yokan sat back down and flicked a wrist before picking up his quill. "I don't believe your future bride cares for me."

The pages before Zhong Ye blurred, and he forced himself to take three full breaths before saying, "I've done everything you've asked of me."

The alchemist smiled and regarded him with flat eyes. "Yes. And hasn't it worked out well for us both?"

"Your eyes, they're changing color." Silver Phoenix pressed closer, her face hovering over his.

He closed his eyes and kissed her. "I don't know what you mean." They had lost color with each soul he had eaten; the change was barely perceptible. But of course Silver Phoenix would notice.

"They've always been dark brown, like the earth after a rain." She cupped his face, forcing their eyes to meet. His heart pounded faster, with guilt and desire. He wondered if she could feel it. "They're becoming lighter."

"You can barely see in here," he said. Two lanterns shimmered dimly in the far corners of his bedchamber. He trailed his fingers down her back. "And if so, it's probably from the love spell."

She sat up. He reached for her, but she spun away in one fluid motion, like the graceful dancer that she was. She climbed from his bed and pulled on a brocaded robe.

"I've always loved the color of your eyes. I hope it wears off soon." She leaned over and kissed him. "I must return to my mistress." She opened the secret door panel in his bedchamber and slipped into the passageway.

Zhong Ye sat up and buried his face in his hands. How much longer could he keep the truth from her?

* * *

Zhong Ye had drunk too much wine. He couldn't remember the last time he had been so foolish. Tang Er's one-month celebration was a success. The entire court now knew of the Emperor's regard for Mei Gui, as she was given her own throne beside his, with the Empress flanking his other side. The older woman couldn't wipe the sour look from her face.

Silver Phoenix stayed near her mistress the entire evening, her flowing celadon dress accentuating every curve of her body. Zhong Ye studied his love discreetly, but as the night wore on, and as he drank more wine, his stares became blatant. She caught his eye twice, a hint of a smile on the corners of her mouth, before turning her attention back to her mistress.

The full moon perched just above the rooftops of the palace, and he paused on his way back to his quarters to admire it. An autumn breeze swept through the court-yard, and the fallen leaves skittered against the cobble-stone like withered souls. The edge of the moon blurred. He shook his head, trying to clear his vision.

His quarters were dark, and he cursed, wishing that Xiao Mao had lit a lantern for him. He stumbled into the reception hall and tensed, the hairs on his arms rising. Something was wrong. He pulled the dagger from his waist in one swift motion.

Zhong Ye heard the intruder jump at him but could see nothing in the darkness. The assassin jabbed a weapon, tearing his tunic and slicing his arm. The wound burned instantly. Poison! The stinging snapped Zhong Ye to full alertness. He twisted away, thrusting his dagger toward the sound of the man's shifting feet. A loud grunt, and the intruder slumped to the ground.

Zhong Ye was crouching over the body, wrenching his weapon free, when someone else grabbed him from behind in a chokehold. He couldn't breathe, and his head began to spin. Suddenly a lantern flared at the hall entrance. He threw a backfisted punch and heard the sickening crunch of the assassin's nose. The bastard groaned but only tightened his grip.

"Zhong!" Silver Phoenix cried from behind him.

He would have shouted if he could, would have told her to run. His attacker tried to twist him around to face her, but Zhong Ye planted his feet and wrenched him in the other direction. Then the assassin loosened his hold and slit Zhong Ye's throat.

Zhong Ye woke to Silver Phoenix's sobbing over him, her silk dress pressed against his neck. Her eyes widened when they met his. He tried to speak but gagged on the taste of blood, thick in his throat.

"I—I thought you were dead," she managed to stutter.

He struggled to sit up, pushing her hand away. Her dress was soaked crimson. He coughed, splattering more blood on himself and her. "Water," he gurgled.

Silver Phoenix quickly gave him a cup, and he rinsed his mouth and spit on the floor.

"Are you all right?" he asked. The words came in croaks. He ran his eyes over her, searching for injuries. His throat burned.

"Me?" She laughed through her tears. "Stay still. The royal physician is on his way."

He glanced around the hall, blazing now with light. The assassins were gone.

"The guards hauled them away," she said, as if reading his thoughts.

"What happened?"

"I bashed my lantern against his head," she said. "It knocked him out, but not before—" She lowered her face for a moment. "I was trying to stop the blood when Xiao Mao arrived. I sent him to get the physician and guards."

Interesting that the physician was not yet here. Had he been bribed to stay away?

He reached over to clasp her hand. Their fingers were sticky with his blood. "Did the assassins live?"

"I believe so."

"They must be kept alive, so I can interrogate them." He took another sip of water and swallowed, his throat feeling bruised.

Silver Phoenix began wiping his neck with a damp cloth. He tried to jerk away, but she steadied him. "You've stopped bleeding. There's only a scar where he had cut you."

Zhong Ye gingerly touched his throat. A jagged scab ran from ear to ear.

"How is it possible?" she whispered, staring into his eyes. "You should be dead."

His temples throbbed, and he could not meet her gaze.

"The immortality spell—you're still doing the ritual?"

"Yes."

"Are you using the dark arts?" she whispered.

"What do you know of it?" he rasped.

"I'm not a learned scholar. But I know that such a thing cannot be achieved without cost."

Valor and sacrifice—those were the costs. "I would be dead now if it weren't for the immortality spell. Would you have preferred that?" He spit out the words, knowing how cruel he sounded, unable to stop himself.

Silver Phoenix covered her face, her shoulders shaking. "I was so afraid I had lost you."

Zhong Ye pulled her into his arms and stroked her hair. "I'm sorry, love."

"Promise me you'll stop," she murmured against his ear, and he felt her hot tears on his cheek. "It saved you, I know. But it's wrong. Please stop."

"I'll stop," he whispered, and held her until she was no longer trembling.

Finally, it was the eighth moon and a week before their wedding banquet. The Emperor was on progress and wouldn't be back for another month yet, after the harvest of empress roots.

Zhong Ye had risen late that morning. Silver Phoenix had been spending her nights with him since Mei Gui was also on progress with her son, Tang Er, whom the Emperor doted on. He realized when he kissed her good-bye that they would be sharing quarters permanently after the wedding, and he grinned at the thought.

"You look like you've sneaked a forbidden treat," she said, teasing.

"Better. I stole a kiss from you." He leaned in for another, and she whirled away, laughing

"I'm late in meeting the royal chef to discuss our banquet menu. You'll look at it before we decide?"

"Bring a copy to me, love." Zhong Ye was now within

the Emperor's inner circle as one of his most trusted advisers, and the palace was abuzz over the arrival of his and Silver Phoenix's lavish wedding banquet.

She spun on the tips of her toes, the pink silk panels of her gown fluttering like butterfly wings. "And you'll be closeted with that alchemist all day?"

"I'll try to leave early." He watched as she flitted away. Zhong Ye couldn't fathom how he had become so fortunate. His thoughts were filled with her and their future together as he walked through the palace grounds. He would request bigger quarters, one that could allow for a family. He'd ask when he gave the Emperor the precious empress roots.

Yokan wasn't there when he entered the study. He'd been gone more often in the past month, making short forays into the countryside to collect the herbs native to Xia. But he'd left a note: "A prisoner is waiting. You can do this alone. Be sure to record everything."

Zhong Ye had promised Silver Phoenix he'd stop. And he hadn't. But he would, today. He paused, read Yokan's words again. How could this one last time hurt?

He crumpled the paper and threw it in the bronze bowl, already set out for him. This would be his thirteenth time, and each time he had required less of the empress root, as the immortality spell grew stronger within him, accumulated. Yokan had left him a small, thinly sliced portion. It would be the first time he'd have to kill the prisoner himself. He held up the vial of poison, the green liquid catching the sunlight streaming through the study's lattice windows. It was painless, the alchemist had assured him.

The guards brought the prisoner early. This one was older, in his fifties by the looks of him. His shorn hair was a shock of white, his bedraggled beard tinged with gray. Prison life had not been kind to him. "Leave us," Zhong Ye said.

He lit the concoction in the bronze bowl. He could never quite pinpoint the odor, but today, he realized it was death: ancient graves with the dead already dust, recent corpses, swollen and ripe beneath the sun. It was all this.

The old man didn't speak, did not beg for his life. But he shook so violently it was hard for Zhong Ye to grip his face. "This won't hurt at all," he cooed, sounding exactly like Yokan. It wasn't until he forced the prisoner's mouth open that he saw that his tongue had been cut out. He poured the poison into his mouth, and the prisoner dropped to the ground. Zhong Ye placed his fingertips at the man's temples, beginning to recite the words of the incantation he knew by heart.

The rush was stronger every time; the pleasure bordered on pain. Almost intolerable. Fully divine. Zhong Ye lost himself in the feeling, and the world ceased to exist.

CHAPTER THIRTEEN

Chen Yong wasn't at the morning meal. Neither was Ah Na. Nik sat at the table in uncharacteristic silence, casting wary glances Ai Ling's way. Ai Ling, tasting nothing, went through the motions of eating. As soon as she could, she bolted and flung her senses wide. Chen Yong was by the fountain with Ah Na. Determined to speak with him, she began walking toward them.

She stopped midway there, hidden behind the maze of tall hedges. It was a cloudless day, and the air was heavy with the scent of honeysuckle. Ah Na was walking back to the manor.

Ai Ling burst into the courtyard. Chen Yong, sitting on the edge of the marble fountain, was staring at the cascading water flowing from urns propped high by statues. He lifted his head surprised. "Ai Ling," he said, for the briefest moment glad to see her. Then his features hardened, and his expression crushed the breath from her.

Her spirit, tightly wound, thrummed. She held herself away from Chen Yong's brightness and his thoughts, even though she ached to know exactly what he was thinking, what he was feeling. She approached, and he remained hunched over the water like a statue himself. She touched his shoulder. "Chen Yong?"

His eyes were shadowed, his face strained.

"I'm so sorry," she whispered.

"I don't know if I can ever forgive you."

She couldn't find her voice but instead stared into the fountain as well. Their reflections wavered, distorted in the water.

"I've been thinking about Deen—my father's offer to me. To stay in Jiang and inherit the estate."

Which parent would he oblige? The only mother he'd ever known in Xia or his birth father in Jiang? Neither involved a future with her.

"And you would marry Ah Na?" she blurted.

"What?"

"I heard Ah Na and Nik talking. She would have you

as her husband." Her heart hurt so much she wanted to curl up, make herself smaller and smaller until she disappeared. Until she couldn't feel. Instead, she blathered on, as if saying these things would exorcise her pain. "It would be perfect. Your father would be delighted by the union. The family fortune would remain within the family."

"You eavesdropped on them, too?" He shook his head in disbelief. Or disgust.

She lifted her chin. "It was the only way I could understand what they were saying."

"But they weren't talking to you," Chen Yong said.

If her pain was a wound, she was gouging her fingers into it. "They were talking about us," she replied.

He met her eyes, and what had once been so familiar to her was unreadable. He had closed himself to her. "What you did to Nik yesterday . . . it feels like I don't even know you anymore."

She fought her gathering tears. She was losing him. Perhaps had already lost him. "Will you stay here? In Jiang?"

He rose to his feet. "I must go meet with my father." His voice was low, tired.

"Chen Yong, wait!"

But he was already walking away. In desperation, she

flung her spirit toward him, allowed herself to anchor and latch. What was he thinking? What had he decided?

He was trying hard to control his emotions. Anger choked him. The sense of betrayal was something solid pressed against his chest. Yet it took every fraction of his willpower to keep walking, not to turn back to her. Because beneath all the jumbled emotions—

Ai Ling gasped as she felt something slip from her, slither toward Chen Yong. She snapped back within herself, confused and feeling an inexplicable sense of dread. Chen Yong disappeared into the maze of hedges. She didn't follow.

Ai Ling was relieved when Chen Yong didn't come to dinner or the morning meal the following day. Relieved, too, when Nik averted his face and did not speak with her. Seeing him, she only felt shame and regret for what she had done. Ah Na was also quiet. Had Nik told her what had happened? He must have. Had he told his uncle? Master Deen appeared the same, kind but alert. He knew something was amiss.

She retreated to her bedchamber, flung the windows wide open, and stared out into the expanse of rolling hills, beautiful and foreign. She had never felt so alone.

A soft knock. She was hopeful for a moment that it was Chen Yong, but then sensed Peng standing outside. She had not seen him since he had come to ask for the details of her wedding night with Zhong Ye. That seemed months ago, instead of days.

"Come in."

He ran his fingers through his short black hair, newly cut, and grinned at her. His smile disappeared after a moment. "What's wrong?"

"Chen Yong and I had a fight," she said in a quiet voice, so it wouldn't tremble.

"A lover's quarrel?" He teased. When she didn't respond, he sat beside her. "What happened?"

"Deen is offering Chen Yong the estate," she said.

"Yes. Deen regards him as a son."

"And Ah Na would like to have him as her husband."

Peng's eyes widened; then he laughed. "I guess I shouldn't be surprised. It makes sense in a way, but surely Chen Yong wouldn't—"

Another knock. Ai Ling gave Peng a puzzled look. "It's Ah Na."

"How do—" he began, but then stopped short.

She pulled the door open. Ah Na was dressed in a tight bodice of bronze satin with a flowing silk skirt a shade lighter. Her thick hair was pulled back, pinned with several bejeweled hair clips. She was undeniably beautiful. Ai Ling wanted to shut the door in her face.

"Have you seen Chen Yong?" she asked. She gripped the folds of her skirt, wrinkling the fabric.

Not wanting to sense anything from him, Ai Ling had closed herself to him entirely after their last meeting. His disappointment and anger were too painful. But now she opened herself up and didn't like what she gathered: his presence, dimmed, but nothing more. "He's—I think he's in his bedchamber."

"We've knocked several times. He doesn't answer, and I assumed he wasn't in," Ah Na said. "Although it's locked and he was never given the key."

Ai Ling threw one glance at Peng, and they bounded to the bath chamber connecting the two rooms. She burst into Chen Yong's bedchamber. He was lying on his bed, in the same clothes he had worn when she saw him. His arms were at his sides, and he was as still as death.

"Chen Yong!" She ran to him and touched his shoulder, then shook him in her panic. She stroked his cheek. "He's so cold." Helpless, she turned to Peng.

Peng was beside her, and Ah Na hovered behind him. He placed a hand on Chen Yong's brow, then leaned close over his face. "His breath is shallow. Who was the last to see him?"

"I—I saw him in the garden yesterday morning," Ai Ling said.

"As did I," Ah Na replied. "Uncle met with him before the midday meal, but he didn't come down to eat."

Ai Ling had skipped that meal as well, to avoid seeing Chen Yong.

"Ah Na, could you tell Yen to come? To bring my incense box and the book beside it?"

Looking pale and shaken, Ah Na swept out of the room.

The moment the door shut, Peng turned to Ai Ling. "What happened yesterday?"

It was hard for her to think. To speak. Why was he so still? Why had he fallen ill? "We argued. Over—over whether he would stay in Jiang."

She sat down heavily by Chen Yong's side and dropped her head into her hands.

"And you didn't speak of anything else?" Peng asked. "Didn't do anything else?"

The last question was like a jolt through her hazy mind. She raised her eyes. "I touched his spirit. I latched on, so I could know what he was thinking."

Peng slammed his fist against the bedpost. "I should have come to see you sooner."

She didn't understand what he was saying, and panic smothered her. "What?"

"You and Zhong Ye's spirits have been inextricably tied. From all that I've read and could deduce, you're part of each other."

She gasped. She hadn't told Peng what had happened in the woods. Her vision of Zhong Ye, of herself, and the other tortured souls. How Zhong Ye's life seemed to mix with her own, how it was getting worse. She hadn't told anyone. "But what does it mean?"

"It means that you are his link to this living realm. I don't think any other spirit in the underworld would be capable of it, but Zhong Ye wasn't a mere mortal. I think he may have possessed Chen Yong . . . through you."

It was as if he had struck her. She doubled over, choking back the bile in her throat. "*I* did this?"

Yen entered the bedchamber without knocking. He gave Peng a carved camphor wood box and a leather-bound book. Ah Na hovered in the doorway.

"Yen, if you could tell Master Deen that Chen Yong has taken ill, but we are treating him and he'll soon recover . . ." His eyes locked with Yen's, and something seemed to pass between the two men. "Ah Na, would you please take Yen to your uncle?"

Yen shut the door, and Peng turned the brass lock. He lit incense and set it beside the bed. "It helps to cleanse," he said.

"What can you do?" she whispered.

"I'm not certain. I've studied various cases of demon possession in *The Book of the Dead*. But this situation is unique. Zhong Ye isn't a demon."

He was far worse.

"I think Chen Yong is fighting him." Peng had been pacing but now stopped to consider her. "Zhong Ye isn't as strong as he was when he lived in this mortal realm. He couldn't have sent his entire being into Chen Yong; part of him, probably most of him, still resides within the underworld."

"How can you be certain? Perhaps he's just sick . . . perhaps someone poisoned him," said Ai Ling. She couldn't believe she was responsible for this, that she had put Chen Yong in danger because she had been unable to bear his rejection.

Peng nodded toward the incense. "Look."

She watched the slow curl of the smoke, smelled the scent of sandalwood spreading through the chamber. At first, she didn't understand what Peng meant. Then she followed the trail of the smoke and realized with horrified understanding that it was making its way directly to Chen Yong's pillow.

"It goes to where there is spiritual corruption," Peng said.

"No!" She reached to touch Chen Yong's cold face. "Come back. I'm so sorry." She whipped around toward Peng, anguished. Furious. "What can we do? How can we save him?"

Peng opened the heavy book. "I can try some of the mantras used to exorcise demons, but I have little hope they'll work."

"Do it." She turned back to Chen Yong, biting her lip so violently her vision blurred. "We'll do whatever it takes."

Sometime later, when it was dark and the lanterns were lit, Master Deen came to see Chen Yong himself, accompanied by a physician. The physician examined him as Ai Ling hovered on the other side of the bed. Then Peng, Master Deen, and the physician clustered in the corner of the bedchamber, whispering in serious tones. Ai Ling pressed her palm against Chen Yong's chest. His heartbeat felt far away. Faint.

She stroked his cold hands, trying to bring warmth, murmured to him in coaxing tones. *Come back to me.* Ah Na and Nik visited in the morning, when light poured through the jeweled windows. They stood solemnly over Chen Yong, and Ai Ling could feel their concern and worry. She wanted to shove them out of the room.

The only presence she could tolerate was Peng's. He hung small mirrors around the bedchamber, burned more incense, and struck a bronze bowl filled with water, the pure tone carrying her back home to Xia. And constantly he chanted the mantras in his strong voice.

Peng implored her to eat, to sleep. She refused but would sometimes doze off unintentionally on the cushioned bench by the window. It was dark again when Peng drew her away from Chen Yong's bedside and sat her down in an ornate chair in the corner. She didn't know how much time had passed. Peng's clothes were rumpled; his face was dark with stubble.

"Nothing is working." Peng spoke quietly. He lifted his eyes. "I'm so sorry."

Her hands trembled in her lap. "What will happen to him?"

Peng rubbed his face, his own hand shaking. "I cannot say for certain. I believe Chen Yong is fighting Zhong Ye's spirit. I think . . . I believe—"

"What?" Ai Ling dug her nails into her thighs.

"If he cannot conquer Zhong Ye, he may die."

"No!" Ai Ling leaped to her feet, but Peng caught her by the wrist.

"Or he may wake and be possessed by Zhong Ye."

She buckled to the ground. "No," she whispered. She gripped Peng's arm. "Chen Yong is strong."

"He is. He's still alive, fighting. But he is only mortal. And Zhong Ye is . . ."

"Is there nothing more we can do?"

Peng's silence was answer enough.

"I could enter Chen Yong's spirit. I can fight Zhong Ye!"

"But that was how Chen Yong was possessed in the first place. You are a conduit for Zhong Ye. Would you risk making it worse?"

She pushed herself up. "No, I can help him. I've done it before."

"Don't." He clasped her shoulder. "It's too dangerous."

Ai Ling flung her spirit into Chen Yong. She instantly felt his soul. It was crushed to a wisp, but still shone brilliantly. She enveloped him with her own spirit, drawn to him as if he were the sun. The cord at her navel suddenly tightened, dragging her away. She would have cried out if she'd had a voice. She felt for one more heartbeat his familiar warmth and the power of her love for him before plunging into a black abyss.

Zhong Ye's eyes snapped open, and life surged through him. He heard small gasps, as if someone were having difficulty breathing. Surely the old man was dead. He had consumed his soul. A sudden sense of horror slammed into his gut, and he jumped up. Silver Phoenix stood in the doorway, one hand covering her mouth, the other clutching a parchment. She was trembling, and when she met his eyes, they were filled with terror. Before he could speak, she turned and fled.

"Silver Phoenix! No!" He tripped over the corpse as he ran after her. She was no match for him, and he caught her before she was halfway across the courtyard. She whirled like a wildcat and slapped his face. His ears rang.

"Let me go!" she screamed.

He would not. He tried to embrace her. She slammed his chest with her fists. "How could you, Zhong? What have you done?"

"Nothing, love. It's nothing," he murmured against her neck. She pushed him away so violently she almost fell backward. He grabbed her wrist to steady her.

"You took his life." It came out in a whisper. Her face was blotchy, wet with sweat and tears. Wisps of raven hair stuck to her cheeks. She was so young. One look into her beautiful eyes, and his heart broke.

"He was a criminal. He would have died anyway." She was silent, and he captured her other hand. "If you would just try it once. For me . . . for us."

"Why can't you be content with what we already have? All that we've been given?" Tears continued to streak down her face.

He would never have escaped the family farm if he had been content with his lot. Never have come to the palace, never have met her. "But we could have so much more," he said.

She stared hard at the ground, and when she lifted her head, something in her face had changed. "Isn't our love enough?"

"It's everything to me." He pressed a palm over his heart. She seemed a world away.

"You lied to me."

He hesitated only a moment. "How can I change your mind?"

"You can't." She leaned over to retrieve the parchment she had dropped, their banquet menu.

"I love you." He opened his hands to the heavens to beseech her. "I won't lose you."

"I love you, too." She touched his cheek. "I won't lose you either. You'll stop working with that wretched alchemist. This won't go on if I'm to be your wife."

Her black eyes were fierce when they met his. And it was as if they were seeing each other for the first time.

Their wedding day arrived at last, and all the preparations were in order. Zhong Ye and Silver Phoenix had spent the previous evening apart, and he had missed her. Manservants helped him dress, hooking the front of his black groom's tunic. Dusk neared. The wedding sedan would soon be making its way to Silver Phoenix's bridal quarters.

He heard the shrill scream of his name before the panicked footsteps. A handmaid tripped into his chamber without knocking and threw herself at his feet. "Master Zhong, it's the mistress we only left for a brief moment she asked for some time alone—"

Dread settled like stone in his stomach. "What is it?" He restrained himself from shaking the teeth from her head. "Is Silver Phoenix ill?"

The girl hid her face in her hands.

Zhong Ye ran.

He ran the entire way to Silver Phoenix's bridal quarters and crashed into her bedchamber. Silver Phoenix lay on the sumptuous wedding bed, her hands resting on her stomach. Inexplicably, a crimson breast binder was wrapped like a scarf around her neck.

Two other handmaids hovered near her, sobbing.

"What happened?" He pushed them aside. "Did she faint?"

"She-she h-hanged herself. I-I think she's d-dead."

Zhong Ye, enraged, turned on the girl, as she continued to hiccup incoherently. His mind couldn't understand the words that she spoke. Wouldn't accept them. "Get the royal physician!" he roared. "Get out!"

They scrambled from the chamber.

"Silver Phoenix?" He touched her forehead. She was warm, certainly asleep. The excitement had exhausted her.

He took her hand, and it felt heavy, unresponsive. *She hanged herself.* He choked back a sob and wrenched her robe open, pressing a palm over her heart.

Nothing.

He kissed her mouth. Cool. Listened for her breath.

Silence.

"No." He stroked her arms.

"No." Her cheeks.

"No. Nonononono." Zhong Ye threw his head back and howled, in fury and in pain. In disbelief. He gathered her in his arms and clutched her to him, her head against his shoulder, perfect, like so many times before. The scent of jasmine filled him.

He rocked her, caressing the hair that had fallen

across her soft shoulders, sobbing until her locks were wet with his tears.

When the royal physician arrived, it took him an hour to convince Zhong Ye to let her go.

Royal Physician Chu had replaced Physician Kang while the Emperor was away on progress. He confirmed that Silver Phoenix was dead, most likely from asphyxia when she hanged herself from the bedpost with the breast binder. The details were given haltingly by the handmaids, and Zhong Ye had to clench his fists so he wouldn't strike them. Or smash the physician in the face for pronouncing the cause of death so plainly, as if he were discussing the weather. Zhong Ye, his breath coming in rasps, forced everyone out of the chamber.

"I could give you a sedative," the physician said, turning as he left.

Zhong Ye slammed the door in his face.

He sat beside Silver Phoenix as the evening cooled and the darkness deepened. He ignored the gentle knock on the door. It slid open. Yokan entered, holding a lantern. Zhong Ye turned, wincing at the light.

"I've sent all the wedding guests away." Yokan walked to the bedside. "I'm so sorry."

Zhong Ye couldn't speak for long moments. "Why? Why would she do this?" His throat was hoarse, closed, and sore. He was empty, as if someone had slit his wrists and bled him dry of everything that mattered to him in life.

"Such a tragedy," Yokan murmured. "She was lovely." He reached out to touch her hair.

Zhong Ye caught Yokan's open palm and squeezed so hard the foreigner's knuckles cracked. For the briefest moment, an angry bruise bloomed on Yokan's cheekbone. Zhong Ye blinked, and it was gone. He narrowed his eyes and shoved the man's hand away.

Yokan met his gaze, his features composed. "Did you argue? Was she upset over something?"

Zhong Ye felt as if he'd been struck in the chest, remembering Silver Phoenix's anger, her disappointment in him. *Had he caused this?* He drew in a shaking sob; there were no tears left. "The Calling Ritual," he said, and his heart swelled with hope.

Yokan set the lantern on a table beside the bed. "You would do that?" he asked in a quiet voice.

Zhong Ye couldn't understand the question.

"You would have to remove her heart." The alchemist's head was bowed as he studied Silver Phoenix in the lantern light.

She looked alive still in its soft glow. "I'll do it," Zhong Ye whispered.

"And a full bronze bowl of your own blood." Yokan slanted his head to look at him, the shadows obscuring his pale eyes.

"I have enough to give her."

Yokan pursed his lips. "You would need an entire empress root. We have none."

"What?"

"You used the last of it."

"But the harvest! They are growing now." Zhong Ye felt his spirit lift. It was meant to be. He could bring her back. But how could he bear to leave her?

As if sensing his thoughts, Yokan nodded. "I'll do it. I'll go harvest the roots in your stead. The trip shouldn't take me more than six days. I will make haste."

"You would do this for me?"

Yokan gripped his shoulder. "I have all the notes from your last journey. I'll leave before dawn tomorrow."

CHAPTER FOURTEEN

It was as if she had been thrown from the skies. Ai Ling clutched her head and doubled over to protect herself from the cacophony of noise and color. She stayed on the hard ground, her eyes squeezed shut, until a searing hotness pierced her chest.

"This one isn't whole," a voice like gravel grumbled.

Her eyes snapped open, and she saw a man with the head of an ox, his horns magnificent and curved, his skin a dusty blue. "Did you feel that?" He jabbed a sharp spear at her torso. She cried out, feeling again the stabbing pain.

"She can make noises, too!" Ox head's mouth stretched into a grotesque sneer. "Have you seen the like, Horse?"

Ai Ling jumped to her feet. She was surrounded by normal people, most looking terrified, confused, or sorrowful. But the ox man towered over her, his powerful body twice her size. A man with a horse's head, wielding a gleaming scythe, approached. His skin was a sick green, and he was not as bulky as Ox; but he looked just as dangerous.

"I can see through her," Horse said. He raised his scythe as if to test it, and Ai Ling stumbled back. Suddenly a voice boomed over them. Many in the crowd dropped to their knees, knocking their heads to the dirt. She fought the impulse to do the same and turned toward the speaker.

A magistrate sat at an ebony table decorated with jade, his backdrop the sheer cliff of a mountain. He had a long black beard that reached past his rotund stomach. His robe was a rusted red, like dried blood. He stood and was twice the height of any mortal man. He towered over the hundreds of people cowering in front of him.

"Stop your stupid squawking, Horse and Ox. Get back to sorting!" His words rattled her teeth, and her hands did nothing to protect her ears. It was as if he had spoken from within her.

"We've got a see-through one here, hell lord," the demons cried in unison.

A deep rumbling from the back of the magistrate's throat shook the ground they stood on. "Let me see."

Horse raised his scythe, and Ai Ling ran. She tripped through the crowd toward the magistrate, feeling shivers of cold when she brushed against the others. These men and women seemed to be real, solid. She was like a ghost.

The magistrate's thick brows drew together when she finally stood before the massive table. She tipped her head back so she could see his face; he looked like a man in every way, except for his immense size. "You don't belong here." His voice reverberated, and she heard those around her whimper. "What is your name?"

"I am called Wen Ai Ling," she said, as forcefully as she could manage. Wisps of clouds drifted past the jagged cliffs that surrounded them.

The magistrate leaned forward and squinted down at her. His breath whipped through her. His black eyes narrowed. "Silver Phoenix's incarnation," he said.

Ai Ling let out a small gasp that was obliterated by the mewling and terrified clamor from the others.

"You aren't welcome here." He curled a thick finger, and an old man stepped forward to stand in front of a giant oval mirror beside the table. The Mirror of Retribution, she realized.

"I have to see Zhong Ye!" Her words were almost inaudible. She repeated herself, shouting this time.

"That wretch? He's not taking visitors." The magistrate's laugh boomed, knocking her off her feet. "Be gone now!"

She turned her head, the dirt beneath her cheek like ash. The old man in front of the mirror, like a withered leaf clinging to a tree, trembled at whatever images he saw. She knew that he was being judged and that all his life's sins were displayed in the mirror's reflection. He tilted toward the shining glass and vanished, his fate determined.

"Next!" The magistrate waved another person forward.

Ai Ling lurched to her feet, felt as if she would float away if she didn't concentrate. It was impossible to move quickly. Her body lacked substance and momentum.

"What are you doing, girl? Stop her!" The magistrate pounded on the table, and everyone bounced from the force of it.

She fell. Ox and Horse careened toward her, their weapons extended. She lunged for the mirror. They stabbed her, their thrusts like a sizzling branding iron on her heart. She thought she cried out when she touched the glowing glass. She saw her ghostly face, then Silver Phoenix's reflected back at her. The images merged into

one, and the mirror splintered into a thousand shards as
dazzling white light exploded around her.

The ground was damp, slick. She could hear a steady
dripping. Ai Ling blinked, trying to adjust to the darkness. The curved walls began to glimmer with a blue
phosphorescence. She stood and turned in a circle and
saw that she was in a massive cave. Alone. Echoes of
screaming, sobbing, and shouting floated to her from a
great distance.

A sudden tug at her navel, and she glanced down. A
glowing white cord as thick as her finger and as insubstantial as air shimmered from her stomach and disappeared into the shadows of the cave. She followed its
faint pull. Ai Ling knew who would be at the other end:
Zhong Ye was waiting for her.

Water dripped from the ceiling, at times through her. It
was cold, like a streak of ice. She didn't know how long she
walked. She saw no one. The cord led her through a small
opening at the back of the cavern, one she could barely
fit through. She placed a palm against the wall. Although
her hand slid beneath the rock's surface, there was resistance. She couldn't simply walk through the stone.

A blur of motion, and Ox was bounding toward her.
"Stop! You don't belong here!"

She dropped to her stomach and began wiggling through the small opening. Ox tried to grab her legs, but his fingers slipped through her, his touch scalding. She cried out as she pulled herself to the other side. She could hear Ox hurling himself against the wall.

She stood on a small landing, with nowhere to go except down into a wide river of molten lava. Beyond the river she could see a warren of endless catacombs, a wasp's nest hewn from rock. The screams and cries were louder here. A plume of lava, taking the shape of a clawed hand, bubbled from the river. Another burst of molten heat formed a skull with long fangs. It surged high enough for her to stare at fiery eye sockets.

Ox crashed onto the landing. He seized her by the throat, his fingers passing through her, and she choked. She scrambled back, teetering on the edge of the small landing.

"There's nowhere to go, fool," Ox jeered. "You're keeping me from my tasks." Arms wide, he pounced again.

Ai Ling glanced down. She followed the shimmering cord from her navel all the way across the river to the catacombs. That was where she needed to go, where Zhong Ye was.

She jumped.

Ox sprang after her, shouting, "No!" His hand cut

through her chest, stabbing like a thousand needles, but it was too late.

Instead of falling, she drifted, weightless, buffeted by the hot air. A serpent-shaped spiral of lava shot upward and through her. Heat blazed across her body. But the river couldn't stop her. She swung her arms as if she were swimming and followed the glowing cord as it plunged into the catacombs.

The closer Ai Ling got to the river, the more unbearable the heat. She was almost there. She landed in the magma, burning her feet to the ankles, and screamed. The sound was swallowed by the roar of lava that bubbled in jagged knifelike formations from the riverbed. She stumbled forward through the boiling hot current.

Finally, she climbed onto solid rock and, consumed with pain, pulled her knees to her chest. She stared down at her feet, phantomlike and charred but still there. She stood and took a tentative step. It was like walking on hot glass. She gritted her teeth and continued, one agonizing step at a time.

The cord snaked through a crevice and into a vast cavern. Giant hooks hung from the ceiling, many swinging with human bodies strung upside down or with parts of bodies. She sank to her knees and recognized the demons of hell, with their strange blue, gray, or green-colored skin and their towering height. Just like the illustrations from *The Book of the Dead*.

Two demons laughed hysterically as they pulled a sharp-toothed saw between them, back and forth, while the victim, impaled on a hook, his hair hanging over his face, screamed. Even when he was halved, and his blood and innards had spilled to the floor, he kept screaming. One of the demons hacked at the rope, and both sides of the man crashed to the floor. They moved even then, squirming like bloodied worms.

Ai Ling stood and tried to run, but her feet wouldn't allow it. Instead, she kept her eyes on the glowing cord and walked at an infuriatingly slow pace through the cavern. Groans and wails and screams surrounded her, convulsed through her.

The air reeked of blood, guts, and urine and the salty sweat of terror. Passages from *The Book of the Dead* returned to her. The punishment of vertical rending was given to those who had destroyed marriages to satisfy their own lust. She pushed against the cord. Faster, she needed to move faster! It was like thrusting a knife into her own gut. She clenched her fists and forced herself forward.

A gust of hot wind seared through her as she entered a new chamber. This one was lit by hundreds of fires, the flames as tall as she was. Massive black cauldrons were suspended above the fires. Ai Ling screamed when she saw a demon with the head of a goat toss a man over the rim of the cauldron and into the scalding oil. His entire body blistered instantly, and his hair burst into fire. These men and women, who had helped cheat the poor during their lifetimes, would never die, would be made whole again and again to suffer for their transgressions.

She pressed forward, impaling herself on the cord. The air was thick with grease and the nauseating stench of burned flesh. She gasped with relief when she saw the shimmering cord curve through another opening in the cavern wall.

This chamber was small, circular, the walls a glowing milk white stone. The air was cool. She wiped the sweat from her brow, relieved, even as something tickled the back of her mind like a stray spider silk. The cold stone soothed her feet. The room was empty, and she saw no exit, although the glowing cord shot through the opaque wall. Quivering, she collapsed to the ground.

The cave shimmered. A rainbow of light swirled in the air above her: beautiful and mesmerizing. She saw herself in the light crouched on the floor, next to Li Rong's body. The blood unfurled beneath him, staining the white stone floor a deep crimson. She watched as her other self reached into the gaping wound of his chest, slicing his heart out with her dagger.

"Forgive me, Li Rong. I will make it right again."

"No!" she shouted, and lunged at the vision, lunged at herself, and crashed to the ground, empty-handed.

The cavern glimmered in brilliant colors again, and this time she was in an opulent bedchamber. Festive red lanterns were strung from the ceiling and bouquets of fragrant lilies filled the room. She could smell the steam rising from a jasmine bath. Ai Ling blinked hard, her heart still hammering from seeing Li Rong again, from the memory and the guilt. She watched Silver Phoenix, uncomprehending. She looked older, even more stunning, her hair braided and looped elaborately, threaded with pearls and rubies. A gold brocaded robe was pulled over her shoulders, and she stroked a crimson breast binder with slender fingers.

Ai Ling suddenly understood and tried to turn away, but she couldn't. She was being forced to watch. Silver Phoenix's wedding night, so like the one she had endured with Zhong Ye. Soon, Ai Ling knew, she would hang herself. Silver Phoenix dropped the binder on the bed next to her gorgeous wedding dress, the same gown Ai Ling had been made to wear. She glided to the bronzed mirror and gazed at her reflection and adjusted her ruby earrings.

Ai Ling gasped when she saw Yokan flicker into view. Silver Phoenix spun to face him, drawing her robe tight around herself. "What are you doing here?"

The alchemist didn't reply. He stalked forward, and Silver Phoenix backed away, until she bumped against the lacquered vanity. Yokan paused, standing as close as a lover.

"Get away from me," Silver Phoenix said.

He pressed closer, never speaking. Silver Phoenix's arm shot out, an etched gold and silver dagger glinting in her hand. The alchemist wrenched her arm back, the motion so swift it was a blur. He shoved Silver Phoenix hard against the vanity, and the dagger clattered to the floor.

He released her wrist and jammed his hand to her throat. Silver Phoenix thrashed, fought with all her strength. But Ai Ling could see that it was like struggling against an immovable statue. Yokan lifted her off the ground, his pale face expressionless.

Silver Phoenix swung at him. Her jade phoenix ring slammed into his cheekbone. Yokan's head snapped back, and he lifted his brows in amusement before wrapping his other hand around her throat and crushing the life from her.

Ai Ling watched, frozen, as the minutes dragged into

eternity. Finally, the alchemist let go, and Silver Phoenix slid like a broken butterfly to the floor. He flicked his fingers and smiled. The crimson breast binder snaked through the air and tied itself neatly around Silver Phoenix's neck.

Ai Ling screamed and tried to lunge forward again. But the scene dispersed, gone like a breath of mist. She was as cold as ice and lying on the floor of the white stone chamber, staring at the illuminated ceiling. Stunned and horrified by Silver Phoenix's fate, she tried to speak the handmaid's name aloud but could only whimper. Her hand flew to her neck. She was afraid she'd find it bruised. Broken.

She forced herself onto her ruined feet, her being as diaphanous as dragonfly wings, and allowed the glowing cord to tug her to the cavern wall, where a gaping hole had opened from nowhere.

A deep pit dominated the center of this cavern. The odor of burned hair and flesh trailed her every step. She climbed down and stopped in front of a rough rock, where Zhong Ye sat, alone. He was naked, and the cord was connected to his navel. She dropped her eyes, unwilling to look at him.

The glimmering cord thrummed, then disappeared.

"You've come to me, Ai Ling," he said in that smooth, rich voice.

She looked at him then. This wasn't the pale-eyed Zhong Ye she had met, the one she had wed. This was Silver Phoenix's Zhong Ye: nineteen years, handsome, his eyes a deep brown, like the earth after a rain.

Corpses swayed overhead, hanging between spiked rocks from a ceiling that reminded her of sharp fangs. She didn't want to look, but a dreadful sense of familiarity forced her to. It was Zhong Ye. They all were Zhong Ye: dozens of identical corpses, dead from every kind of torture, dripping blood and guts. She covered her mouth, gagging.

"The demons are keeping score," he said with a wry smile, not bothering to glance up. "I'm losing."

He was glad to see her; she could sense his pleasure. It only terrified her more.

Zhong Ye stood, unabashed in his nakedness. His legs were shackled, and the chains clanked. She remembered how easily, how perfectly Silver Phoenix could tuck herself against him, his chin touching the top of her head. "I sent you that dream of Li Rong."

"What?" she whispered, her entire being cold.

"I needed you to go to Chen Yong. To take this journey."

"Release him!" she screamed. "You're killing him!"

Zhong Ye brushed the hair from his eyes. "I knew I could lure you here." He cocked a dark brow at her. "You love him enough to risk everything to save him."

Anger exploded within her. "Haven't you caused enough harm? All this for vengeance, because I would not love you?"

His laugh was mirthless. "If I wanted vengeance, Chen Yong would already be dead." His eyes burned with pain, with anger and sorrow. "I only wanted to bring Silver Phoenix back." He dropped his head, as if it were too heavy to hold up any longer.

She hated him for what he had done to Chen Yong. Hated herself for understanding him so completely. His life had been opened to her like a book well studied. "I know," she whispered. "It was wrong."

"You." He stepped closer, and she had to force herself to meet his gaze. "You, of all people, know why I did it. *You* cannot judge me."

Her heart was in her throat.

"Ah, yes." Zhong Ye continued, scrutinizing her as if he could read her thoughts. "I've lived your entire life— more than once. I know that you have your mother's hands but despise embroidering. That you have your father's eyes, his stubbornness and drive. His acute mind for books and his artistic talent. I know that you miss your cat, Taro. That you stole candy from the sweets jar when you were seven years and felt terribly repentant for far too long. I know—"

"Stop." She would have fallen to her knees, but her body was too insubstantial. "Stop!" It was as if he had plundered her head of memories. Just as she had plundered his. How he had caught a toad for a pet at nine years and named it Smudge, only to have his older brother toss it into a lake out of spite. How he had done extra chores for a drunken scholar, starting at eleven years, in exchange for reading and writing lessons. How he had stayed up past the thieving hour to study, begging for candle stubs. How ruthless he had become after he had lost Silver Phoenix, driven only by rage and grief, guilt and betrayal. But she hadn't wanted any of these memories. She hadn't wanted to know.

"You *did* send Chen Yong that dream," she said.

"I only showed him the truth." His glittering eyes narrowed. "I could smell the guilt you carried even in the underworld. Did you truly think you could hide something like that from him?" He snorted. "From Chen Yong?"

Furious, her vision spotted, for a moment went black. "Don't lecture me about guilt or keeping secrets!" Ai

Ling stomped toward him, slapping her hands against his chest. His skin sparked at the contact, and Zhong Ye, surprised, took a step back. "Silver Phoenix would never have died if you hadn't lied to her. She warned you about Yokan!"

He seemed to crumple before her. Her words had hit their mark. She only wished she could feel some satisfaction, but there was no triumph in it.

"I only wanted to protect her," he said in a rough voice. He sat down again on the hard rock, his shackles jarring against it. "Would you have fared better?" He met her eyes, his soul laid bare, concealing nothing.

Ai Ling recalled living those moments of Zhong Ye's life: the ecstatic pleasure overwhelming her body; the exuberance of life's essence flooding every fraction of her soul. Each time more powerful and potent than the one before. She couldn't answer him truthfully.

"I know how I appeared to you." He regarded her with an unreadable expression on his handsome face. "Like a monster. Just as she had feared—"

"I am not Silver Phoenix," Ai Ling whispered. It was all that she could muster.

"No. You're not. I thought—" Suddenly his shackles seemed to morph into giant snakes, their scales like emeralds. He didn't notice. "I could make things right through you. You were her incarnation. If you loved me as she had . . ." He clenched his jaw, the cords of his neck taut. "I need your help, Ai Ling."

"My help?" she asked, unable to keep the incredulity from her voice. Frantic for Chen Yong, she was fighting hard not to cry, to scream. She'd lost track of time. How much time had passed? Was it already too late? The cavern pulsed a sickly orange, and the corpses above spun in a lurid dance as if taunting her.

Zhong Ye had tucked his head between his fists. "I realize I have no right to ask it," he said.

Ai Ling felt her being shiver, vibrate like a lute string plucked. It was as if she had stepped away from herself toward Zhong Ye, as if she had split in two. The snakes binding his wrists reared their heads and hissed. She stroked his shoulder. Her fingers glided across his bare skin. He raised his eyes and gasped, caressing her face. His touch left a flourish of warmth on her cheek. "Silver Phoenix," he whispered, "I'm so sorry. I tried. I tried to bring you back."

Silver Phoenix brushed her hand over his. "I know." She smiled at him, radiant, although her eyes shone with sorrow like his. "I know."

"He lied. Yokan never returned with the empress root. I went after him, but there was nothing left. He had taken it all." His words spilled one on top of the other, as if he had clutched them inside for too long. "Why? Why did you kill yourself?"

She shook her head sadly. "He tricked you, Zhong. He used you. He wanted to be certain the immortality spell was"—she pursed her lips—"safe. He tested it on you first."

"No. I saw him. He showed me how to do it."

Silver Phoenix dropped gracefully to her knees. "He never ingested the empress root," she said.

"But he appeared younger!"

"Minor spells, to alter his appearance. Artifice." She paused. "He killed me."

Zhong Ye leaped to his feet. "What!" His body seemed to expand with his wrath.

She pressed her fingertips to his wrist, and Zhong Ye sank back on the rock. "How could I have ever believed it?" He gazed at her, his eyes shining with tears. "Does Yokan still live?" he growled.

"He drowned centuries ago. Swept overboard on a return journey to Xia." Silver Phoenix's beautiful face had turned cold and hard. "The gods do not often meddle in the lives of man, but I only asked for one well-placed storm. Yokan was strong, but he could not survive an angry sea." She lifted her chin to meet Zhong Ye's gaze.

"I don't regret my request. The gods would kill Yokan for me, and I would end your life."

Zhong Ye brought her hand to his lips. "I was a fool." He stared at her, as if trying to memorize her face. "Is that why you killed me? A pact with the gods?"

She placed her palm against his chest. "I wandered the underworld for years without reincarnating, a restless spirit. Then the Goddess of Records gave me the gift to watch you on earth—"

"You don't have to say more." He drew a fist over his eyes.

"I offered myself to the task. I couldn't bear to see you become less and less of the man I love. The goddess granted me this one last chance, brought me back so I could see you, speak with you. I latched on to Ai Ling's spirit when she touched the Mirror of Retribution and entered the underworld. I needed to explain in person. I killed you because I love you, Zhong, please believe me. It had to end." Silver Phoenix's image shimmered, grew brighter as she spoke.

"I do." He clasped her hands in his. "I've failed you, love."

Silver Phoenix's full lips curved into a soft smile. "Do you . . . forgive me?" she asked.

"There's nothing to forgive." He drew Silver Phoenix to him. "Thank you."

They stood together, his solid body embracing her insubstantial one, oblivious of everything except each other. Ai Ling couldn't look away.

"We've had our time, my heart," Silver Phoenix said in a quiet voice. "Let Chen Yong go. Let Ai Ling go."

Zhong Ye glanced beyond Silver Phoenix. He was suddenly aware of Ai Ling's spirit in the flickering shadows.

"Give her her life back." Silver Phoenix leaned in to touch her lips to Zhong Ye's. He closed his eyes for one heartbeat, then snapped them open, as if afraid she'd disappear. "Give her her love back," she whispered.

Ai Ling realized as Silver Phoenix gazed into Zhong Ye's eyes that she would always see her as more than a handmaid. She was an earthly goddess, an empress. It was how Zhong Ye had seen her.

"We don't have much time," Silver Phoenix said. "Chen Yong is dying. But Ai Ling is closer to death than he is."

Even as she heard those words, Ai Ling felt her body crackle, from her heart outward. She gasped and pressed a hand to her breast. Her flesh was slowly solidifying. She felt no heartbeat.

Silver Phoenix was gone.

Zhong Ye leaped toward Ai Ling. He raised his arms like a mad prophet, and she shrank from him. She saw the tears in his dark brown eyes before he covered her face with his hands. "Go, Ai Ling." His palms were calloused. "You don't belong here," he said, and shoved her so hard she screamed and careened backward into nothing.

"Burn my remains." His voice trailed after her into the abyss. "You know where."

CHAPTER FIFTEEN

Ai Ling woke to a soft chanting. Peng. Her body was stiff, bruised all over. It hurt to breathe, and she could not draw a full breath. She whimpered. The chanting stopped, and she heard footsteps, felt someone lean against the bed.

"Ai Ling?" Peng whispered. He touched her brow.

She tried to speak and managed a small grunt.

Then Peng was propping her up, stacking thick cushions behind her. It was impossible to open her eyes; it was as if they had been sewn shut.

"Drink," Peng said.

She felt steam on her cheeks, smelled jasmine and medicinal herbs. She managed to part her lips, and the cup was brought to her mouth. She took a small sip. It was the best thing she had ever tasted.

Peng's hand was firm on her shoulder. "More."

She obliged, then sank back into the cushions, feeling the tea and medicine spreading warmth and a sense of calm through her body. She fought hard to open her eyes. It was daytime; she could tell by the crack of sunlight slanting through the drawn curtains.

She saw Peng's face, rough with stubble. "Chen Yong," she croaked.

"Awake and well. I made him leave awhile ago. He's pacing outside like a caged tiger." His face broke into a grin. "He was driving me mad and makes a terrible patient."

Ai Ling laughed, but it came out as an odd hiccup. She winced.

"You've been asleep for four days. I wasn't sure if you'd return to us."

"Thank you," she rasped.

"Do you want to see him?" Peng asked.

No. She couldn't bear to face Chen Yong just yet.

When she woke again, the lantern was burning by the bedside and the window had been thrown open to let in the mild evening air. Chen Yong sat beside her on the bed, holding her hand.

"Ai Ling," he said when she opened her eyes. "Thank the goddess."

"I couldn't keep him away." Peng appeared behind his shoulder and shrugged. "I'll leave you now."

Chen Yong spoke before the door even clicked shut. "You foolish, rash, mad—" He paused. "Stubborn, impetuous, foolish girl."

"You already said foolish," she whispered.

He smiled. He looked haggard, unshaved, like Peng, his clothes rumpled. But alive. His hand clasping hers, strong and alive.

A knot rose to her throat, and she had no strength to swallow it. "I'm so sorry." She could barely hear her own words, as the tears came, running from the corners of her eyes, sliding into her ears.

He wiped them away with gentle fingers. "Don't cry." His own voice was rough. "I'm sorry, too."

Her eyebrows drew together. "Why?"

"I was so angry with you." He held her gaze, and she couldn't look away.

"You had the right to be. Chen Yong, I know what I did was wrong."

He squeezed her hand and stroked the hair from her face. Ai Ling forgot to breathe.

"I was a fool, for not accepting the truth sooner. A

coward, for not telling you sooner."

She didn't understand. But it didn't matter as long as he held her hand. "Do you mean about your father?" Two shallow breaths. "And staying in Jiang Dao?"

He was tracing slow circles against her inner wrist with his thumb, the sensation sparking her to life. "I spoke with my father right before . . . it happened. I told him that I would be returning to Xia with Peng but I would visit as often as I could in the future."

She loosened her grip on the satin sheet and let out a sigh. At least he would return to Xia and not spend the rest of his life a world away from her.

"It was you, Ai Ling."

She blinked. Why was Chen Yong speaking in riddles? "What?"

"The Sea Shifter. Taking on the image of someone you loved. It was you that night." He leaned closer, until she could feel the warmth of his body, until she could see the copper flecks in his eyes.

She tried to sink deeper into the bed, her heart beating hard. He dipped lower. Ai Ling shut her eyes and wondered if she was dreaming.

It was almost two weeks before Ai Ling began to feel like herself again. The days melded together, and Chen

Yong's bedchamber bustled with people and activity. Chen Yong himself was a constant visitor, although he often lingered in the background, like some stoic statue. Whenever she woke, she sought him out first, and he would smile—almost tentatively. This confused her. She realized within a few days of waking that her power was gone. There was only her own voice in her mind, her own feelings, and blissful silence beyond.

Everyone visited her. Nik brought flowers from the garden, their fragrance filling the chamber. Peng had explained to Nik that Ai Ling had been possessed, sick.

"We hear old wives' tales of such things. I had never taken them for truth." Nik encircled her wrist with a chain of tiny purple blossoms. "This flower is called fairy laughter," he said.

"Thank you." Not knowing how to express herself, she fingered the delicate petals. "I apologize for what happened. I was not me . . . not myself."

"I knew it couldn't have been you, truly." He smiled.

She didn't need her power to feel his interest, to see that he desired her. "I cannot—" She struggled with the language. "We can be friends?"

His grin faltered for an instant. She gathered enough courage to meet his gaze. He deserved that much. "Friends. Of course."

When he left, she thought she glimpsed the shadow of someone in the corridor. Ah Na, she assumed, spying again. Not yet trusting the guests from Xia.

The Jiang doctor gave Ai Ling tonics to drink, their consistency as thick as honey and just as sweet. Ah Na visited by herself twice, sitting primly on the side of the bed, speaking with her about the latest Jiang fashions and asking her what the women wore in Xia.

Master Deen would chat about his new stained glass designs, their shapes and colors. Ai Ling truly enjoyed his visits, as he didn't seem to expect anything from her except her company. She studied his face and mannerisms unabashedly, discovering more that reminded her of Chen Yong each time.

His gray eyes held hers for a long moment now, as if he were seeing her clearly, and embarrassed, she glanced away. "Chen Yong told me the truth."

"The truth?"

Master Deen smiled. "That you are not siblings."

"Ah," she said with sudden understanding. "I'm sorry we spoke wrong. It was the best way to travel on ship." Without her power, she had to rely on her limited knowledge of Jiang, although she realized with surprise that she had improved greatly.

"I remember well the rules of decorum in Xia. You seem to break many of them." Taking her off guard, he spoke in Xian.

She laughed. "You speak the language so well," she said, genuinely impressed.

His gentle eyes lost their focus, and it was as if he were looking into the past. "It is like remembering a favorite song. It feels good to speak it again; it feels right."

She stretched her legs. Aching for fresh air and sunshine, she wondered when she could run through the garden.

As if reading her thoughts, Master Deen said, "Physician Kas has deemed you strong enough to venture outdoors. Fresh air and exercise would do you good."

She grinned, and the older man smiled back at her, knowing the news made her happy.

"Should I ask Chen Yong to walk with you?" he asked.

Although she had seen Chen Yong often, Ai Ling had barely spoken with him since she'd woken and never in private. "I would enjoy it," she said.

Master Deen stood. "He's told me about his situation, and perhaps I'm not the best example of following Xian decorum when it comes to the rules of love." He gazed down at her. "But Chen Yong is my son. All I want for him is happiness."

Distracted, she nodded in agreement. "Of course, Master Deen."

"Please, call me Deen. I'll let Chen Yong know you'd like a stroll in the gardens."

Ai Ling stared at herself in the gilded mirror in the bath chamber. Her cheekbones were more prominent, and her coloring had paled in the weeks she'd spent indoors. She looked older. She ran her wooden comb through her hair, finding comfort in the familiar routine. She wove into her single braid a vivid green ribbon, one that Chen Yong had bought for her at the market in Seta.

He was waiting for her in his bedchamber when she returned. His face lit up, and she felt herself smiling back at him. He was thinner, too, the angles of his face more defined. Chen Yong offered his arm, and she took it. He guided them through the manor and into the garden.

She tilted her face into the sun, inhaling deeply. The colors were so stunning: the lush greens of the curved leaves and the prickly hedge, the grays, blues, and pinks of the smooth stones covering the path. "I feel alive again," she said, wanting to see, hear, and smell everything at once.

Chen Yong led her along the path. For almost the first time since she'd known him, she didn't have to anchor her spirit. "Do you remember what happened?" she asked, after a companionable silence.

He glanced at her and covered her hand with his. "I don't. I remember feeling very sick after speaking with my father. I went to my bedchamber to lie down, and the next moment I woke up, with you beside me."

They walked on without speaking. "Do you remember?" he asked finally.

She couldn't look at him, so she admired a bed of vermilion starbursts instead. "I do," she whispered.

Chen Yong stopped and turned to her. "How could you risk yourself? I didn't even know if you would live—" His voice cracked.

"It was my fault. I had done that to you. I couldn't . . ." Her throat closed, and she glared at the ground.

He touched her cheek, but she still would not look at him. "Thank the goddess you're all right." He dropped his hand awkwardly. "Peng said we can set sail in a week's time. He wants to return before the end of autumn."

She glanced up then. "I thought you were staying here in Jiang?"

His dark brows drew together, and he looked at her, puzzled. "Don't you remember? I had told my father I would return to Xia." Understanding flitted across his handsome features then, and his face softened. "You don't remember."

He wouldn't be staying in Jiang Dao? She searched her memory, feeling as if something had been misplaced. He stepped closer. "I told you right after you first woke. I told you—" He closed his eyes for a brief moment. "I kissed you."

She almost laughed. "You did?"

They stared at each other until Chen Yong began to smile. "I did. And you fainted . . . or fell asleep." He laughed. "I couldn't decide which possibility was worse."

She laughed with him, although she didn't know how she was able to draw enough breath. Then the memory returned, revealing itself like clean brushstrokes. He was still chuckling when she wound both hands behind his neck and rose onto tiptoes to press her mouth to his. She drew back immediately, embarrassed.

"Ai Ling." His voice was low, hoarse. Chen Yong reached for her. He ran his hands along the curve of her spine and crushed her body to his. He dipped his head and kissed her throat, marking a hot path with his lips to a sensitive spot behind her ear. He whispered her name again, his breath warm against her skin.

She would have crumpled to the ground if it weren't for his tight embrace.

He pulled back to gaze at her. "I've wanted to do that for a long time." His eyes had deepened to a burnished amber. "And this."

Then his mouth was on hers, soft and firm. She gasped and drew in his breath, tasted him on her lips and her tongue. He caressed her; then his fingers were buried in her hair, loosening her braid. She wound her arms around his neck, pulled him to her, deepening their kiss. He couldn't be closer. Or close enough. Chen Yong stroked her arms, his hands trailed down her sides to her hips and lingered there before cupping her face, his exquisite lips never leaving hers.

They kissed until her knees trembled and she became light-headed. But she didn't faint a second time, as she would never have forgiven herself if she had been the first, again, to end it.

Peng knocked on her door just as she was beginning to pack for the journey to Xia. She dropped a tunic onto the bed and went to him to squeeze his hand. "I still don't know how I can possibly thank you. You saved both our lives."

He smiled, ever gracious, and sat on her bed. "Yen

helped. He prayed with me through those long hours, brought any items I needed. I would be lying if I said I knew for certain the outcome would be a happy one."

Ai Ling shivered. She realized how fortunate she was, how fortunate they all were. "I know," she whispered. "I can never repay you for your kindness."

"You can, perhaps."

She looked at him questioningly as she folded her clothes.

"Do you remember what happened?" Peng asked.

She laughed, shaking her head.

"I didn't want to ask earlier, you weren't recovered yet, but—"

"You remind me of my cat, Taro," she said. "You're so curious about everything."

It was his turn to laugh. "You can't fault me for wondering."

"I do remember." Her mood was suddenly serious. "It is my curse to remember everything."

Peng stared out the window, his black eyes intense. He glanced at her, and she smiled. "Would you be willing to tell me, perhaps during our trip back to Xia?"

She sat beside him. "I would."

He grinned, appearing even more charming. "How are things with Chen Yong?"

She blushed. "They are well." Ai Ling almost brought her fingers to her lips, full and bruised from kissing. Instead, she ran a hand over the tunic Peng had given her, then folded it, smiling.

"He doesn't remember anything," Peng said.

"Thank the goddess for that," she murmured.

"When he awoke and saw you . . . like that"—Peng gave a slight shake of his head—"he was incoherent, frantic. Yen had to restrain him, then drag him out of the bedchamber."

She tried to envision the scene and knew how Chen Yong had felt. She had felt exactly the same when she had seen him so still on his bed. "I must make offerings to the Goddess of Mercy when I return to Xia," she finally said in a soft voice.

"We'll be back before all the leaves have fallen," Peng replied.

CHAPTER SIXTEEN

Ai Ling set forth to the Palace of Fragrant Dreams within two weeks of returning to the kingdom of Xia. Her father accompanied her and understood her urgency. Master Cao, one of the Emperor's closest advisers and an old colleague of her father's, received them as honored guests. Her father was visiting in the outer court, but she had especially requested entrance to the inner court, where the Emperor's concubines resided.

As she crossed the courtyard, her embroidered slippers crunched over golden leaves, and she drew in the crisp scent of autumn. Chrysanthemums bloomed in vibrant reds and pinks, in bursts of bright orange. She walked along the various paths as if she'd had a map in her mind. The palace had changed little in these last three centuries.

Memories, both hers and Zhong Ye's, tangled and chaotic, haunted her. Her heart raced. She looked down, almost expecting to see the resplendent dress of an unwilling bride. Or the sapphire blue of an adviser's robe. She paused before some rosebushes, barren now but for a few withered leaves. They couldn't possibly be the same roses planted in front of Mei Gui's old quarters, but the crescent-shaped stone bench, the one Zhong Ye had sat on as Silver Phoenix danced for him three centuries past, appeared the same.

Ai Ling knelt by the bush nearest to the rising sun and began to dig with the wooden spade she had brought with her. It was sometime before she struck something hard. The square box she retrieved was dark with grit, and she rubbed her thumb over the carved side, revealing a lotus. The box was jade. Her hands trembled, and she struggled a little to lift the lid. It opened with a popping sound. Ai Ling placed the box on the ground, then wiped her hands on her trousers, not caring if she dirtied them.

A tortoiseshell comb decorated with plum blossoms lay nestled in a bed of lavender silk. She picked it up and brought it to her lips without thinking. It was the

comb Silver Phoenix had dropped on that first evening
she had spent with Zhong Ye. There was more, she
knew. Ai Ling lifted the silk and removed a small square
of yellowed parchment. Afraid the fragile paper would
crumble, she unfolded it with care. She smelled jasmine,
but it was so faint she wondered if she imagined it. She
read the poem written in Zhong Ye's assured hand, the
calligraphy neat and concise, like a scholar's:

> The promise of an evening past
> Without fragrant orchids and lilies wreathing
> my chamber or pinned to your locks
> Without the emeralds and pearls I wanted to bestow
> on your slender wrists or exquisite throat
> Instead only talk and laughter—
> the warmth of your eyes and your hand
> clasped in mine
> The delicate scent of jasmine on your skin
> You did not realize you left a gift behind
> as we wandered to your quarters by moonlight
> I await the day I can fasten this comb into
> your thick hair again, love

Ai Ling returned the comb and poem to the jade box,
then reached again into the ground for what she had

come for. She dug with her fingers and finally freed the glass jar containing Zhong Ye's last remains. Ai Ling would burn this, and he would finally be reincarnated, as the gods saw fitting. She almost returned the jade box to the ground but on a whim took it with her. She wanted to have something that had belonged to Silver Phoenix. And although she would never admit it aloud, something from Zhong Ye as well.

Their carriage clacked to a stop before the massive walls of the Deen manor in Gao Tung, and the driver began to unload their boxes. Her father pounded on the thick wooden door that had been plastered with new paper door gods, and it opened almost at once. Chen Yong greeted them, his grin so boyishly wide she laughed. Instinctively, even months after losing her power, she still tried to close herself at the sight of him.

"Master Wen, Ai Ling! Did you journey well?" Chen Yong clasped her father's hand, then her own, holding it longer than was proper. He had cut his hair short, in the Jiang style. She flushed when her eyes rested on his mouth, her heart expanding until it felt as if it would burst. She dropped her gaze from his throat to his shoulders. That didn't help. She felt his pull stronger now than ever, even without her power.

Her father cleared his throat, and Chen Yong released her hand, his face also coloring as he turned to lead them into the manor.

"The journey was a smooth one. We were honored to receive your father's invitation," Ai Ling's father said as they followed Chen Yong through the expansive courtyards. She glimpsed a pond tucked behind pomegranate trees exploding with ruby fruit, and the air was thick with the sweet scent of gardenias. Chen Yong ushered them into spacious quarters, with bedchambers on either side of a reception hall. The walls were papered in pale sage and decorated with brush paintings of the four seasons.

"It's incredible my father was able to buy a manor so close to my family. I'm still helping him settle in, but he acts as if he'd never left Xia." Chen Yong's contentment was obvious. He had written to Ai Ling immediately after he'd arrived home. His betrothal had been broken. "It wouldn't be right," he wrote, "as I'm in love with someone else." She had pressed her lips to his signature the first time she had read it.

"Where is Wai Sen?" her father asked.

"My father is waiting for you in the main hall, Master Wen. He is anxious to see you."

Ai Ling's father shook his head in wonder. "Twenty years passed so quickly. I'm eager to see my old friend again." He smiled at them, tapping his closed fan against his palm. "I saw the main hall at the other end of the courtyard. I'll find my way back."

Autumn sunshine filtered through the lattice panels. She could hear the slow trickling of a waterfall.

They were alone.

Chen Yong swept her into his arms, kissed her hair, then burrowed his face into her neck. "You smell amazing." He drew back, his eyes taking on that golden glow that had always stolen her breath away. "I've missed you."

This past month apart had been agony.

"I know," she said.

He released her and laughed. "I see."

"I meant—you know what I meant!" She felt foolish and tongue-tied. "I missed you more than anything." The words seemed a mockery, too inadequate to express her feelings. Her world had dulled, as if it had been robbed of color and light without him.

"More than a missed meal?"

She grabbed his tunic and pulled him close, tipping her face so she could see into his eyes. "I would fast for you, Li Chen Yong."

It was supposed to make him laugh, but although a faint smile touched his lips, the look he gave her was tender and serious. "That's saying a lot, Wen Ai Ling." He rested his forehead against hers, so their noses touched.

Her heart skipped a beat.

"Come with me." Chen Yong grasped her hand and led her into the courtyard. "I want to show you something."

They strolled through the gardens, which were rich with gold and vermilion. She smelled the pungent sweetness of tuberose, and songbirds serenaded them from their perches in the plum trees. "Where are we going?" she finally asked.

He squeezed her hand and, grinning, winked. "You'll see."

They stopped before a grand hall. He slid the door open and let her enter first. There was one large chamber with dark wooden beams running the length of the ceiling. Eight worktables took up half the room's space. The scent of wet sand and metal lingered in the air. Large clear glass lanterns hung from the ceiling.

Chen Yong waved his arm with a flourish. "Our own stained glass studio. Probably the first in Xia." His eyes gleamed with excitement. "We're still setting it up, but my father seems pleased by it."

Ai Ling walked between the worktables, recognizing tools and materials from Master Deen's workspace in Jiang Dao. "It's wonderful. Have you made anything yet?"

"I have. My first stained glass project." He stepped behind her and covered her eyes. "But it's a surprise, a gift for you."

She laughed as they walked like wooden puppets, his chest pressed against her back, until Chen Yong stopped. "Ready?" He dropped his hands. They were standing in front of a stained glass panel framed with silver birch wood. It was nearly the length of her arm, and it hung from the ceiling so that light from the lattice windows glimmered through the jeweled panes. Two silver bamboo stalks with leaves were set against a background of deep indigo and pale lavender. A round pearl moon and golden stars shone above the bamboo.

She lifted a hand and traced her fingertips above the glass, too afraid to touch it. "Chen Yong, you made this?"

"I did. Do you like it?" He was studying her intensely.

"It's beautiful." She kissed him. "Thank you," she said, breathless when they finally drew apart.

Chen Yong leaned against one of the worktables, lacing his fingers through hers. "I designed it with my father's help. Getting the colors right was the most difficult part." He nodded at the panel. "This was my third attempt."

She circled the stained glass, admiring it from different angles, and he followed her, their hands clasped.

"A belated birthday gift, Ai Ling. Bamboo for your strength."

She smiled up at him. "I thought it was oak for strength?"

"This one has Xian symbolism," he said. "I remembered how the Moon and Fertility goddesses were your favorite. I mimicked the colors. And I always think of you when I see the night sky."

As she always thought of him. "I love it, Chen Yong."

He flushed with pleasure, and it took considerable restraint for her not to throw herself into his arms.

"I'm glad. The studio is fairly well stocked, but we still need more supplies and equipment from Jiang Dao." He drew her to him and slid his hands down to her hips. "My father wants to travel back next spring. I want you to come with us."

"What?"

The distinct song of an ardor bird filtered through the workshop windows, its notes passionate and sweet.

"You can have your own cabin this time," he said.

"Well. No, then."

Chen Yong threw back his head and laughed.

She blushed, resting her palms against his chest. "It's not that I don't want to, but what would people think? It wouldn't be—"

"Proper?" He cocked an eyebrow. "Like this?" He bit her throat gently, then pressed his lips to the same spot.

"Chen Yong!" She pounded his shoulder with a fist, even as she leaned into him, her entire body responding.

"It's not as if you haven't already taken the journey—"

"But that was because I thought you were in danger," she said.

"There's no point in justifying something no one else can possibly understand. What happened to us was incredible, Ai Ling. What happened to you is incomprehensible. The people who would judge us already have." His expression was intent, pensive. "Besides, do you really care what people think?"

"I care what my parents think," she said after a pause.

Chen Yong nodded. Fascinated by the way the colors from the stained glass danced across his handsome face, she couldn't look away from him. "My father is speaking to yours right now. He is saying that you and your family are always welcome at the Deen manor. This one and the one in Jiang Dao. Considering how your father saved my life, we're almost like family." He glanced around the studio. "There's nowhere to sit in here. Let me show you the garden."

They followed the ardor bird's crisp melody along a stone path that led to a deep oval pool surrounded by dramatic rocks, the same pool that she had spied earlier. A secluded pavilion was nestled beyond the pomegranate trees, but Chen Yong went to the pond and sat on a flat stone, his back to the waterfall.

She stood in front of him, enjoying the sun's warmth on her back. "It's a beautiful manor."

His eyes crinkled against the light, and he wrapped his arms around her waist. "I think it suits my father's needs." Silver and orange fish darted in the pond behind him, their mouths tasting the water's surface.

"I want to go with you, Chen Yong." She gazed down at him. "I do. But it would be selfish."

"And if we were betrothed?" he asked in a low voice.

She backed away then, shrugging from his touch. "Are you—is your father asking for us to wed?" She suddenly felt faint, unsteady. "What does your mother say?"

"My mother was very upset when I broke the betrothal she had arranged." Chen Yong rested his elbows on his thighs, then clasped his hands as if he didn't know what to do with them. "I explained to her my feelings for you. She finally relented, after accusing me of being a hopeless romantic."

"And what does your father want?" Her mouth had gone dry. She needed to sit down.

"He wants what I want, Ai Ling. And I want what you

want. I'm hoping that never being apart again . . . Is what you want, too?" He cleared his throat. "A day is too long. A month is intolerable." He raked a hand through his hair, his eyes downcast.

"You cut your hair," she whispered, not knowing what else to say.

"Only because it's easier for when I'm working in the studio." He sat motionless as she ran her fingers through his hair; it was soft and thick. She didn't need her power to feel his desire and his love for her.

"Do you remember the first time we met?" he asked.

She laughed softly at the memory. "I liked you despite myself. You said you wanted a bride to sweep the front courtyard and spoon-feed you broth."

The corners of his mouth twitched. "You said it. And I agreed."

"I didn't think I'd ever see you again." Her hands were still buried in his hair. His were gripping the stone's edge, as if he were afraid she would bolt with any sudden movements.

"I'm not the same person you met that day, Ai Ling."

Neither was she.

His expression took on that serious intensity so familiar to her. The one that always made her wonder what he was thinking. The one that she loved. "What does it mean for you to be betrothed?" he asked.

"You know what it means," she whispered. "You're speaking to a girl who ran from it. It means to wed and be kept in the inner quarters, embroidering slippers and making babies." She dropped her hands and took a step back. She loved him—couldn't possibly love anyone more—but the thought of being sequestered in the inner quarters for her remaining days was as oppressive and terrifying as a yoke around her neck.

He stood, and she was keenly aware of the hand's width separating them. "It's not what I'd expect from you if we were to wed one day," he said. He lowered his head, as if the sun were too bright in his eyes. "How could I when I've seen you slay monsters? Be called on by Immortals? Sneak on a ship and sail to distant kingdoms? Go to the underworld to save my life?" He caught her fingers and studied her palm, as if he could decipher the future in the lines etched there. "It'd be as wrong as finding a phoenix and trapping her in a gilded cage. Or capturing a dragon. I want you by my side, Ai Ling, not tucked away and hidden somewhere."

The waterfall splashed on behind them, and she drew his hand to her cheek, her heart beating too fast. He finally met her eyes and smiled. "Your parents could come?"

She hesitated, confused. "To our wedding?"

Chen Yong grinned wider. "I meant, to Jiang Dao."

"I can't keep up with you." She laughed, feeling giddy and out of breath.

"I think you have that turned around." He captured her single braid and ran a palm down its length, pulling her to him for a kiss.

Voices startled them apart.

"They must have wandered off for a stroll." She heard her father say from somewhere up the path.

"Well, they'll miss the midday meal then," Master Deen replied, with a laugh.

"Ah, good," she said, her lips tingling from their near kiss. "I'm hungry."

"When aren't you hungry?" He chuckled when she pinched his arm in retribution. Still, she couldn't help laughing with him as he grasped her hand, and they went to greet their fathers beyond the pomegranate trees.

ACKNOWLEDGMENTS

The Kingdom of Xia is inspired by ancient China, but my stories do not take place in an actual place or time in Chinese history. Jiang Dao is completely fabricated and not based on any particular countries in Europe.

Several books were essential in my research for this novel: *Daughter of Heaven*, by Nigel Cawthorne; *Chinese Junks on the Pacific*, by Hans K. Van Tilburg; *A Thousand Years of Stained Glass*, by Catherine Brisac; and *A Chinese Bestiary: Strange Creatures from the Guideways Through Mountains and Seas*, edited and translated by Richard E. Strassberg. Also this website, http://people.reed.edu/~brashiek/scrolls.html, for fantastic information on Taizong's hell.

My gratitude to my agent, Bill. And to my editor, Virginia: this novel is as much yours as it is mine. Thank you for pushing and challenging me as a writer, just enough so I could improve on my story and prose, but not so much that I needed to seek therapy! That storm and the kiss were written for you. Cupcakes and cookies to everyone at Greenwillow Books, you are all wonderful!

Hugs to Malinda Lo and Megan Whalen Turner, two author friends who made 2010 especially fun and memorable for me. To the Brat Pack: Aaron, Amy, and Heather, I love all our lunches together and hilarious chitchats. And much gratitude to my old college roommate, Dr. Natalie Grunkemeier, who patiently and thoroughly answered random and weird medical questions from castration to goring to heart removal.

Thank you to my critique-group friends, who offer me encouragement, laughter, and insight: Tudy, Kirsten, Mark, Janice, Eveie, and John. Rich and Rachel, I miss you. Special thanks to Jean, my Chinese brush painting teacher, who is always there to guide and inspire. And to my fellow brush painting classmates, I look forward to both our art and your company each week.

To my online friends, so many of whom have become real-life friends: the debs, the inkies, the undies, and blueboarders! To my hedgies, who were there from the start. And a special bootay shake for my puglets, who are always there for me and gave advice on the hot smooch when I needed it. (Can you tell I like pet names?)

Last but not least, to my crazy little family, Mark, Sweet Pea, and Munchkin: I love you!

Please visit my website, cindypon.com, to find out more about my novels, my Chinese brush art, the books I read, and general ramblings. I adore comments and emails from readers! I hope you enjoyed reading *Fury of the Phoenix* as much as I enjoyed writing it.